# Before You Sleep

# Before You Sleep

# Linn Ullmann

Translated from the Norwegian by
Tiina Nunnally

VIKING

VIKING
Published by the Penguin Group
Penguin Putnam Inc., 375 Hudson Street,
New York, New York 10014, U.S.A.
Penguin Books Ltd, 27 Wrights Lane, London W8 5TZ, England
Penguin Books Australia Ltd, Ringwood, Victoria, Australia
Penguin Books Canada Ltd, 10 Alcorn Avenue,
Toronto, Ontario, Canada M4V 3B2
Penguin Books (N.Z.) Ltd, 182–190 Wairau Road,
Auckland 10, New Zealand

Penguin Books Ltd, Registered Offices:
Harmondsworth, Middlesex, England

First published in 1999 by Viking Penguin,
a member of Penguin Putnam Inc.

1 3 5 7 9 10 8 6 4 2

Translation copyright © Tiina Nunnally, 1999
All rights reserved

Originally published in Norwegian by Tiden Norsk Forlag A/S. Copyright © 1998 Tiden
Norsk Forlag A/S, Oslo.

Publisher's Note
This is a work of fiction. Names, characters, places, and incidents either are the product of
the author's imagination or are used fictitiously, and any resemblance to actual persons,
living or dead, business establishments, events, or locales is entirely coincidental.

CIP data available.

This book is printed on acid-free paper.
∞

Printed in the United States of America
Set in Stemple Garamond  •  Designed by Jaye Zimet

To Niels

I'd like to sing someone to sleep,
by someone sit, and be still.
I'd like to rock you and murmur a song,
be with you on the fringes of sleep.
Be the one and only awake in the house
who would know that the night is cold.
I'd like to listen both inside and out,
into you, and the world, and the woods.
The clocks call out with their tolling bells,
and you can see to the bottom of time.
Down in the street a stranger goes by
and bothers a passing dog.
Behind comes silence. I've laid my eyes
on you like an open hand,
and they hold you lightly and let you go,
when something moves in the dark.

—RAINER MARIA RILKE
*(translated by Cal Kinnear)*

I don't want to knock my opponent out. I want to hit him, step away, and watch him hurt. I want his heart.

—JOE FRAZIER

# Before You Sleep

Sander is quiet. Karin is quiet too. That alone should tell you that something isn't the way it's supposed to be. Normally Karin talks all the time. But when two people are lying in bed in the middle of the night, waiting for a phone that doesn't ring, things tend to get quiet. What they hear is: the alarm clock on the nightstand, which is not ticking but droning. The creaking in the walls. The rush of the wind and snow outside the window. The insomniac neighbor next door who turns off the radio and gets ready to go to bed one more time.

Karin has promised Sander that he doesn't have to go to sleep until Julie calls to say good night.

Sander is seven and a half.

Julie should have called several hours ago.

At this very moment Karin and Sander are lying close together in bed. Only their faces are sticking up over the comforter, along with a little tousled hair. Now and then Karin tells him a story. That's what she's doing right now.

Want to know something, Sander? she says.

What?

Remember that picture of your great-grandfather and all the others standing in front of the monument in Queens—in front of the time capsule of Cupaloy? Remember how we talked about all the things inside the time capsule? Things they lowered into the ground, stuff that no one can touch for five thousand years?

Yes, says Sander.

There's a story in there too.

In the ground?

Yes.

Why?

The people who buried the capsule probably wanted the people who dig it up in 6939 to have something to read to their children.

Can you read it to me?

Karin brushes his hair out of his eyes.

I don't have to read it, I know it by heart.

Really?

Just listen, she says softly, listen to this: Once upon a time the North Wind and the Sun were fighting over which of them was stronger, and one day a man came by wearing a warm cape. When they caught sight of the man, they agreed that the first one who managed to make the man take off his cape would be, forever and always, the strongest.

So then what happened? says Sander. He yawns, he curls up under the comforter. So then what happened? His voice is barely audible.

Is he asleep yet?

Karin leans over him, places her ear close to his face.

No. Not yet.

Sander sits up again. Puts his arms around her neck. His head against her breast. He wants her to say something. About why the phone isn't ringing. About the silence in the room. About the night.

What time is it now? he whispers.

It's late, Sander, she says, but doesn't say how late. It's really late. I don't think you've ever been up this late before.

# Wedding, August 1990

Once upon a time, almost nine years ago. It was the year I turned twenty, Anni went to America, and Julie married Aleksander.

I might as well start there.

I'll start with your wedding day, Julie—a sunny afternoon, August 27, 1990. Later, much later, no one could say that it wasn't a splendid wedding, oh no, you were lovely, Julie, you were so lovely. No one could say, with their hand on their heart, that you weren't a lovely bride. I wasn't lovely, I knew that. I've never been lovely. Short and thin and dark-haired with a little too pudgy nose. But it didn't matter, I could sing.

No one was home when I woke up that morning. Julie and Anni were out, taking care of last-minute things before Julie put on her wedding gown and Father came to pick her up, according to tradition, of course. I remember that I woke up and walked barefoot across the rough hardwood floor, down the hallway, into the living room, and over to Anni's bar. I opened the liquor cabinet and took a little of her whisky, mixing it with a cup of cocoa.

I had moved out of the apartment on Jacob Aall Street several years before, but Anni thought we should be together, all three of us on "the last night," as she put it. *I want to be with you on the last night before Julie gets married,* she sniffled, *it'll be like when you were little, oh how quickly time passes . . .*

I'll tell more about Anni later on. Anni is my mother. She's not quite right in the head.

Putting the whisky in the cocoa was something I did because I'm a nostalgic sort of girl—as the years go by I'll become responsible, mature, a survivor, and truthful enough, but on this day I'm mostly nostalgic—and putting whisky in the cocoa was something I used to do when I was a little girl. Not that I was anything as depressing as an alcoholic child. This isn't that sort of story. No, you were much sadder than I was, Julie.

If I tried to describe my family, and that's exactly what I'm going to do, you could probably say that Anni drank to forget. I drank to be happy. Father drank just to keep going. Grandma drank to sleep better at night. Aunt Selma drank to be even meaner than she already was. Rikard, my grandfather, claimed that he didn't drink at all, even though people say he made a fortune in America by selling liquor—but that was a long time ago.

Julie was the only one in the family who was—what do they call it?—a moderate and sensible drinker. Unfortunately! It did her no good. She didn't forget, she wasn't happy, she couldn't sleep, and she was never mean. And she didn't get rich either.

It was your wedding day, Julie. I remember seeing you up there at the altar, the tiny white flowers in your hair, the long pearl-embroidered, cream-colored, and much too princesslike silk gown. You looked lost in that gown, lovely and lost, and that endless long veil trailing behind, that veil that stretched down the middle aisle of the church, out onto the steps, down the street, across the fjord, through the sky like the stroke of a brush. Yes, I saw you up there at the altar and thought: This must be the most godforsaken proof of love that two people can give each other, promise their love forever and always, as if that's even possible—what is the minister saying? Do you hear what he's saying, Julie? He's saying that if the time should come when the two of you aren't strong enough to love each other, when you can't find the strength to love each other anymore, then you should know that love, love itself, is greater than any individual person's ability to love, because love comes from God, and God's love is eternal, he says, and you say yes, and Aleksander says yes, but Aleksander doesn't look at you, Julie, he doesn't look at you, he looks straight ahead, like the impeccable man that he is.

I drank Anni's whisky, added water to the bottle so she wouldn't notice that I'd taken any—just like I used to do. I put the glass and bottle back and closed the liquor cabinet.

Afterwards I got into my splendid red dress, stepped into my red shoes, and put on red lipstick. I turned around and looked at myself in the mirror:

*Is that you, Karin? Is that you?*

Of course. Even today. Not bad.

I turned around and looked at myself, yes don't you look fine, I said to the girl in the mirror, and the girl nodded, and the girl said: Don't come back tonight and say that you couldn't go through with it after all.

And I wasn't exactly drunk when I arrived at the church on that late summer afternoon to bear witness to the impeccable Aleksander Lange Bakke marrying my sister Julie.

I was happy and light and just a little bit too hot in that prickly red dress—and somewhere inside me a touch of nausea.

Anni is standing on the steps outside Uranienborg Church, all silky fine in a long green dress. Standing there Anni reminds me of the Caribbean Sea, big and cool and inviting. I don't think either Julie or I would trade our mother for any other mother if we had the chance. I at least wouldn't trade her in. Not Anni, our own glamour girl, Oslo's best hairdresser. Our own Anni, who didn't really want to be Anni at all, but somebody else entirely. Anni wanted to bathe in the Trevi Fountain in Rome, kiss blue-eyed movie stars on the lips, pat adorable and grateful children on the head, run her fingers through her own thick, long reddish-blonde hair while the world looked on and gasped. She wanted to get out and away, Oslo wasn't good enough, she wanted to go back to America— that same Anni, brought up in Trondheim but born in Brooklyn, daughter of Rikard Blom. Little Anni who at the age of eight could stand on her bicycle seat across Lexington Avenue in New York with one leg in the air and one hand on the handlebars: Hurray for Anni, they all shout. *Hey, all of you, look at me look at me look at me*, shouts little Anni, *hey, all of you, look at me look at me look at me*. And Anni turns around to see if everyone is watching, and the ground crashes up toward her, the ground crashes up toward her, and the bicycle topples over, and Anni turns toward me on the church steps and says: Karin, stay here with me for a while and greet the wedding guests.

Anni is what you call an irresistible woman. That's what men say to her. Anni did not become famous or celebrated, Federico Fellini did not come to Trondheim to whisk her away, the journey back to America had to wait. But she was utterly irresistible all the same. Unhappy, yes. Bitter, yes. Drunk, yes. Stark raving mad, yes. But irresistible. Nobody can take that away from her.

I remember once, a long time ago. Anni, Julie, and I and Anni's boyfriend Zlatko Dragovic from Yugoslavia were on our way to Zagreb by train. Zlatko Dragovic was Anni's first boyfriend after Father. It was summer vacation. We sat in a train compartment, the train rolled on, there were no other passengers in the compartment. Zlatko Dragovic said in that dark voice of his, in his broken English he said: Your mother in that light, can you see? Look at your mother. Karin! Julie! Look at your mother! Her eyes, my God, her eyes. Have you ever seen such eyes?

Then he quietly wept because he was so moved.

Julie and I gaped.

Anni licked her paws and glanced at us. *I see that you're looking at my eyes, aren't you? He's right, you know. I am simply unbelievable.* That's not the kind of mother you want to trade.

And Anni is standing on the steps outside the church, receiving the wedding guests; the sun is shining in her eyes, on her thick reddish-blonde hair, which she has put up with shiny gold barrettes; it's gleaming on her dark-green high heels that are scraping the ground.

Karin, she says, gripping my arm before I have a chance to sneak into the church, which is dark and cool. Help me out here, she says, stand here with me for a while and greet the guests. *Oh look!* Look who's there! she cries loudly, pointing at

Aunt Edel and Uncle Fritz. She's still holding my arm tight, it's unclear which of us is more drunk, but don't think anyone will notice.

I've learned three things from Anni. I've learned that some people play their roles with care, while others play them sloppily. And you must learn to play yours with care, Anni used to say.

That was the first thing.

The second thing is something she told me when I was little, only seven or eight, and feeling sad. She said that you mustn't show them how sad you are. Don't give them that advantage.

I was sad because a boy in my class had promised to kiss me if I ate a worm. He held a worm in his hand, it dangled from his fingers, long and thin and gray and slippery, I remember thinking it was a disgusting worm. But all right, I said, fine, I'll eat it, and I let him put the worm on my tongue. It lay completely still in my mouth, and when I sank my teeth into it, I noticed how it softly, with almost no resistance, split in two. I felt a prickling sensation all over, there was sweat on my forehead and on the palms of my hands. You have to chew it properly, said the boy, who was following the whole thing with interest. We were squatting down behind a bush. You can't just swallow it, said the boy. That's cheating, said the boy.

I looked at the boy and thought: I'll do anything to kiss you.

I chewed the worm. I chewed it properly. I didn't open my mouth. I didn't throw up. I kept my part of the bargain. When the worm had turned to mush in my mouth, I opened wide and said: Is this good enough? The boy peeked into my mouth and said okay, you can swallow now, and I swallowed. I opened wide again and showed him.

Can we kiss now? I asked.

Shit no, said the boy, you think I'd kiss a girl who's dumb enough to eat a worm?

I cried for days. I cried because the boy wouldn't kiss me. I cried because I'd been tricked. I cried because I wasn't strong enough or brave enough to strike back.

That's when Anni said, after days and nights of crying: You mustn't show them how sad you are. Don't give them that advantage.

That was the second thing.

The third was a refrain that originally came from Grandma, but it was Anni who made it her life's motto. *Never look back, just cross it out and keep going*—that's what Grandma always said. The first time I heard her say it was when she moved into our apartment with us on Jacob Aall Street after Father had moved out. She took up a stance, ramrod-straight, in the middle of the living room, a tiny giant of a woman, and said, not without a considerable amount of dramatic flair: *Never look back, just cross it out and keep going.*

No way, said Anni after a few days, climbing out of bed; no way am I going to lie here a second longer and cry over that man, a goddamn mediocre middle-aged drunk who never made me happy anyway, that goddamn fucking rat prick, she said and blew her nose.

See that? said Grandma, pointing at Anni. A good soldier never looks back.

Anni isn't a soldier, I said.

Oh yes she is, said Grandma.

Julie didn't hear any of this. Julie was sitting on a chair next to the window in her room, keeping an eye out for Father's white Mazda. The only thing Grandma could do was stroke her hair and say that he hasn't stopped loving you, Julie, he hasn't stopped loving you.

That was the third thing.

Oh, look who's here, says Anni. Here comes Uncle Fritz and Aunt Edel. Here comes Uncle Fritz and Aunt Edel, all right, and Anni lets go of my arm so I can greet them politely, the way she wants me to. Hello, hello, how nice you look today, Aunt Edel, oh, thank you, and Uncle Fritz, how are you? I said, how are you? HOW ARE YOU, UNCLE FRITZ? No, I haven't seen the bride yet. Julie and Father wanted to be alone for the last hour. He had some good advice he wanted to give her about marriage before all hell broke loose.

Uncle Fritz is Aunt Edel's son. I don't know how they happened to be called uncle and aunt, I know that in some way or other we're related. Edel has taken care of her son Fritz ever since he was born fifty-four years ago, they live together in a three-room apartment on Schønning Street in Majorstua not far from Anni's apartment on Jacob Aall Street, they take vacations together in the south, they run a little pastry business together, with the kitchen on Schønning Street as their base. Edel bakes cakes, the best cakes in town, as a matter of fact; she baked today's wedding cake, a cream cake with eight layers, just like she baked Anni's wedding cake twenty years ago. Uncle Fritz's job is to deliver the cakes to the customers. When Uncle Fritz was thirty-seven he moved into his own apartment, quit his job as Edel's cake driver, and told his mother that it was time for him to start out on his own.

Eight days later he moved back in with Edel.

The sun is prickling my scalp and cheeks. I'll be sitting next to Uncle Fritz at dinner. Anni doesn't dare seat anyone else next to him; sometimes he throws up with no warning when he's at a family function. He threw up on Anni at Grandma's funeral a year ago. Anni took it well. It was worse on Christmas Eve three years ago. That time he threw up all over the dinner table, it splattered on everybody, it's one of the pictures that didn't make it into Edel's photo album: a long white table, arms and hands outstretched, palms turned outward, trying to fend off the vomit; save us from that, save us from that, we don't want that on us, stop it, man! I see pale faces, one after the other after the other, all around the fancy white table, their eyes closed. I see disgust, so much disgust around a dinner table can't be found in even the most unhappy of families, and we weren't even a particularly unhappy family, but there were a lot of us. Unhappy or not, who can tell? There was a little of this and a little of that. But I can safely say that there were a lot of us.

am Karin. I was born in the summer of 1970 at Aker Hospital in Oslo. Anni said she didn't think giving birth to me was especially painful, but she threw a glass of water on the floor and howled for the sake of appearances. Then the doctor leaned over her and whispered *now, now, now.* Julie came into the world three years earlier. I've heard that her birth was quite a bit tougher. The midwife groaned, Anni was brave. Julie showed up feet first, and never before had the midwife seen such big feet on a newborn. Julie's body was tiny and blue and looked more like part of a body than a whole one. Her feet were unusually big and smooth, not covered with little wrinkles like the feet of most babies, but well shaped, like salmon heads. Yet seen in relation to the rest of her body, they were grotesque. And Anni knew it: Julie's feet *were* grotesque, and every time she changed Julie she tried to avoid looking at them.

Anni loved her children. I *love* my children, she used to say. That's how she was brought up: A mother loves her children. She used to say it out loud, often for no reason at all, to anyone who would listen: I love my children. Grandma also loved her children, she loved her daughter Anni and she loved her daughter Else, who lives in Wisconsin. I'm sure that

Grandma's mother loved Grandma the way Grandma loved our mother and the way our mother loved us.

We were a loving family.

That's why the thing with Julie's feet was hard for Anni. She hadn't counted on her vanity being as powerful as her love. And Anni could never admit that she felt anything but love for her children. She couldn't say to herself that I'm ashamed of Julie's feet, of the way Julie lumbers across the floor, of Julie's much too jerky movements—it was all wrong—her arms were too long, her body was too skinny, her face was too pale. She couldn't say to herself that she was ashamed of Julie. Such a statement would be absurd. Totally unthinkable. Absolutely impossible. And yet Anni couldn't help staring at Julie's feet every time Julie did something clumsy, like dropping her cup of milk on the floor on her way from the refrigerator to the dinner table. Or tipping over a bowl of apples. Or stumbling on the street. Or stepping on Anni's toes. Then Anni, against her will, would envision herself in childbirth, her legs spread apart, and Julie's giant feet sticking out of her. So Anni, because of the shame she felt every time she looked at Julie, would kiss her and kiss her and kiss her. Anni wanted the shame to disappear. She didn't understand it. A mother loves her children.

Julie was always stumbling, often for no reason at all. Suddenly she would simply crumple and be stretched out full-length on the ground. She was a thin child, and she did all she could to hide her nakedness. She didn't cry. Julie never cried. Anni cried, I cried, but Julie never cried. Only once, before she disappeared, did I ever see her cry.

Anni and Father lived together for almost ten years, and then Father left. He didn't go far, he got in his car and drove for a quarter of an hour, from Majorstua to Tøyen. He bought an apartment near the University Press, where he was an editor for the types of reference books that nobody really cared about or read, not even his colleagues at the publishing company, and sometimes when I called him at work the receptionist would say: He doesn't work here anymore, but of course he did.

Father got in his car and drove for a quarter of an hour from Majorstua to Tøyen and said he was through with women. Anni may very well have been irresistible, but the men never stuck around. There are plenty of things you can have too much of. Irresistible is one of those things.

I can't anymore, said Father. I just can't anymore.

Father had been married once before he met Anni, and I remember when Julie and I met Father's firstborn from his first marriage. Our brother, Father's son. Anni and Father were still living together in the apartment on Jacob Aall Street. Suddenly one day, a Sunday, a strange boy was sitting at our dinner table at home. The boy was big and skinny and he sat with his head bowed. His hair was wet and needed cutting. He was wearing a red shirt with a thin burgundy tie hanging over his stomach. His neck was sweaty. Anni flitted around him, around Father, around us, around the table, around the kitchen, and the smell of her skin, her hair, a lovely blend of perfume, chamomile, apples, and papaya filled the room. In addition to the smell of dinner: little spicy meatballs, corn on the cob, homemade mashed potatoes, and gravy with goat cheese. You have to eat, said Anni, and flitted some more. It's so good to see you eating, she said, look how the boy can eat. The boy grunted and turned red in the face. Father didn't say anything, he raised and lowered his fork, up and down, chewing his food. The boy looked at Father. Father looked at the boy. They didn't say a word to each other. Anni was the one who carried the conversation. Father said Hmmm, the boy said Hmmm. Julie and I were just plain scared and couldn't manage to say a thing because we suddenly had a brother, a real-life big brother with a tie who was sitting there eating spicy meatballs at our dinner table with our father and mother. Nobody talked, try as hard as Anni might, trying to make this into an ordinary, pleasant Sunday dinner with the family. Nobody talked, it was so quiet that we could hear the sound of the silverware clinking, and that's way too quiet for Anni.

Yes, that's way too quiet for Anni. This is why she started to sing. Not exactly sing, but hum, and after a while she began tapping out the beat with her fork. *Baby it's cold outside*, she hummed. She had a dreamy, veiled look in her eyes, and she tried to catch the boy's glance, the dark, scared-stiff glance of our brother, our father's son. *Baby it's cold outside . . . but I really can't stay . . . but baby it's cold outside*, she hummed. The boy looked down at his food and blushed even more. Anni hummed louder and stretched her arm across the table to stroke his hair. The boy flinched and dropped his fork on the floor. Anni stopped abruptly and fell silent. Everyone looked at the boy, at the boy bending down to pick up his fork from the floor, at him mumbling an apology. I'm sorry, he mumbled. I'm sorry, I'm sorry.

No one said a word around the table. Father looked at the boy. Father looked at us. Father looked at Anni.

Maybe we could eat the rest of the meal on Jacob Aall Street and not in a Hollywood movie, said Father, what do you say, Anni?

Go to hell, said Anni, and smiled at the boy.

When it was time for the boy to leave, Father followed him out to the hallway. Father squatted down and watched the boy put on his down jacket and cap. When he was ready, Father stood up and hugged the boy the way men hug other men, with a pat or a thump on the back, and Father said: So we'll see you next week, right? Fine, it's a date then. The boy nodded and ran out the door and down the stairs.

The following Sunday the boy was back in his place at the dinner table. He was wearing the same red shirt, with the same thin tie hanging over his stomach. His neck was sweaty, just like before. The only difference was that he had gotten a haircut. The boy had been to the barber and gotten a haircut so that now we could see his forehead, and his eyes were much bigger than I thought. Father looked at the boy. The boy looked at Father. Dinner was eaten. Afterwards they went out to the hallway, Father squatted down, the boy got ready to leave. They hugged each other, and Father invited him back the next Sunday. And so it went. Every Sunday the boy would be sitting at the dinner table. He never came late. He never came early. He never stayed long. Once I tried to talk to the boy: It's strange that you're our brother, I said. Yes, said the boy, it's strange.

Then came a Sunday when the boy wasn't sitting at the dinner table anymore. Father didn't explain. And we didn't ask. That's how things were with Father. People disappeared.

People disappeared. When Father got in his car and drove away from the apartment on Jacob Aall Street to the apartment in Tøyen, Julie and I stood in the window and waved. Anni lay in bed in the next room and cried. Good God how she cried. All day and all night and all the next day after Father left, she cried. I've read that there are lots of different words for wind, somewhere else I read a description of all the different kinds of thunder: rolling thunder, rumbling thunder, thunder that crashes, thunder that crackles across the sky. On Jacob Aall Street we could have put together our own dictionary for Anni's tears.

Anni's tears aren't always genuine, aren't always an expression of sorrow or joy, aren't always prolonged, aren't always comprehensible. Anni's tears occupy her whole body, her eyes, her mouth, her stomach, between her legs, her fingertips, her throat. Anni cries when she's caught off guard. It might be sick children lying on cots on TV, children with wide-open eyes, flies on their faces, swollen bellies—like little pregnant children, Anni thinks, little pregnant boys and girls—and Anni sees a thousand-year-old child's face turn toward the TV camera, turn toward Anni, a thousand-year-old child's face that says: Help me, Anni, can't you help me either, Anni? And then

Anni cries. These are tears that sit in her stomach, that start out as a low whimper, *can't you help me either, Anni?* and the tears spill out of her mouth, nose, and eyes, like vomit, and it's unbelievable, but then it's over. Anni looks up at the TV screen again, and it's over. It's over now. Other times Anni cries for no reason, sits down calmly at the kitchen table under the cold blue ceiling lamp and cries. *It's really nothing, Karin, it's nothing, Julie, I'm just crying, it's the tears inside me, it'll be over soon.* And sometimes Anni cries because she's moved. Then her eyes fill with little spring-rain tears that trickle down her face. Out of her mouth come hiccups that sound like laughter. Anni can be moved and start to cry over anything: an obituary in the newspaper, a very old or very young person whom she's never met, but *someone* actually did know them, and that's sad enough. She can also cry quietly, without a sound, with tears running, literally running, down her cheeks. When Anni cries like that, her glittery blue eyes get even more glittery and blue, she knows that. She knows that this type of crying arouses tenderness, compassion, and helplessness, because the men in her life can't stand to see a woman's tears. Anything but that, say the men, not a woman's tears. But don't think Anni doesn't cry when she's mad; then she cries loud, she squeals, she slings her tears at you, and I know that's when the worn-out phrase "like a stuck pig" is totally wrong. It's impossible to say that Anni squeals "like a stuck pig"; there's something helpless and weak about a "stuck pig," and Anni's anger is neither helpless nor weak, Anni screams like an enraged child *I hate you I hate you I hate you I hate you I hate you,* then so many foul words come out of Anni's mouth that they're hard to forget afterwards, even though she's forgotten them all long ago, and it's not her eyes but her mouth that is full of tears, spit, foam, and slime. Completely different from Anni's tears at night, when Fear comes in. Then she moans softly, without even opening her mouth. Her eyelids are wet, her cheeks are wet, her lips are wet, the back of her hand is wet, but the tears don't come from her eyes, the tears come from someplace deep inside her body. And Anni is so exhausted that the only thing she can do is pray: Make them go away now, make it go away, make what's inside me go away. And sleep is impossible, Anni knows that, it's impossible to sleep. Can't sleep until dawn. Unless she foresaw it all the night before and drank enough so she'd be brave. But sometimes she wakes up and is scared anyway: scared that the liquor hasn't worked the way it was supposed to, scared of the Fear that isn't there but might come at any moment, and it's dark outside, it's dark outside and Anni is lying on her back in bed and crying into the pillow that she's pressing against her face.

When Father got into his car and drove off from the apartment on Jacob Aall Street and over to the apartment in Tøyen, Anni cried in a way she had never cried before. Everything opened up in her and tumbled out. There was no stopping it. Anni cried because she knew that from now on she was nothing to Father. Nothing. Zero. Nada. Try to understand nothing. Father didn't disappear. Father moved, Father left, Father took off, but he didn't *disappear*. It was the others who disappeared. Just like the boy, and the boy's mother, and now our mother.

I can't anymore, said Father. You *are* no more.

Julie and I were Father's twin hearts. That's what he told us when he left. You're my twin hearts, he said and stroked our hair like he used to do. We hadn't disappeared. We weren't *nothing*. I think that Julie and I, or Julie at any rate, lived with the realization through our whole childhood, and even later on, that we hadn't disappeared, that no matter what we did, we mustn't disappear. That's why we stood and waved to Father from the window, smiled and waved, as he drove away in his car, and I had to pinch Julie's arm so she wouldn't collapse. Can you please stand up straight, Julie? And Anni was crying in the next room, but we were little children, and she was a grown-up, so that was her problem, I thought.

'm standing on the church steps with Anni. I've put on my red dress, I'm wearing red lipstick, I've twisted and turned in front of the mirror, and it's not just for the fun of it that I've decked myself out this way. The thing is, I'm going to seduce a man. It's a secret game that I've played ever since I began seducing men at the age of twelve. (Well, maybe not actually twelve, but somewhere around there.) I don't know exactly how to explain it. I'm not going to *make love*. No, spare me words like that. It's not about love. Don't talk to me about intimacy. I'm not in love. I don't even know which one of the men now on their way to church I'm going to seduce; that's what makes it a game. I haven't chosen him yet.

I'm thinking about Grandma. Her name was June. I'm thinking about the photo I have of her: short, curly gray hair, her face full of wrinkles, with stern eyebrows, startling green eyes.

Grandma, I asked her, are you a soldier too?

Yes, you can damn well bet I am. I was a damn good soldier, said Grandma.

What about me, am I a soldier?

I think so, Karin. But not Julie. She's no soldier, and never will be. But you, Karin, are going to be a good soldier, better than Anni. I'll bet a hundred kroner on it.

And here comes the world's angriest old woman, Aunt Selma, Grandma's eighty-two-year-old little sister, wearing a long dress with red flowers and red high heels, her thin, white baby-hair done up for the occasion. Usually her little white wisps of hair stick straight up from her head, making her look as batty as she really is. Ice-cold, pale blue eyes, a crooked nose, witchy hands, lopsided hips, thick ankles. One detail about Selma's face: It's impossible not to notice the soft, sensual skin around her mouth; her lips are full, naturally red, and as kissable as a young girl's.

When Grandma died, Aunt Selma opened a bottle of cognac to celebrate; she wasted no time telling everyone who came to the funeral that it was an exceptionally good bottle of cognac, nine hundred and fifty kroner, she would add. Grandma and Selma couldn't stand the sight of each other; it had to do with something that happened in Brooklyn a long time ago, before the war, when they were both young and living in America.

When it comes right down to it, Selma can't stand the sight of anyone. She thinks people are contemptible, weak, stupid, ridiculous, petty—but she's not some kind of morose misanthrope. On the contrary. It's rage that keeps her alive. Selma laughs louder and longer and more maliciously than anyone else in the family. She smokes forty cigarettes a day and can drink anybody under the table. When she's drunk she howls like no eighty-two-year-old would ever howl, and she makes long speeches about foreign countries she's been to. She never passes up a chance to yell at Anni, who she *really* can't stand the sight of.

Hi, Aunt Selma, I say, and can't help snickering because I know what's coming next.

Hi, Aunt Selma, says Anni.

Don't talk to me, Anni, says Aunt Selma.

She lights a cigarette, grips Anni by the arm with her dazzling white claw of a hand, and whispers into her ear: Have you looked at yourself in the mirror lately, Anni? Do you know that the older you get, the more repulsive you look? You're not one of those who ages gracefully, Anni. Admit that it's over, girl. Over!

Yes, Selma thrives on her hatred, her contempt, her sarcastic remarks. She enjoys it. She enjoys her role as the witch in the gingerbread house, the wolf in the bed, the troll in the mountain. BOO! says Aunt Selma. Are you scared yet?

Selma peers into the dim light of the church.

Oh look, there's Fritz and Edel, she shouts suddenly, stubbing out her cigarette and hobbling into the church.

Fritz and Edel have sat down in the third row, sitting close together like two eggs in an egg carton. Edel cautiously turns around, sees Selma come hobbling up the aisle, sees the shadow of her little, lopsided body, a glimpse of her face, an expectant, wide, and mean-spirited smile on her face. Edel sees it and knows what's coming, she slips her hand into her son's hand. Fritz sits motionless and stares at the floor, hunching his shoulders up around his ears. Selma enjoys this, enjoys the fact that everyone is afraid of her, enjoys hobbling right up to Edel and Fritz in the third row, enjoys giving Fritz a chummy pat on the shoulder, saying that if you throw up on me today, I'm going to throw up on you too.

They arrive one after the other, all dressed up and happy, coming to celebrate Julie and Aleksander's wedding. Here comes Else, Anni's sister, along with her husband and their four grown-up children. Else has a face like a bird. She has a loud voice and laughs a lot. She's come with her family all the way from Wisconsin. *Beautiful, beautiful, what a beautiful day for a wedding,* is what I hear. They disappear into the church in a rush of sloppy kisses, laughter, potent perfume.

A moment later Julie's maid of honor, Val Bryn, arrives. At every wedding, in every story, in every family there's always a young woman who's more like a siren than a human being. Val Bryn is that kind of young woman. Pretty, with long hair, and so sweet that you just want to eat her with whipped cream.

And there's something about her voice.

She can say how do you do and hello and nice weather and how are you, but what's she's really saying is something altogether different. Her voice has a dark resonance to it, a kind of music, a merry promise of good things to come.

What she's actually saying is: If you stick with me—and you're the special one I've chosen—exciting and wonderful things will happen in your life.

First she greets Anni, then me.

A kiss on the cheek for each of us.

No, Anni whispers as Val Bryn disappears into the church, no, no, no, I don't trust that girl.

And then Aleksander's mother and father arrive. They're coming up the steps. Aleksander's mother is wearing her *bunad,* the traditional Norwegian national costume, and Aleksander's father is wearing a dark suit.

Hello, hello, says Anni.

Hello, I say.

Let me introduce Hannah and Harald: parents of the impeccable Aleksander. They're both short, both thin, both old, they have the same rosy red cheeks, the same kind blue eyes, and the same short, glossy white hair. Anni smiles, I smile. Hannah says it's a lovely day for a wedding—and of course no one can disagree with her about that.

It certainly is a lovely day, says Anni, raising her eyes to the sun.

Everyone else raises their eyes to look at the sun too.

Yes sir, says Harald thoughtfully, the sun sure is bright today, isn't it?

Yes, says Anni.

Everyone looks at her.

I think it's a lovely day for a wedding, says Hannah again.

Darn right it's a lovely day for a wedding, shouts Aleksander's brother Arvid, who comes panting up the church steps with his wife Torild and their three pale children in tow.

Let me introduce Arvid and Torild: two unhappy, infuriated people who wonder why they got married twenty years ago, right after high school, why they stayed married when Arvid fell in love with a girl named Karoline sixteen years ago, and why they're still married today when all that's left is so pure: pure hatred, pure dread, pure contempt, pure despair.

I page back to a dinner party right before the wedding. *A dinner party for Julie and Aleksander's closest family members,* said Torild, *so we can all get to know each other a little better.* Torild invited Julie, me, Aleksander, Aleksander's parents, Anni, and Father, but Father didn't come. The dinner was eaten, the wine drunk; and I haven't had a better roast lamb in a long time, sighed Anni with satisfaction. Afterwards they served coffee, cheesecake, layer cake, napoleons, port, and cognac in the living room.

Two sliding doors separated the dining room from the living room, the sliding doors were closed almost all the way except for a tiny crack in the middle. I was sitting so that I could see Arvid and Torild through the crack: Arvid was sitting all alone at the littered table in the dining room, sitting alone and fiddling with his whisky glass. Torild was clearing off the table while she waited for the coffee to brew. Arvid ran one hand over his stomach and tried to grab hold of Torild with the other. I feel so good, he said sadly. I feel so good. He gulped down the rest of his whisky. Want to fuck, Torild?

*Shhh,* murmured Torild and pointed to the sliding doors.

Hush, shush, you don't have to tell me to hush, whined Arvid, reaching out for her. He lurched in his chair.

*Shhh,* whispered Torild, a little louder this time.

In the living room her mother-in-law Hannah cast an anxious glance toward the crack. Her whole little body tensed, her earlobes turned red. She looked like a chipmunk.

Please, not tonight, murmured Torild, not when we have guests, don't be so pathetic, Arvid.

Don't be so what, my precious? muttered Arvid, pursing his lips for a kiss.

Don't be so *pathetic,* sneered Torild as she picked up the coffee pot and the last plate of cakes.

With a rolling sound she opened and then closed the sliding doors. Torild came into the living room: More cake! she exclaimed, beaming at her guests.

The guests applauded enthusiastically.

And behind the closed doors: The hell if I'm pathetic, whispered Arvid. The hell if I'm pathetic, but you! You're a cunt, he hissed and fell off his chair.

I close my eyes and open them again: At that very moment a man comes around the corner down the street and starts walking toward the church hill. I know it's him. It has to be him. He's the one I want. I've found him. He's the one I'm going to seduce. I look up at Anni, who's standing next to me in the sunshine.

There he is! I say. I didn't mean to say it out loud, but Anni hears me.

There's who? she asks.

Oh, I don't know, I say, confused, and look at the man approaching the church.

Who is it, Karin? asks Anni again. She's so green and elegant standing there.

Nobody, I say.

Anni is standing in the light, I'm standing in the shade. Isn't that just typical, I say, and move closer to her.

————

I remember one time when Anni, Julie, and I were sitting in a train on our way from Trondheim to Oslo. Anni's Swedish boyfriend Bertil Svensson was there too. Bertil Svensson was boyfriend number two after Father. Anni wouldn't have been Anni if during the course of the trip she hadn't looked at her lover and asked him: Are you in love with me?

Yes, of course I am, replied Bertil Svensson sincerely.

Do you know that every man who sees me falls in love with me? All I have to do is give them a little look, said Anni, making her eyes wide.

Bertil Svensson looked at Anni.

Well well, that was quite a nice look, he said.

Julie sighed, I stared at Anni, the train rolled on.

Just wait, I'll show you, said Anni. The next man who comes in and sits down in this compartment, regardless of who he is, will fall in love with me. I swear it.

Well well, repeated Bertil Svensson and closed his eyes.

The train rolled on.

The door to the compartment was shoved aside and a plump, sweaty little man with plastered-down hair came into the compartment, looked around anxiously, and sat down right across from me. He was out of breath and red in the face, his whole body looked like it was one big apology.

The man didn't look at any of us, I don't think he dared. I heard only his despondent breathing behind the pages of his *Evening Post*. Did he realize even then that he was a tiny creature that Anni was about to devour?

Anni stood up, changed places with me, and sat down right across from him. She cleared her throat. The man looked up, and Anni smiled at him.

On Jacob Aall Street we could have compiled a whole dictionary of words describing Anni's tears. It wasn't the same way with Anni's smile. Anni has only one smile and when she smiles men die. It was her father's smile, Rikard Blom's.

Anni smiled at the man on the train and the man tried to smile back before he ducked behind his newspaper again.

Anni cleared her throat a second time. The man tried to hide his whole body behind his *Evening Post*.

Anni cleared her throat a third time and went so far as to touch his foot with her own. The man gave a start and looked at Anni. She smiled at him. The man blushed and looked around the compartment. Julie, Bertil Svensson, and I pretended nothing was happening. The train rolled on.

The man looked at Anni, she smiled at him. He looked up at the ceiling, then at Anni—she smiled at him. He looked down at his newspaper, looked at Anni—she smiled at him. He looked at the door, looked at Anni—she smiled at him. He looked out the window, looked at Anni—but this time she didn't smile at him. Anni didn't look at him. Anni looked out the window. The man looked and looked at Anni, but she didn't look at him. The man collapsed behind his *Evening Post*, yes, he literally collapsed behind his *Evening Post*. (What did you think? Did you think this marvelous woman would drop everything and leave the train with you? Did you really think that?)

Anni let him wait. The train rolled on. She let him wait for a long time. But then she did it. She turned her head. The light from the window followed her. Anni turned her head and the light from the window followed her. The man looked up from his newspaper in disbelief, looked at Anni, saw that Anni was smiling. Anni smiled. Anni looked at the man and smiled. But it was more than that. It wasn't only that she was looking at him and smiling, she looked through him, saw all of him, saw him the way no one had ever seen him before, and he didn't blush. He didn't try to hide. He put his newspaper aside. He smiled back. He opened his lips to say something. Now he would tell her everything. He would tell her everything about himself. He would share everything with this woman, this empress, this angel on the train. He opened his lips to say something.

Julie saw it. I saw it. Bertil Svensson saw it. It was impossible not to see it: this plump, little man with the parted lips who had fallen in love on the train from Trondheim to Oslo. Anni nodded as if to say well, there you have it, it's a snap for me, just a little look, just a little smile, and it's done. The man opened his lips to say something, but Anni was finished with him. Anni wasn't smiling anymore. Anni paid no attention to him. He no longer existed. You no longer exist. It's as simple as that, you no longer exist.

Anni took out a hairbrush from her bag and brushed her golden hair, over and over and over again she brushed her golden hair with long, calm strokes, and the train rolled on.

I don't know who he is, he's coming closer, is he a friend of Aleksander's, a relative? His face tells me nothing. I see that he has a blonde woman at his side and he's carrying a little child, a little girl. That can't be helped. He's the one I want. He could be anybody, the man on the corner, the man in the car driving past, the man in the café, the man in the window. Thirty years old. Forty. Maybe thirty-five. His face tells me nothing about who he is. But if you look at him closely, and I'm look-ing at him closely, there's something about his face—the taut skin across his cheekbones, his chin, and those big blue-green eyes—that tells me everything about how he looked as a child, and everything about how he's going to look as an old man. He's coming closer. The blonde woman takes his hand, says something and laughs. She shifts her glance to the little girl he's carrying, takes out a lemon-yellow handkerchief and wipes off something around the child's nose and mouth. She smiles at the child, she pats the child gently on the cheek, and the little girl opens her mouth and laughs with her whole face. I see that she has two baby teeth on top. The man kisses the woman on the forehead. The man kisses the little girl on the fingertips. He's coming closer. He walks up the church steps. He and the woman get ready to greet Anni.

How do you do, says Anni.

How do you do, says the man and puts out his hand. He says his name is Aaron. He says he's the bridegroom's childhood friend. He introduces the woman and the child.

Anni smiles at the child and tries to stroke her hair, but she turns away. The grown-ups laugh, the way grown-ups always laugh at children who protect their integrity when meeting strangers. I put out my hand and offer a greeting. The man doesn't pay any attention to me. The blonde woman takes my hand and says hi, her smile is friendly but her gaze wavers. I don't interest her. In the next instant she's forgotten all about me. I say that I'm the bride's sister. The blonde woman says oh yes, how nice, and isn't it a lovely day for a wedding, you never know about August, it could be quite cold and rainy. She laughs sweetly.

I certainly agree with you about that, I say in a low voice and force her to look at me again, you really never do know about August, it could suddenly begin to rain, and then it rains and rains and rains, and what are you supposed to do then? What do you think? Do you cancel the wedding? Do you say to hell with everything? It's raining!

The blonde woman gives me a strange look and says, oh, I didn't mean anything in particular, I was just trying to make conversation. I don't know many people here.

The man glances over at us, smiles broadly, but he doesn't pay any attention to me. *He still isn't paying any attention to me.* But I'll show him. I don't know exactly how yet. I can see this is going to be more difficult than I thought. In contrast to Anni, I'm not irresistible. I don't have Anni's eyes. I know that. I open my eyes wide and look at the man, look at him the way Anni looks at men, but nothing happens. Nothing. Zero. Nada. In his eyes I'm just some twenty-year-old girl standing on the church steps with her mother. Nothing more, and I'm going to have to do something about that. He has no choice. I've made up my mind. This is the man I want, and I want him now, tonight, before the wedding banquet is over.

Father and I once saw a film by the French director Eric Rohmer called *Chloe in the Afternoon*. Father and I often go to the movies. We feel more comfortable in a movie theater than anywhere else. Every week he waits for me outside the Saga or Klingenberg or Gimle or Frogner or Eldorado or Cinematek. By then he has already bought the tickets and two milk chocolate bars, one for me and one for himself. I remember one evening I was running down Bygdøy Allé to meet him outside the Frogner Theater, it was winter, the sky was dark, the streetlights were on, and I was late. Father was standing outside the movie theater wearing his worn-out, oversized coat and smoking one last cigarette. When he turned around and saw me come running, he threw out his arms and shouted: Welcome to the temple of the escapists.

*Chloe in the Afternoon* is about a married man who loves his wife. Even so, he starts meeting a woman he used to know slightly in the past. The other woman falls in love with him and tries to seduce him but doesn't succeed. They always meet in the afternoon. The man is a lawyer in Paris, but doesn't have a lot to do in the office. The firm's two female secretaries, two pretty young things who keep track of everything the man does, handle the telephones and take messages.

The man's wife is lovely, there's nothing wrong with her or with their marriage. The other woman is pretty too, but in a whole different way. The other woman has a much more assertive presence in the picture, more chaotic, more direct, more open about her sorrow and her desire.

What should the man do? Should he indulge himself and make love to the other woman, thereby betraying his wife, or should he resist temptation and rejoice over his faithfulness and his own spotless conscience?

On our way out of the theater my father threw on his coat and said that if it had been him, he wouldn't have said no to the other woman. Not because she was pretty, but because she had refused to give up.

It's impossible to say no to women who refuse to give up, said Father.

Were you unfaithful to Anni? I asked.

I'm going to give you a piece of good advice when it comes to infidelity, Karin, said Father. You'll appreciate this advice when you're grown up. Don't forget that it was me, your father who loves you, who taught you this. I want to make a contribution to your upbringing with this advice.

What's the advice, Father?

The advice is: Never admit to being unfaithful! If you're confronted with accusations, reproaches, suspicions, hard evidence—never admit to it! That's when you have to lie as if your life depends on it, and then most likely it does.

The man in the Rohmer film didn't want to lie, that was the whole point, I said.

But that was just a movie, said Father, and Rohmer is a Catholic moralist. Ask Anni. If she's in the proper mood, she'll tell you I'm right.

We kept walking, past the cab stand on Thomas Heftye Square, toward the bus stop on the corner of Bygdøy Allé and Hafrsfjord Street. Puffs of cold air rolled out of our mouths.

Well, maybe not, he said. She'd never tell her children that it's good to lie. I don't think Anni herself knows how many lies she tells in the course of a day. She believes them herself. Anni is the most sincere hypocrite I know.

Do you still love Anni? I asked.

When something is over, then it's over, said Father, it's behind you. That's true about love too. I love you and Julie, that will have to do. A human heart isn't any bigger than this, said Father, taking his hand out of his pocket and showing me his clenched right fist. The knuckles were white.

You shouldn't ask for too much, he said.

———

The wedding is going to start soon, and the man I've chosen, the man I'm going to seduce before the day's over, he's not paying any attention to me. He hasn't even glanced at me once. He's not making it easy for himself. And he's not making it easy for me either.

I'm thinking about a scene in the movie *Chloe in the Afternoon*: The married man is sitting on the Métro and thinking about beautiful women. He's thinking that almost all the women he sees are beautiful. All the women he sees have something special about them. (The camera zooms in on one woman's face after another on the Métro.) Every single woman possesses something mysterious, he thinks, something only that woman has, something different, something that can't be found in any other woman.

Later in the day the man is sitting in a café in the middle of Paris. He's still thinking about beautiful women. Sometimes, the man thinks, he wishes he had a little medallion around his neck that had the power to make it impossible for women to refuse him. If he went up to a total stranger on the street and asked her: Will you come with me? Well, then she could only nod, let go of whatever she was holding, even her husband, and come with him.

That's the kind of medallion I wish I had now. Then the man I'm going to seduce today wouldn't have a thing to say about it. He'd have to drop everything and come with me.

I turn around and watch him go: He's on his way up the church aisle with his blond-haired woman and his little child in his arms, and the situation doesn't look promising. My head prickles, my eyes are running, it's hot. My red dress is scratchy on the inside. Anni takes my hand and says: It's time for us to take our places, Karin. Julie and Father will be here soon. It's ten minutes to twelve, and the wedding starts at twelve sharp.

Julie and I were alike when we were children. Not so much in appearance, she was tall, thin, blonde, and dreamy with broad, stooped shoulders. I was short, thin, and dark. And yet I always stood up straight. Always!

No, Julie and I were alike in other ways. We had the same easy laugh, we liked the same secret games, we read the same books. The age difference of three years didn't bother Julie, she'd rather spend time with me than with children her own age. When she turned seventeen everything changed, of course. Then she wasn't interested in anything.

The biggest difference between Julie and me was that I lied and she didn't. For instance, if I felt like I was about to fall over, I'd tell myself: I'm not falling. And then I wouldn't.

I've always lied, ever since I was little, and long before Father told me that in some situations it was all right to lie as if your life depended on it. I've always lied as if my life depended on it. It was easier that way. And more fun. I didn't see it as a problem. I was fully aware that I was lying, I did it on purpose, still do it on purpose, and even though everyone but Father said it was wrong to lie, nobody could tell me why. Only that it was wrong. But as long as I knew that I was lying—and that was of course a given—then no one was hurt by it.

There are many ways to lie. The first time I thought about

my lies as being lies, I was eleven years old, a year after Father got in his car and drove away from the apartment on Jacob Aall Street to the apartment in Tøyen.

Anni had a little short-haired, light-brown dachshund that she loved, truly loved, there was a love between Anni and the dachshund that astounded many of her lovers. I think the dachshund reminded her of Father. Or rather: I think it reminded her of the years she lived with Father. The years when she, by her own admission, was *truly happy*. Father bought the dachshund from a kennel outside Oslo and gave it to Anni.

Here, he said, here's a dachshund for you. I love you, Anni. The dachshund is proof of my eternal love for you.

I hated the dachshund. It barked all the time, it slept in Anni's bed, it licked Anni's face; it was called Pete, named after the Norwegian boxer Pete Sanstøl, Grandfather's great hero.

One day Julie was out walking Pete. Three times a day Pete had to be walked, this was Julie's chore and mine. Every time we came home from one of these walks, Anni would yell from the kitchen or the living room or her bedroom: Kaaaaarin! Juuuulie! Did Pete do her duty, number one and number two? If we replied truthfully that no, maybe Pete would do it later, but Pete hadn't done it yet, then we had to turn right around and go back out. It might be raining, it might be snowing, it might be thundering, it might be hailing: Pete had to go out. Pete had to be walked. And Pete had to do number one and number two.

I don't think even Pete appreciated how much we did for her. She was way too fat, her belly swept the ground, which meant that she had problems with her long, sausagelike back. She hated getting water on her coat or her paws and always resisted if it was raining or there were puddles on the sidewalk: Then she would dig her disproportionately tiny legs into the ground, lay her ears back, clamp the leash in her jaws, and look up at us with her big, oval, chocolate-brown eyes, which Anni said were *utterly human*.

I was eleven when I realized the situation was intolerable. I realized it one icy-cold January afternoon as I walked through the streets of Majorstua with a reluctant, squeaking, resisting Pete who wouldn't do what she was supposed to do, neither number one nor number two. I was freezing, and if there's one thing I can't stand, it's being cold. That's when I decided to lie. Instead of going up the four flights to our apartment on Jacob Aall Street and saying no, it was no good that day, Pete wouldn't do it, I went up the four flights to our apartment and said: Pete did it all, Mother, several times, in fact!

It was an odd feeling to be eleven and discover that it paid to lie. Instead of being sent down the stairs and back out onto the street, Anni drew me into the warmth and light and said: Good girl, my Karin.

I told Julie about it. I said all you have to do is tell Anni what she *wants* to hear, it doesn't really matter whether it's true or not. I said you have to try it too, but Julie just stared at me and said I can't very well do that.

The next day it was Julie's turn to go out with Pete. I watched them leave the building, walk up Jacob Aall Street and over to Suhm Street: Julie in her too-tight shoes and Pete on her too-short legs, and it was such a pitiful sight. It was so pitiful and cold and awful and I got so mad at Anni for forcing us to go through this every day that I ran into her room and told her that I'd killed Pete. I said I'd crushed her skull with a rock and thrown her into Oslo Fjord. Anni stood motionless in front of me, motionless and gaping—it's the only time in my life that I've ever seen Anni gape—and then she grabbed hold of me. You goddamn little brat, what are you standing there telling me? she yelled. Anni grabbed hold of me and shook me so hard I got dizzy. After she'd given me a good shake I started to cry and said I didn't really kill Pete, don't you know that?

Anni let me go. Anni stood motionless.

Then she started shaking me some more.

That's not the point, she screamed, the point is that you're a naughty, lying little girl. She stopped for a minute, got control of her voice, which was all over the room. Then she whispered: Karin, I love you because I'm your mother, but I don't particularly *like* you very much.

That day I understood the difference between a lie that paid (that Pete had done number one and number two) and a lie that didn't pay (that I had killed Pete with a rock and thrown her into Oslo Fjord). A lie that had to be taken back and replaced with the truth was a useless lie that didn't pay. But a lie that didn't have to be taken back, that might, with time, be replaced by a new lie, but never—never!—with the truth, that was a lie that paid.

Since I had now learned the difference between a lie that paid and a lie that didn't, I decided to lie as much as possible for the rest of my life. And that's how it turned out.

The verger opens and closes the church doors, the organist lifts her hands, the congregation rises, the minister folds his hands, and everyone fixes their eyes on the aisle of the church. No one looks at the groom now, no one looks at Aleksander, who is standing up near the altar and wiping away an invisible drop of sweat from under one spectacled eye. Or at the best man, Terje Nedtun, or at the maid of honor, Val Bryn. No, no one is looking at them now. Everyone's eyes are fixed on the aisle of the church, because there she comes: Julie, my Julie. Arm in arm with Father she glides—yes, she glides!—toward the altar. She lifts her head, she's the only one in the church who's looking straight ahead, she's looking at the groom, looking at Aleksander standing up near the altar, waiting for her.

I can't bear to take her all in, all of Julie, at one time. The bridal scene comes to me in a succession of rapidly edited close-ups: the tiny white flowers in her hair, the long, pearl-embroidered, cream-colored, and much too princesslike silk gown, the endless long veil.

Julie is walking on Father's right, she's gripping his arm tight, she wants him to walk slower; Father would prefer to run up the aisle and be done with it. That's how it looks from where I'm standing, at any rate. He doesn't feel comfortable in his black tux with a red flower in his buttonhole and a bow tie around his neck. I know that. I know he misses his regular coat, his whisky glass, and his pack of cigarettes, but he's doing this for Julie, he's playing the role of the bride's father and slows his step. Now he looks almost dignified as he walks up the aisle of the church, and as they near the altar Julie lays her head on his shoulder and closes her eyes. Not for long, only for a moment, and I can see Father looking down at Julie. If her hair hadn't been adorned with flowers, he would have stroked it like when she was little. Julie opens her eyes and lifts her head. Both of them seem to rise to the occasion to walk the last stretch up the aisle of the church. Father looks at Aleksander, catches his eye, gives him a long look, and Aleksander isn't used to being looked at in that way, he knows that something is expected of him, but he's not entirely sure what. He smiles at Father, and Father looks as if he's thinking: That was a friendly smile—it wasn't exactly the kind of smile I wanted for Julie, I guess I wanted more . . . *courage,* but it was a friendly smile, and you can't ask for too much.

With one last look at Aleksander he lets go of Julie's arm, he even makes an elegant little gesture with his hand, as if to say: I now give her to you.

Julie and Aleksander sit down on the tall gilded chairs across from each other, next to the maid of honor and best man. Everybody in the church sits down. The wedding guests sing "Lovely Is the Earth," and the minister turns to face the congregation and says: In the name of the Father, the Son, and the Holy Ghost. Val Bryn cautiously gets up to straighten out Julie's veil. The light from one of the stained-glass windows falls on the pulpit, a child in one of the last pews says oops look at that, someone laughs softly, the minister spreads out his arms and says: Dearly beloved. Julie raises her eyes and looks at Aleksander. He's fidgeting with something in his hands, it looks like a stem or a twig that he plucked from somewhere outside. The minister says: God has created us to live in communion with Him and with one another. He has arranged it so that man and woman shall be one, and He has confirmed this fellowship with His blessing. Marriage is God's magnificent gift. In this way our will is tested to share joys and sorrows, to give and receive, to understand and forgive. In this way man and woman shall grow closer to each other and reach out in faith and hope toward all that God has to give.

The congregation is silent.

The best man, Terje Nedtun, raises his hand to his mouth and coughs cautiously. A woman I don't know rummages through her purse and smiles at the man sitting next to her as he offers her a cough drop. Aunt Selma stares at the ceiling and seems to be thinking of something funny. I turn around and catch sight of the man I'm going to seduce. He's sitting several pews behind me, with his gaze fixed on the minister and holding the blonde woman's hand. I try to catch his eye, but he pays no attention to me.

The minister says: According to the Word of God marriage is sacred and inviolable.

It is written in the first book of the Old Testament: God created man in His own image, in the image of God created He him; male and female created He them. And God blessed them, and God said unto them, Be fruitful and multiply, and replenish the earth, and subdue it.

Val Bryn raises her eyes and smiles at Terje Nedtun. I turn around to see if Terje Nedtun's wife saw it. Val Bryn's smile could not be misinterpreted. It was an Anni-smile. Terje Nedtun's dark-haired wife is sitting way back in the church and whispering something in a little girl's ear, and the little girl whispers something in her ear, and they both laugh. It looks like they're playing some sort of game.

The minister says: And our Lord Jesus Christ says: Have ye not read, that He which made them at the beginning made them male and female, And God said, For this cause shall a man leave father and mother, and shall cleave to his wife: and they twain shall be one flesh? Wherefore they have no more twain, but one flesh. They are one. What therefore God hath joined together, let not man put asunder.

The minister takes a step back and lowers his gaze. He gestures for the next person to come forward. Torild gets up from her seat and walks up the aisle and sits down at the piano to the right of the altar. She clears her throat softly and says that this song may not be totally appropriate for a wedding, but I think it's a nice song. To me it tells us that we shouldn't laugh at love; love won't stand for that, I don't think. Torild blushes and looks down at the keys. Then she lifts her hands, plays the first chord, and begins to sing. Torild in her blue dress. Torild with her sad, thin, quiet song. It's as if someone has put a plunger down her throat and sucked out most of her voice. But she has a little left, only a little, and Torild sings Nat King Cole's "This Will Make You Laugh."

Julie looks down at the floor and bites her lip. Aleksander smiles more than he really should, and Torild sings:

> *This will make you laugh*
> *I staked my dreams on you*
> *This will make you laugh*
> *They never did come true*
> *I took a chance on the one romance*
> *and vowed it couldn't miss*
> *But I should have known*
> *to never judge*
> *a heart by a kiss.*

Arvid told a story the evening that Anni, Julie, and I had dinner with Torild and him at their house. He told the story about back in the late sixties when Torild and Arvid were going to Nissen High School, and Torild was the sweetest and funniest and bluesiest girl in the city. He actually said bluesiest. He said

41

that he knew he was in love with her when she rose to her feet and sang for him. They were at a late-night party somewhere in Asker, it was a warm summer night, and all the other guests were out in the garden. It was the first real warm summer night of the year, Arvid told us: We were eighteen and finished with high school and suddenly Torild rose to her feet and said to me, Now you sit right there, Arvid, and I'm going to sing for you. And Torild rose to her feet, Torild smiled, Torild sang.

Arvid chuckled and took a gulp of his whisky.

Torild blushed when he told the story, and it could very well have ended there, but Anni couldn't let it end there. Anni couldn't let it rest. Anni never knows when enough is enough. Anni looked at both of them and smiled tenderly. Anni put her arm around Arvid's shoulders and gave him a hug. Anni practically shed a tear. Anni raised her glass and said: I want us to drink a toast to Arvid and Torild. I want us to drink a toast to the upcoming wedding. I want us to—and here Anni looked each and every one of us in the eye and smiled warmly—I want us to drink a toast to Love.

Everyone drank a toast without really wanting to.

Then silence.

Arvid didn't say a word. He looked at Anni. He looked at his wife and he looked at Anni. Then he started to laugh. Arvid laughed and said: What I didn't fathom that night was that I was so damned drunk I could have fallen in love with anybody. Anybody—it made no difference, don't you see? he said. *You sounded better with every beer I drank, darling*, he added, and raised his glass to Torild.

I think at last she's done, and no one applauds, but I guess that's okay, of course; we're in church. The minister steps forward again, and makes a little gesture with his hand to signal the congregation to rise.

Everyone stands up.

The minister makes a new gesture with his hand to signal

the happy couple to step forward. Julie and Aleksander stand up and walk to the altar.

Julie turns to face Aleksander and smiles. Aleksander stares at the minister, looking as if he's wondering whether there are more instructions he doesn't know about yet.

The minister looks at both of them, the minister smiles, the minister is the kind of minister who never feels indifference, not when it comes to precisely this moment, when two people are about to give themselves to each other in love.

The minister says: Before God, our Creator, and in the presence of these witnesses, I ask you, Aleksander Lange Bakke: Do you take Julie Blom, who is standing beside you, to be your wife?

Aleksander looks at the minister. I do, he says. Not very loudly, but not particularly softly either. But that's the way Aleksander is, I think. The minister says: Will you love and honor her and remain faithful to her until death do you part?

Yes, says Aleksander.

The minister says: And I ask you, Julie Blom: Do you take Aleksander Lange Bakke, who is standing beside you, to be your husband?

Julie turns to face Aleksander, Aleksander looks at the minister, and Julie says I do.

The minister says: Will you love and honor him and remain faithful to him, in good times and bad, until death do you part?

Yes.

The congregation is silent.

The minister says: Then you may now give each other the traditional handshake.

Aleksander and Julie turn to face each other and shake hands.

How should I describe the minister?

The minister is not an indifferent man. The minister is a good minister, but he can't suppress the actor, the showman, the dramatist, the storyteller in himself. He can't resist making a deliberate little pause at just this moment, right before he delivers the words of redemption. A deliberate pause is the secret of every successful performance; the minister knows that. The deliberate pause emphasizes the very drama of the situation; he knows that too. He looks out at the congregation and takes in the silence, the tension in the nave, the fact that everyone is waiting for his next words. It's a good feeling, thinks the minister.

Everyone is silent. The bride and groom are silent. The wedding guests are silent. Even the children are silent. A light falls on Aleksander and Julie in front of the altar.

The minister makes a deliberate little pause and looks out at the congregation. He doesn't say a word.

What in the world is the minister doing? What is he waiting for?

*I'm waiting for all of you to understand what I'm actually doing standing here. I'm waiting for you to understand.*

Understand what?

The seriousness, perhaps. Yes, that's right: the seriousness.

But dear minister, I say and stand up from the church pew. You're an intelligent and old man, I'm sure you've seen a little of everything and you've been around a lot longer than I have. How can you still take this so seriously, how can you expect *us* to take it seriously? Everyone here knows what happens to married couples. They shred each other to pieces or they torment each other with silence. I don't know if it's worth it.

What are you talking about? replies the minister. Are you talking about what things are worth? Aren't you a little young to be so cynical?

I'm not cynical, just smart, I say. I'm not like my sister. Blindly in love with some impeccable man, a man who doesn't know her inside and out. I'm not like my mother, I don't thrive on being seen and loved and adored at all times. That's not me. I'll play my cards better than that.

The minister chuckles: It doesn't look as if it's going very well with that man you're thinking of seducing today. He's not paying any attention to you. Have you noticed that?

Forget about it, I say. I don't have a lot of practice yet. Just wait, I'll work it out. Maybe I'm not as irresistible as Anni or as captivating as Julie, but I'm a much better tactician. And besides, I can sing. He'll be mine before the evening's over.

Love's little Machiavelli, snickers the minister.

You haven't answered my question, I say. How can you keep standing there marrying people, and even expect it to be taken seriously, when you know how much grief and unhappiness and disappointment are going to follow?

When I listen to you, says the minister, and then he stops for a moment. When I listen to you I think that you talk like a child, think like a child, dream like a child, and that one day something will shatter inside you, and only then will you no longer be a child.

You're not answering my question, I say.

There's a voice inside you that can't lie, Karin, that doesn't weigh the consequences. The minister lowers his voice. Look at Julie's face, he whispers, look at her, don't look at me, look at her. What you see is hope. Do you know what hope is, Karin? Or are the little lines around your mouth—quite unusual for a twenty-year-old—a sign of indifference? In that case, I feel sorry for you. Let me tell you something, says the minister: If the time comes when Julie and Aleksander aren't strong enough to love each other anymore—people's ability to love each other is fragile, you know—then I'll tell them that love is greater than any individual person's ability to love, because love comes from God, and God's love is eternal.

I look at the minister standing there and taking his deliberate little pause. He's done this before, I think, he likes standing in front of the congregation and listening to the silence in the church, looking at the faces, knowing that everyone is waiting for his next words.

Can he say them yet?

Yes, now he can say them. Now he can say them.

The minister first smiles at Julie, then at Aleksander.

The minister says: Before God and in the presence of these witnesses you have promised each other to live together in marriage and you have shaken hands, according to tradition. Therefore I now pronounce you husband and wife.

The minister says: Now give each other the rings, which will be a sign of your vow of faithfulness.

Julie and Aleksander exchange rings.

Julie places her hands on either side of Aleksander's face. Aleksander bends down and kisses her.

At precisely that moment someone snaps a picture.

There's still plenty of time left before the gong sounds and Anni invites everyone to the table: Some of the guests are frolicking under the huge, clinking chandelier in the foyer, some are on their way out to the garden, others are surveying the long, festively decked table in the dining room to find out where they're going to sit. The little red place cards are all lined up, Anni and Julie have decided who's going to sit where. Some people are waiting in line for the bathroom, some are sitting and talking on the purple chaise longue in the hallway, some are roaming from group to group, smiling, saying hi, how are you, hello, let me introduce myself. Ingeborg has let Anni borrow her house, this is where the wedding banquet will be held, in a big white wooden villa built in the 1800s. Red velvet drapes on either side of each tall window, pale red wallpaper in the rooms, thick old carpets in red, lavender, and gold. Ingeborg is Father's companion, but they don't live together. He doesn't want to live in Ingeborg's big house. He wants to live in Tøyen.

Anni is standing out in the kitchen, crying because the cook she hired for the occasion has forgotten that she asked for sugar peas; and I refuse to serve roast veal without sugar peas, she whimpers.

Julie and Val Bryn are whispering together in a corner of the living room. Julie waves to me and her face is hot and flushed and her wedding dress is already slightly wrinkled. Father is sitting on a chair in the corner and he shuts his eyes and drinks whisky and says: Karin, how about if you and I get away from all this and go to the movies instead? Just a minute, I say, I'll be right back and then we can talk. Somewhere far away I hear Arvid's roaring laughter. And in the living room Terje Nedtun lifts his daughter high up in the air and twirls her around and around and around under the crystal chandelier. Uncle Fritz has sat down on a spindle-back chair and is staring straight ahead with his mouth open and his eyes half-closed.

Hi, Uncle Fritz, I say.

Oh boy, says Uncle Fritz.

Hi, Aunt Edel, I say.

Oh Karin, she whispers and waves me over. I've lost a tooth.

What did you say, Aunt Edel?

I've lost a tooth, she says, clutching a red cocktail napkin.

Which tooth? I ask.

My front tooth, she says, cautiously opening her mouth to show me.

I peer inside her mouth. A black hole where the tooth should have been.

Is there anything I can do for you? I ask.

Edel presses her lips together and shakes her head.

Do you want someone to take you home?

Edel shakes her head.

Do you think they can put it back, or do I have to get a new tooth? she asks.

I don't know, I say.

I'm keeping it here just in case, she says, showing me the crumpled cocktail napkin.

You do that, I say and move on.

Out in the kitchen Anni is still crying, the cook is threatening to quit, and Ingeborg is trying to calm both of them down. Anni and Ingeborg don't like each other much, but they tolerate each other, and occasionally they meet at a pastry shop. Ingeborg is Anni's only connection to Father. What Ingeborg gets out of their peculiar friendship I have no idea.

Brussels sprouts are actually better than sugar peas, Ingeborg says in a way that only Ingeborg can. It's hard to have doubts or objections whenever Ingeborg makes a pronouncement.

I don't know, cries Anni doubtfully, I don't know.

But I do know, says Ingeborg. She gives the cook a smile of acknowledgment and pulls Anni along with her out of the kitchen.

I move on. I'm looking for someone. I'm looking for him. I'm looking for Aaron.

I see the blonde woman first, she's talking to Aleksander, and Aaron is on his way over to them with glasses of champagne. I go up to them. Hello, I say. Hi, says Aleksander. Have you met my friend Aaron?

Yes, I say.

Yes, of course, you're the bride's sister, says Aaron.

Hi again, says the blonde woman uncertainly.

Everyone looks at me. Everyone looks right through me. No one has a thing to say as long as I'm standing there. I'm not welcome. Could you please leave, Karin? You're not welcome. Can't you find someone else to talk to?

I think I'll go and find some champagne, I say.

But aren't you under eighteen? asks Aaron.

I smile at him.

I think that now's the time I should have given him an answer that would really make him notice me. Now's the time I should have said—well, what should I have said? All I managed was an insipid smile.

I get a glass of champagne. I drink a glass of champagne. I get another glass of champagne. Someone turns on the stereo in the living room, someone dims the lights, and suddenly the wedding banquet turns all Ella Fitzgerald.

Someone comes up behind me.

*Hi, Karin.*

I recognize the voice.

I turn around.

It's Val Bryn.

Val Bryn is older than Julie, thirty-one or thirty-two, I think, maybe even older. She asks me if I want to go out to the garden; sure, why not, I say. Let's go, then, she says. It had just rained a little, only a sun shower. There's a fresh smell of grass and summer and ripe apples. Val Bryn takes my hand, we sit down on a bench under an apple tree.

I don't like weddings, she says.

Me neither, I say.

I once met a man at a wedding.

Who was that?

His name was Frank Andersen.

Mmmm, I say, I don't know him.

Frank was weak and quite sentimental, she says, and starts telling the story. Val Bryn has a quality that makes you stay and listen, you feel honored, specially chosen, that she wants to share something with you—anything.

I was quite fond of him, she says. When I met him he was blessed with a beautiful little wife—everybody loved her and said nice things about her, especially that she was so *genuine* . . . her name was Lina.

I had met Frank and Lina a few times before, at other parties, but never really talked to either of them. And I don't know what it was exactly that made me fall in love with Frank, maybe it was because of Lina, the commendable Lina, good Lina, beautiful Lina, genuine Lina. The urge to *obliterate* this lovely creature that everyone said was so beautiful and gifted, and yet so *weak*—you know what I mean?—the urge was so overwhelming that I had to hold onto the wall and close my eyes every time Lina's name was mentioned. I felt like going right up to her, right up to Lina, and *hitting her hard in the face,* says Val Bryn.

At first I didn't really think it was Frank I wanted at all, I just wanted to see if it could be done. I wanted to see if it was possible to destroy . . . I wanted to see if anything was sacred. Yes, that's it! Sacred! she said. Later I grew quite fond of him, but by then it was too late.

So did you find out? Was anything sacred? I ask.

I don't know what to tell you, says Val Bryn, but after eight months of meeting me in secret, he left her.

Congratulations!

(I can picture the whole scene: Frank Andersen standing in the middle of his and Lina's bedroom with his suitcases, two suitcases—one in each hand—declaring that it's all over, I'm leaving for good now, thanks anyway, Lina, but there's nothing I can do, I've met another woman and I can't live without her.

No no no, chirps Lina, you can't just leave like this.

She follows him downstairs, past the kitchen, out to the hallway, out the front door, wearing her nightgown and bathrobe and slippers.

I have enough love inside of me for both of us, she cries. Can't we try a little longer? Just give me a chance. Please don't go, no not like this, don't leave me.

Frank has to stuff both hands in his coat pockets in order to keep from turning around and hitting her as hard as he can. He barely manages to get into the car. Lina says she wants to come with him. He can't just leave like this, she says. He can't.

He shoves her out of the car, but even then she doesn't get the message. She runs after him, in her slippers and bathrobe, runs after the car which is turning onto the street.

But then, finally, when he can't see her anymore, he stomps on the gas pedal, turns up the music, plays the steering wheel like a drum, and races down Sørkedal Road. I'm a free man, Frank thinks.)

All of this conveniently coincides with Frank's planned business trip to Japan, Val Bryn continues. We simply catch the first plane to Tokyo and go to a hotel downtown, the Hotel Okura.

Val Bryn stubs out her cigarette in the grass and lights another one.

Do you want to know what happened before we landed in Tokyo?

Of course.

Somewhere along the way, she says, during the flight, Frank is looking out the window, chewing on a peanut, waiting for the tray of food and more red wine. I'm asleep next to him, or pretending to sleep. The truth is I was pretending to sleep because we suddenly didn't have anything to talk about, and it seems so awkward, you know, when you're madly in love and suddenly have nothing to talk about. Anyway, Frank was looking out the window at the wispy clouds below, the massive plane wing, the white air that was so thin you could drink it, and he was thinking—because he was a man who had just walked out on his family, left, moved on, not looked back, made a decision that would affect him for the rest of his life—he was thinking: Yes! This is heaven! I am a man who is flying through heaven. And that's when God showed His face to him.

What did you just say? I ask.

I said that's when God showed His face to him, says Val Bryn. Or rather: not His whole face, which would be so big that it would be impossible to see it. No, God showed him a tiny portion of His forehead, the corner of His right eye and a smidgen of nostril—which in fact was more than enough to scare the hell out of Frank, who wasn't a particularly religious man, not really, not until that day, not until he thought about himself as a man flying through heaven. And God stared at him through the plane window, pressed the corner of His right eye against the round window and stared at him, and Frank dropped his peanuts to the floor and screamed. *He screamed.*

And at that moment the plane started shaking, because of turbulence, I guess, and I bolted up in my seat and started screaming because Frank was sitting next to me and screaming, and of course the other passengers panicked and started screaming too.

The flight attendants swarmed around us, running up and down the center aisle and shouting hush, hush, it's just a little turbulence, it's completely normal, there's nothing to be scared of, hush, hush, dear people, hush! There was a terrible commotion. The captain was summoned and came into the cabin and ordered everybody to shut up.

But a woman passenger kept on screaming long after the other passengers had calmed down; finally the captain went over to her seat and hit her in the face to make her stop, says Val Bryn. But it did no good. The woman cried all the way to Tokyo.

n a corner of the entryway Aunt Selma is holding court with herself. She's puffing on a cigarette and listening with raised eyebrows to a small child who has ventured into her presence.

You look like a witch, says the child.

That's because I am a witch, says Selma.

But I bet you're not a mean witch, says the child, politely.

Oh yes I am, says Selma.

Mean in what way? asks the child.

My favorite dish is boiled little girl fists and fried little girl ears, she says softly, reaching for the child's throat, and then I like to have a dish of little girl stew to finish things off.

I don't believe you, howls the child and runs away.

Selma rolls her eyes.

Hi, Aunt Selma, I say.

Is that you? she says peevishly.

Can I bum a smoke? I ask.

Aunt Selma hands me her pack of cigarettes and says: I see you're wandering around staring at a man, the guy with the blonde woman.

You can see that? I say.

Your mother is stupid, your sister is stupid, your grand-mother was as stupid as they get, your grandmother was so stupid that she didn't understand anything, but I'm not stupid. Of course I can see.

I'm planning to seduce him, I say.

I see, says Selma, it doesn't look like you're making much progress.

No, I say. Got any advice?

She takes a drag on her cigarette.

You try charm? she asks.

I think so, I say.

You try looking him deep in the eyes?

Yes. He doesn't pay any attention to me.

You try talking to him?

Yes, just a few minutes ago. It didn't go very well.

You try walking right up to him, telling him you want to sleep with him, and the only thing you expect from him is that he makes himself available for about fifteen minutes?

No. But I don't think that would do any good. I don't think he's the type to fall for that.

He's not, huh? she says. It worked fine for me when I was younger. But I was prettier than you, that helped.

You have any other advice?

You try flattery? she says.

Flattery?

Yes, flattery. It's a sure winner, never fails, she says.

Flattery, I say.

Flattery, says Selma.

But how? I ask. What should I flatter him about? I don't know him.

That's the whole point, she says, the less you know a person, the easier it is to flatter him.

But how? I ask.

Selma takes another drag on her cigarette. She chokes on the smoke, turns red in the face, her tongue shoots out of her mouth, her tongue hangs out of her mouth, she doubles over. Selma doubles over and lets out a gurgling squeaking rattling coughing sound that makes everybody in the vicinity turn around, thinking that she's had it, she's dying, it's definitely over, goodbye and thank you, Aunt Selma, we'll never forget you, bon voyage and give them all our best. A cough like that, I think, so old and so rotten that it's been gurgling in her throat ever since she was young and fabulous; a cough that might possibly date back to a cigarette she lit in a New York café, let's say, in October of 1929 when she was tossing back drinks with three of Wall Street's merriest speculators, drinking them under the table, if truth be told, and forcing them to dance with her afterwards, one after the other, and all three at once, in spite of how drunk they were; and no doubt this contributed to the fact that those same three speculators had terrible headaches the next day and couldn't do their jobs properly, and things didn't improve any when the entire stock market collapsed, bringing about the economic crisis in the U.S. and large parts of Europe for the next ten years. Two of the three speculators committed suicide that very evening; their wives blamed Selma.

She's never been what you might call a spreader of joy, I think—and then she stops coughing. Selma stops coughing. She straightens up, lifts her head, opens her eyes, gives everyone a cross-eyed smile, takes another drag on her cigarette, and lets the smoke seep out of her nostrils: You thought I was going to fall this time, didn't you, you thought I was done for, you thought it was all over. But look! I didn't fall, I'm still standing, I didn't fall. Selma laughs and says you just do what I tell you, Karin, and the boy won't have a chance. That boy there, she says, pointing at Aaron with the long yellow nail of her index finger, that boy there can't resist flattery. It's not his desire you need to stroke, but his vanity, and then all the rest will fall into place.

But how? I ask.

Be an actress, Karin! Act!

Selma coughs again, then she grips my shoulder and whispers: Look at him and make him understand that you can see the big secret he's carrying inside his heart.

What big secret?

That's not the point, she says. It's entirely possible that he's not carrying a damn thing inside his heart, in all probability he isn't. The point is, he'd like to *believe* that he is and that *someone can see that he is*. Everybody wants to be more than they actually are, Karin, and if you give that boy over there the impression that you see he's more than he is, that you see he's carrying a big secret inside his heart, that he's special, Karin, that he's different, that he has been kissed by God, well, then it's done, then he's yours.

I sneak into the dining room, find the place card with Aaron's name on it, and put it next to my own. Then I take the other place card and put it at Aaron's original place, a Daniel K. I read on the card, maybe one of Aleksander's friends, I don't know.

All right! Now it's done. Now he'll *have* to talk to me. Now he can't get out of talking to me. Now we'll sit side by side through the whole long wedding dinner and it would be rude of him not to talk to me. He has no choice, that's all there is to it. He has no choice.

I feel a hand on my shoulder.

What are you doing, Karin?

I turn around. It's Father talking to me.

I'm switching place cards. There's someone I want to sit next to, I say.

I see, says Father. Then he says: Can I leave now? I don't want to be at this party anymore.

No, I say.

Anni's whisky isn't any good. Anni never could tell the difference between good whisky and bad.

Whatever you say, I reply.

I like Johnnie Walker, she likes Upper Ten.

Right, I say.

Anni has no taste.

I don't know about that, I say.

I straighten Father's bow tie, a red rose in his buttonhole.

Aaron is sitting alone on the purple couch with a glass in his hand, drinking a gin and tonic with a slice of lemon. On the round marble table in front of the couch there's a bowl of pretzels. Next to Aaron is Uncle Fritz, he also has a glass in his hand. Fritz is drinking something red.

I sit down on the couch between them.

You two are my dinner companions tonight, I beam.

Oh boy, says Uncle Fritz.

How nice, says Aaron and his eyes flit around the room.

His eyes remind me of a bird that strays into a living room.

I turn toward Fritz. What's that you're drinking, Uncle Fritz?

What did you say, Karin? he mumbles.

I asked you what you're drinking, it's red.

Sexy Sunrise, he mutters.

What's that, Fritz?

Sexy Sunrise, he mumbles.

Sure, I say.

Karin, he says, staring into his glass.

Yes, I say.

Mamma just lost a tooth, he says.

I know.

First she loses her teeth, then she loses her ears, then her nose falls off, then her eyes fall out—LOOK! he says. LOOK AT THIS! says Fritz, pointing at the two green olives floating around in his drink. Mamma! he cries, and you know suddenly one day Mamma is . . . dead.

Yes, but that won't happen for a long time, I say.

Karin, he says.

Yes, I say.

I don't feel so good. I feel sick to my stomach.

Then you shouldn't have any more of that drink, I say.

Oh boy, he says.

Fritz huddles on the couch, his body bends forward, his lips open slightly, in one hand he's holding his glass.

Is everything all right with him? asks Aaron in a low voice.

Uncle Fritz, yes. Everything's all right, I say.

I look at Aaron. He looks back.

I lay my head on his shoulder. I know what you're thinking, I say.

Aaron pulls away.

What? he says.

I know what you're thinking, I say.

You do? he says.

I turn toward him, my face close to his face, his breath against my skin: I'm lying, I say. I don't know what you're thinking. I just wanted you to notice me.

Aaron looks at me for a moment longer than he should. Then he laughs a little. I look down. His hands are pale, thin, small, rather hairy but at the same time girlish, and under his right thumbnail a speck of red paint that he hasn't washed off.

One winter night in early January, the year that Julie turned thirteen and I was ten: I'm walking up Jacob Aall Street, my schoolbag is heavy, it's dark. The snow is blowing sideways along the streets, swirling around my face, white, transparent, wet, almost gone.

Then I see them. Outside our building entrance there's a group of children with their hands stretched up to the sky. Standing on the balcony of the fourth floor is Julie, wearing a long red cotton nightgown with long sleeves. Her long blonde hair is blowing in the wind, the snow is encapsulating her; a red girl in her palace of snow, I remember thinking.

The children's faces grow clearer as I approach. They're boys and girls from the neighborhood and from Julie's class.

Julie is standing on the balcony, and with calm, sweeping movements of her hands she tosses all her things over the railing, down to the children in the street. She throws down her old doll, the one with the eyelids, eyelashes, and big blue glass eyes; the doll whirls through the air and falls softly onto the ground, the doll says Ow, and the big blue glass eyes blink. She throws down her red portable radio, all her records, books, dresses, and sweaters; she even throws down the little gold heart she has around her neck, which was a gift from Father.

The children all yell and cheer and run back and forth, gathering up whatever they can.

More, Julie, they shout.

Sweet, sweet Julie, they shout.

More, they shout.

At first I stand motionless and watch. I remember thinking: Now you've got to do something, Karin, now you've got to do something. Julie can't just stand up there on the balcony and toss out everything she owns.

Then I climb the four flights of stairs to our apartment. Three girls and a fat boy with a downy mustache follow me. Up the stairs, through the door, into Julie's room.

The three girls and the boy look around the room.

Hi, says Julie.

Hi, say the children.

One girl looks at the bookshelf and finds Julie's comic book collection.

Are you going to throw these out? asks the girl, pulling the comics off the shelf and starting to leaf through them.

I don't know, says Julie.

Oh please, says the girl.

I don't know, says Julie.

Why not? says the girl.

Well okay, says Julie. Go downstairs and I'll throw them down to you.

Okay, says the girl.

I leave the room, leave the apartment, go down to the street.

Julie is busy throwing things again.

The children run back and forth.

No, I shout.

Stop it, I shout.

Please stop it.

These aren't your things, these are Julie's things, I shout, and then I try to tear a record and a stuffed rabbit out of the hands of a big hefty girl. The girl holds on tight to the things, and with one hand she punches me hard in the stomach so I fall to the ground.

I get up, tottering for a moment, catch my breath, and try to pull her down into the snowdrift. But the girl slips out of my hands and runs away.

Please, I shout, trudging around in the snow. Snow in my eyes. Snow on my hands. Snow in my boots. Please. Can't you please stop? These are Julie's things, not yours.

n the traditional manner Anni and Ingeborg signal that it's time for everyone to take their places. Ingeborg holds the gong and Anni strikes it. They walk from room to room doing this.

Are you going to offer me your arm? I ask Fritz, who's sitting motionless, completely motionless on the purple chaise longue.

I don't feel so good, says Fritz.

Can't you at least *try* to feel good? I say.

I'll try, I'll try, says Fritz, clutching his stomach with his hands.

The festively set long table stretches through two big rooms; white tablecloths, red roses, newly polished old silver, Ingeborg's hand-painted china: salad plates, dinner plates, serving platters, all of them red. There are thirty-seven of us at the table, everyone finds his place, Aaron finds his, next to mine, and now things are moving along just fine.

The evening's toastmaster gets up, picks up his fork, and clinks it against his glass.

Let me introduce this evening's toastmaster: Uncle Robert.

Uncle Robert is Father's older brother and the only one in the family who could be considered an intellectual. They say he's read an awful lot of books, he's read so many books that he knows the answer to practically everything you could think of to ask. Aunt Selma, of course, says it's all bluff, that he hasn't read much at all, only a couple of books of quotations and the cultural pages of the newspaper *Dagbladet*. Uncle Robert says this will be a memorable evening. He tells us what we're going to eat, and if anyone has anything they want to say, he declares, then just come to me and I'll make a note of it on the list of speakers, and remember: "The Table is the only Place where you are never bored during the first Hour," to quote the French gourmet philosopher Brillat-Savarin, who lived in France during the 1700s. Cheers!

I drink a toast with Fritz on one side of me and I drink a toast with Aaron on the other side, and I think that before dessert we'll have made a date, you and I.

The doors to the kitchen open with a bang and two skinny young women exactly the same height, wearing beautiful red dresses, come into the room, each carrying a large serving platter in her hands.

*An appetizer,* says Uncle Robert, standing up again, as he tastes the word appetizer. An appetizer should be savored, he says, but not gulped; an appetizer shouldn't quell your hunger, merely tease it, flirt with it. An appetizer, my friends, is the only dish that actually satisfies your desire without weakening it at the same time—the same, unfortunately, cannot be said about marriage.

Uncle Robert clears his throat.

Let me remind you of my friend Lucullus, he continues, the Roman general, art lover, and hedonist. Once upon a time he served his dinner guests ninety-nine lark tongues. One of the guests, a woman, asked in dismay whether he didn't think it was a shame that all those larks had to die for the sake of one meal. But no, the larks didn't have to die, replied Lucullus, they just couldn't sing anymore! Cheers!

I drink another toast with Fritz and I drink another toast with Aaron. Then I drink a toast with Arvid, who's sitting right across from me.

Arvid is loud and boisterous.

Torild is seated at the other end of the table, sending Arvid anxious looks, *now don't drink too much, Arvid, please,* her eyes say. He raises his glass and shouts CHEERS! Cheers, Torild, you old whore.

Everybody looks at Arvid. Torild blushes and looks down.

Cheers, Torild, says Anni, who's sitting nearby.

Cheers, Anni, says Torild.

And now we should drink a toast to the happy couple, says Uncle Robert.

Cheers, everyone shouts, and then Uncle Robert stands up and sings in a loud, resounding voice that this is a toast for the happy couple, Hurray! and then everyone sings that this is a toast for the happy couple, Hurray! and shame on anyone who won't drink a toast to the happy couple! Cheers!

And then we eat the appetizer and drink the white wine and the first speaker this evening is Anni, the bride's mother, because the bride's father is much too shy and embarrassed about playing the role of the father at such a big, traditional wedding.

Anni stands up and says: *Dear Julie.*

Dear Julie, she says, I want so much to promise you that everything will go well, that you and Aleksander will be happy and have lots of children and live a good, long life. But I can't promise you anything. Nobody can. You know that as well as I do.

Anni gives her speech. It's a long one.

That was a wonderful speech, says Aaron after she's done.

I don't say anything.

Your mother must have been a very beautiful woman, says Aaron.

I don't say anything.

It only takes a minute.

*Get hold of yourself, Karin!*

*It only takes a minute. It happens. As if I'm falling. Not here.*

*Where are you, Karin?*

*There you are.*

*Get up.*

*Don't lie there floundering.*

*Get up, I said.*

There's something I want to tell you, I say.

What's that? says Aaron.

Now don't take it the wrong way, I say.

Aaron looks at me. I smile. I stand up. I can feel that I'm going to do it. I'm going to do it. I know I'm up to it. I'm definitely up to it.

You're blushing, says Aaron, and I meet his eyes.

Yes, I say.

The kitchen door opens and the two tall red-clad women come in with the main course. Uncle Robert tells us that we're going to have roast veal, new potatoes, Brussels sprouts, and a gravy made from a recipe that Ingeborg lured out of her grandmother on her deathbed. With the roast we're going to drink Chianti, he says, a Riserva from Villa Antinori, from the incomparable vintage of 1985.

Cheers!

Cheers, Karin, says Aaron.

Cheers, I say.

Cheers, bellows Arvid a little farther away.

———————

Uncle Robert clinks his glass, stands up again, and says: I quote my old friend Martin Luther.

He takes a gulp from his glass, letting the guests wait while the wine rolls around in his mouth. His glass is still raised as he continues:

Martin Luther said that since God created lovely big goats and lovely Rhine wine, that means I can eat and drink them. Let me add: Since God has given us lovely calves and a red wine with the same fullness and color as Julie's cheeks this evening— so help me if we can't eat and drink them too. But first—before we begin eating—I give the floor to the bridegroom's parents, Aleksander's parents: It's all yours! Hannah and Harald!

Harald cautiously gets up from his chair, folds up his napkin, and places it on the table. He gives the happy couple a swift glance, then he looks at Hannah, who is nervously staring at the floor. My dear boy, Harald says, dear Aleksander:

I've never been especially good with words, you know that, it's your mother who's the bookworm of the family, and so I won't plague you or anyone else with a speech. But we've written a song, and I hope that everyone will join in and sing it, because this is a day of celebration, a day of love, a joyous day, says Harald, looking down at the floor, surprised by his own flood of words. Then he musters his courage again and says that the song is printed on the red sheets of paper that are rolled up next to each plate. Everyone is sure to know the melody, so that shouldn't be a problem.

The wedding guests unroll the red sheets of paper.

No one speaks. Everybody is listening to Harald. Harald likes everyone listening to him. Harald says: But since I'm already standing here . . . well, it's not my intention to keep you too long . . . a good speaker knows that he should stop while the going is good . . . or the roast is hot . . . ha ha . . . he says and laughs, because by this time everyone has food on their plates. Hannah smiles stiffly and tries to send a secret look to her husband that *now it's enough, now you should sit down and we'll sing the song.* But Harald doesn't want to sit down yet. He wants to say a few words to his son after all, for example that it's not my job to tell the happy couple about life's good and bad days, only that life is certain to offer you both, and you shouldn't be afraid when the time comes for the honeymoon to be over and everyday life begins, because it's in everyday life that love is tested, it's in everyday life that husband and wife get to know each other, it's in everyday life that . . . that . . . that . . . Harald takes a peek at Hannah . . . isn't that right, Hannah . . . we've had our share of everyday life, you and I . . .

Harald clears his throat, takes a gulp of his wine.

. . . and today, says Harald, there are plenty of people who are scared of everyday life, scared of being bored, scared of being sad, scared of being scared, scared of sitting totally still in front of an open window in case they might decide to jump out.

What I'm trying to say is: Don't blame each other for a life that isn't fulfilled, don't waste too much time thinking about how everything could have been different, I could have been somebody else, you could have been somebody else. Maybe everything could have been different, yes, who knows? But don't think about it. Let it go. Let it go. Think instead about the greatness of a *modest* life, says Harald, taking a gulp of water. If you'll forgive me for getting personal for a minute, I want to tell you what I mean by the greatness of a modest life. I mean the sound of the wind in the grove of trees outside my bedroom window, the taste of lightly salted cod, boiled potatoes, and finely chopped egg with butter, the yearly ski trip to the mountains with my family and the charades in front of the fireplace that same evening while damp socks and long underwear are hung up to dry; I mean the warm weight of a sleeping child in your arms, *the thudding sound of a wet leather ball on the hard-packed earth on a June night;* I mean Duke Ellington, Buster Keaton, F. Scott Fitzgerald . . .

Harald looks down, falls silent.

Hannah blinks several times.

But now, Harald suddenly shouts, let's sing the song, and they all rise to their feet, the entire wedding party, and sing.

Val Bryn is sitting on the other side of the table. She leans across the best man, Terje Nedtun, to reach the salt, I see that she's whispering something in his ear. He laughs.

Aaron looks up.

Do you see her? I ask.

Who?

Val Bryn.

The maid of honor?

Yes. She told me a story a while ago, in the apple orchard.

Oh?

In confidence.

I see.

Do you want to hear it?

Sure.

A couple of years ago she fell in love with a married man whose name is Frank, I say, Frank Andersen, do you know him?

No.

It doesn't matter. Just listen: Val Bryn persuaded him to leave his wife and child and run off with her to Tokyo. It's a sad story.

I see, says Aaron.

You know how it is, I say. While they still had their secret meetings, they could talk about everything they were going to do together, how much they would love each other when he was finally free, but when he finally *was* free, they spent lots of time proving to each other that it was all worth it, that they were worth it, that their love was great and genuine, that they hadn't made an insurmountable, irreparable, incomprehensible, enormous mistake. I don't think it took many days before they panicked.

On the fourth day in Tokyo, after they had examined every inch of the shopping centers, the emperor's palace, the fish market, the neon-lit skyscrapers, Val Bryn and Frank Andersen decided to spend the rest of their money at one of Tokyo's fugu restaurants. Fugu, you know, blowfish, as it's called in English; do you know what I'm talking about?

I don't know, I don't think so, says Aaron.

A Japanese fish delicacy, I say, that's so poisonous it can kill you in a matter of minutes if the chef hasn't done his job properly. First you feel a tiny quivering in your mouth, a numbness, like when the dentist's novocaine starts to wear off. The numbness spreads to the rest of your face and into your nervous system, there's not even a last-minute reprieve of insanity; you suffocate so slowly that you have time to think, you have time to turn your head and notice that no one in the restaurant is showing you any sympathy, you see that they're looking at you, that they're wired, practically cheering, that *finally* it's happening, finally a catastrophe is taking place *right here*.

I sip a little wine, drink a toast with Aaron.

That's how it was, I say, lowering my voice, in January of 1975 when the kabuki actor Mitsuguro Bando the Eighth collapsed sideways onto the table and died; of course it was after he had eaten his fourth serving of fugu liver—the liver is considered the most poisonous part of the fish, but it's still regarded as an exquisite dining experience—and then it's not so strange that they would stare at you. It's not so strange that they stare at you as you fall sideways over the table after your fourth serving of fugu liver, and then what should you do, Aaron? Should you blame them for looking at you?

I don't know, says Aaron.

Hush, I say. You've lost the ability to speak and you've got ten minutes left to live. There's no question of sending the food back to the kitchen, yelling at the chef, complaining, screaming, crying, threatening, changing your mind about the choice of restaurant—is there?

I've lost the ability to speak, Aaron smiles and places his index finger to his lips, I can't say a word.

The internal organs are what kill you, I say: the heart, lungs, liver, ovaries, and sex organs. An average blowfish weighing about three kilos contains enough poison to kill off thirty people. There's no antidote.

I guess not, says Aaron.

And I think it was the taste of fate that tempted Val Bryn and Frank Andersen, you know; the thought that they might not survive their meal together was both beautiful and sad. And besides, Frank Andersen was a man who had seen the face of God, or at least parts of it, and it'd be surprising if that hadn't affected him, making him big and brave, and he fucked Val Bryn with greater power than ever before.

Afterwards they left the hotel room and strolled through the streets of Tokyo to the restaurant, I say. The first course consisted of an appetizer. A prawn filled with Russian caviar and a little lobster. Frank gobbled up the prawn in a matter of seconds and washed it down with some sake.

Easy does it, said Val Bryn, placing her hand on top of his, make it last.

And it's here, at this point in the story, that something happens, I say.

I look at Aaron.

What happens? asks Aaron.

The main course is served, I say, beautifully arranged on the plate in the shape of a crane.

I lay my knife and fork on my plate, I set my wineglass back down on the table, I wipe my mouth and neatly fold up my napkin.

That's when it happens.

I lower my voice a little more: After one or two or three bites, Frank Andersen starts howling.

No way, says Aaron, raising his head and looking over at Val Bryn.

I'm not shitting you, I whisper. Frank Andersen starts howling because he feels a faint quivering in his mouth, a warm tingling and quivering in his hands, around his knees and in his feet, sweat pours out of his armpits, and on top of that he's got an erection, a hard-on as big as a monkfish, something that would have consumed his attention if he hadn't been convinced he was about to die at any moment.

Frank Andersen grabs a glass of water, gulps it down, gives Val Bryn a desperate look, and starts to cry. He pinches his lips with his fingers, sticks out his tongue, slaps his cheeks, bares his teeth—the numbness doesn't go away. I'm going to die, he cries, I'm going to die, I'm going to die, I'm going to die. Val Bryn looks around in desperation, yells for the waiter, the chef, the police, for God, and I don't know who else. Then she throws herself down on her knees in front of Frank Andersen, puts her head in his lap, and hugs his legs. The other restaurant guests turn around and look at them in astonishment. HE'S DYING! OH MY GOD HE'S DYING! she shouts, and the tears run down her face.

Jesus, says Aaron.

Fucking incredible, huh? I say. And there's a terrible commotion in the restaurant. The ambulance is on its way, the maître d' is wringing his hands in despair, the restaurant guests are trying to beat each other to the bathroom to throw up in case they've been poisoned too, the chef has locked himself in the kitchen and is planning a swift and honorable end to his life.

But then something else happens: Frank Andersen takes a deep breath and notices the weight of Val Bryn's tearful face in his lap. MMMMMM, thinks Frank Andersen. She's so lovely, he thinks, stroking her hair.

And then he thinks: Her mouth, that lovely mouth of hers on my body, her mouth around my cock, her mouth.

In other words, Frank Andersen is gradually forced to acknowledge . . . what shall I say? To reevaluate the situation—to ask himself the question: Should I die or shouldn't I? The quivering in his mouth has apparently begun to fade, the numbness has released its grip—look at that! But not his erection.

My God, thinks Frank Andersen. Good Lord!

He bends over Val Bryn, rubs his nose in her hair, and whispers: I don't know exactly how to explain this, but I've got the world's biggest hard-on and we've got to get out of here right now.

I take a deep breath and empty my wineglass.

Aaron gives me an astonished look.

Three weeks later, I say, Val Bryn and Frank Andersen come home from Tokyo. They move in together in a red-painted row house in Vinderen which they decorate in nice bright colors with the help of an interior decorator they both know. One winter day a year and a half later, Frank slips on the ice outside their house and falls. Unfortunately he hits his head on a sharp rock that's sticking up from the gutter, he's often thought that he should do something about that rock, have it removed from the site, it's not even a very big rock. No bigger than the fist of a hefty man. Frank squeezes his eyes shut in pain. The rock has bored into his forehead, if he could stand up the rock would stick straight out of his forehead like a horn.

I stop and look at Aaron. I told you it was a sad story.

Yes, but then what?

Nothing, I say. Frank Andersen just manages to say *Ow* a couple of times before he opens his eyes and dies.

Now there's no turning back. We're sitting here eating and talking as if we had nothing else to do. Don't you know, Aaron, that we have something else to do? Now there's no turning back.

*I'm doing it now.*
*Yes, do it now, do it before you change your mind, come on, do it!*
*Yes, I'm doing it now.*

Aaron turns around. Aaron turns around. Aaron turns to face me and says: What's the matter with you, Karin?
I don't know.
You look like you're crying.
Me?
Yes, you look like you're about to burst into tears.
I can't help it.
The tears are running down your cheeks.
Is that really so strange?
Is it Julie? The wedding? Is that why you're crying?
No.
What is it then?

It's you. I don't think I can . . .

What?

I don't think I can stand it anymore. I honestly don't think I can go on living if we don't . . . ever since I saw you outside the church today. I'm not asking you for anything, not a thing, do you hear what I'm saying? Not a thing, believe me . . . I JUST WANT YOU . . . just for a minute, nothing more . . . because you're so different . . . I HAVE TO HAVE YOU, DON'T YOU SEE THAT? . . . because there's something so special about you, I don't know whether you know it yourself, something totally special about you . . . and I can't go on living . . . no one will ever know, I say, nothing has happened, nothing . . . shall we say in half an hour, at exactly seven-thirty, the red room on the left, up the stairs and to the left? . . . as if nothing has happened, I promise.

I turn around and look at him and practically start to cry: *You're simply utterly irresistible.* Yes, I turn around and look at him and say that you're simply utterly irresistible.

And then I see that he's started to grow, he's getting bigger, he's becoming enormous, and I'm overwhelmed because I didn't think it would be that easy, no I didn't think it would be that easy to flatter a man—or what?

I throw out my arms.

OR WHAT? I shout, so that all the wedding guests stop talking and stare.

I point at Aaron and cast an inquisitive look around. Aaron is sitting on the chair beside me and inflating, it's almost embarrassing, he's getting bigger and bigger, soon he's going to look like a sideshow attraction or a freak in the *Guinness Book of Records*: Aaron, the world's biggest man.

LOOK AT HIM, EVERYBODY!

He's as big as a whale, Father snickers, taking a gulp of his whisky.

As big as a mountain, says Anni.

As big as a skyscraper, says Aunt Selma. As big as the Empire State Building back in the days when the Empire State Building really WAS something.

As big as a troll, shout the children. He's just as big as a troll.

But the way Karin made him grow, all that flattery, that was beneath her, says Father. Sentimental exaggeration, if you ask me.

Nobody's asking you, snaps Anni.

She's my daughter too, says Father.

You shouldn't be so sure about that, says Anni, and WHERE WERE YOU WHEN THE CHILDREN NEEDED YOU? Where were you when they were sick, sad, happy, when they missed you? Where were you when Julie . . . ?

Hush, Anni, says Father, hush!

Father reaches across the table and grabs my hand, his big hand grips mine: Karin, listen to me! I've taken you to the movies, ever since you were little I've taken you to the movies. We've seen good films and we've seen bad films. Can't you learn from the good ones and say to hell with the bad ones? If you really insist on seducing this man, you could have done it in a much better way. MUCH BETTER, Karin. Could I ask for a little more *finesse* next time? Don't just go RIGHT TO THE POINT, my dear. The knockout method isn't always the best way.

Yes, but it works, I say. Look here, Father! It worked, it worked. Look at him growing.

And Father raises his head, Father takes another gulp of whisky to see more clearly, Father is dumbfounded: Aaron has grown so big that he's about to burst through the roof and out into the sky.

I turn to face Aaron and Aaron smiles.

I don't know exactly what to say, he says in a low voice.

I'm here with Camilla, Camilla is my wife, she's sitting over there.

Aaron nods at the blonde woman.

I'm here with Camilla, he says, and little Charlotte. I don't know whether you understand?

Shhh, I say, you don't have to say anything. I understand everything. Seven-thirty, the red room. Don't say anything else. We won't say a word about it anymore.

At seven twenty-five, still a long time before the dessert is served, I leave the table and go up the stairs to the red room on the second floor.

It's a big, square room, one of the four guest rooms in the house with its own bathroom. From the ceiling hangs a heavy, dusty crystal chandelier that clinks in the faint draft from the windows. The intricate plaster rosettes were once white, but now they're grayish-black from dirt, dust, wind, and smoke. Ingeborg never had the room redecorated, just left it the way it was. Once, long ago, Ingeborg's grandmother slept in the red room; she moved in after she was widowed and could no longer stand to sleep in the bed she had shared with her husband.

The tall windows, four altogether—and all of them facing the apple orchard—are hung with burgundy silk drapes adorned with tassels, flounces, fringes, and bows, silk drapes that hang all the way down to the floor and gather in small red pools. The velvet wallpaper is also burgundy, lighter than the drapes, faded by the sun. In the middle of the room is the bed, not against the wall, but in the middle of the room: an old-fashioned iron bed with big white down comforters and down pillows, a white hand-crocheted bedspread, and embroidered pillows with alphabet designs, dog designs, flower designs, red stitching on black fabric. On the nightstand an alarm clock is ticking, the clock shows the wrong time, it says five minutes to four. That doesn't seem to bother it in the least; it's ticking merrily as if nothing was wrong. I pick it up, look at it, it's missing all its knobs so I can't reset it. I put it back down. The ticking continues. For a moment I stand still and stare, rocking my head back and forth in time with the ticking, saying tick tock tick tock tick tock, do you know you're showing the wrong time, do you know you're standing there and ticking for no reason at all, in fact you're no longer needed in the state you're now in. I put the clock in the drawer of the nightstand and slam it shut, but that doesn't help. The ticking continues. Tick tock tick tock tick tock, I mimic.

DAMN IT! It's hot. I open the drawer, grab the clock, open the wardrobe next to the door. There are dresses hanging inside, dresses from the 1930s, yellow, violet, red, and turquoise dresses, one even has a snow-white boa. I fling the clock inside with the dresses and shut the door. I stand stock-still and listen. No. It won't give up. It just refuses to give up. The clock is ticking. All right, I say. You win. I open the wardrobe door, pull out the clock, and put it back in its place on the nightstand. Stay there, I say. *Hush!*

On the nightstand there's an oil lamp that I light with a match I find in the matchbox next to it. The matchbox is from the Hotel Raphael in Paris.

Then I open the door to the bathroom and go in. The floor is covered with tiles that are tiny black-and-white squares, the walls are gray, the paint began peeling off long ago. An odor of warm cellar dampness in the walls. The sink has angular faucets of imitation gold, the bathtub has lion's-claw feet. Huge chili-pepper red towels on hooks, a fluffy terry-cloth robe over the bathtub. I turn on the taps. The pipes thud through the house. Hot water gushes out. At that very moment there's a knock on the door of the bedroom, Aaron whispers: Hello, is anyone here? I hear him close the door behind him.

Aaron! I say, going back into the bedroom. There you are.

Well, says Aaron, smiling uncertainly. He waves two bottles of white wine in the air, one in each hand.

Want to take a bath? I ask. It helps in this heat.

Bath? he says.

I stride across the red carpet, and the carpet is so soft that I take off my shoes and stockings, I stride barefoot across the red carpet and stand in front of Aaron. He's much taller than I am, I stand there and look up at him. I stand on my toes, put my arms around his neck, and kiss him on the mouth. He grabs me around the neck and kisses me back, hard. I don't like it, I don't like him holding me tight. No, I don't like it. I take a step back, look at him, he's wiping his forehead with the back of his hand. I step closer again. It's hot. Aaron is sweating on his upper lip and around his eyes. I loosen his bow tie, unbutton his shirt, take off his pants and boxer shorts. He's naked but I'm not yet brave enough to look at all of him . . . I take him by the hand and lead him into the bathroom. I step out of my red dress and panties. I stick my right foot into the gushing water in the bathtub, I turn off the tap, I say it's hot.

It's hot, I say and get into the tub. It's a big mistake to take cold baths in hot weather, I say. You should do the opposite, you should take a scalding hot bath in the heat; my grandmother taught me that.

Aaron is standing naked on the bathroom floor, he takes a swig from one of the bottles.

I don't know about all this, he says.

What is it you don't know? I say, stretching out.

I don't know, he repeats.

Hush, I say. Come on. And give me some wine.

Aaron sticks a toe in the water and yells.

GODDAMN! he yells.

It's way too hot, he says.

You'll get used to it, I say.

I cup my hands into a bowl and fill the bowl with water. I let the water run down over my face.

Aaron sticks his foot into the water again. He shudders. But then, and I'm surprised at his determination, he slides down into the tub. Water splashes onto the floor. Water splashes as he sits down.

He grabs at my hair and tries to kiss my face.

Don't! I say.

What kind of game are you playing? he says.

Water splashes over the edge.

Stop it, I say.

We don't have all night, says Aaron.

He grabs for me again, this time for my arm, but he doesn't get hold of me.

We thrash around in the bathtub.

His face is wet. His hair is too, plastered to his face, brown hair.

We have plenty of time, I say. Downstairs they're not even done with the main course yet, and there's going to be lots more speeches. Come and sit close to me. Come and sit close to me so I can put my arms around you and stroke the back of your neck, like this!

I wrap my legs around his thighs. I take a drink from the bottle.

He lays his head on my shoulder and closes his eyes.

The bathwater is steaming, but the air is cooler now, gentle against my skin.

You were right, he says, about hot baths in the heat.

Yes, I say.

I can feel I've had too much to drink. It's crazy to drink so much in this heat, says Aaron.

Don't think about it, I say.

The bathroom window is open, facing the neighboring courtyard. Somewhere someone is playing the piano.

Do you know that tune? I say, from the movie *La Grande Bouffe*?

What tune? he says.

Someone's playing it on the piano, can you hear it?

Yes. I've never heard it before.

I hum the tune softly for Aaron. Anni can't sing. Julie can't sing. But I can. I can sing. And I sing softly for Aaron, so softly that no one else can hear it, only him.

He turns around to face me, makes his hands wet and strokes my eyes, the water blinds me. He says that now I don't want to take a bath anymore. A little longer, I say. No, he says, now I don't want to take a bath anymore. He grabs my arm and pulls me up out of the tub. I stand naked in front of him, I look at him, he doesn't like it. Doesn't like me looking at him. He shoves me against the bathroom wall, that's it! he says, and I stand with my face against the wall, the wall has no eyes, I want to see your eyes I say, no he says, not now. He holds the back of my neck tight with one hand. He holds himself tight with the other. My head bangs against the wall when he pushes inside me.

I sit on the edge of the bathtub, let my hand glide through the lukewarm water, I look at the thin naked girl against the wall, the man standing over her.

*Dry your tears, I say, it doesn't hurt.*

*I didn't say that it hurt.*

*Get up.*

*You can see that I'm standing.*

*And afterwards, don't ask for anything.*

*All right.*

*And stop crying. We don't like women who cry.*

That tune. Someone is playing the piano, it's the tune from *La Grande Bouffe*. Father and I saw the film two years before the wedding. Afterwards we talked about Julie; Father wanted to know what had happened. It was impossible to get a sensible word out of Anni, he said, she just cried on the phone and kept bitching and moaning.

You could have come to visit, you know, I said.

Don't you go giving me a guilty conscience too, Karin, he said, that won't get you anywhere.

*There are many ways to die.*

In *La Grande Bouffe* four men—played by Marcello Mastroianni, Philippe Noiret, Ugo Tognazzi, and Michel Piccoli—decide to go off and eat themselves to death. They eat and eat and fuck and eat and fuck and eat until they fall over and die, one after the other. They carry out their plan, despairing, obsessed, without a moment of joy, desire, or pleasure.

It's the face of Marcello Mastroianni that I happen to remember, I told Father, the expression on his face: *Can we be done with it now, please, can we be done with it?*

Those are Julie's words, said Father.

Yes, I said. And mine, I added.

No no no, said Father, those aren't your words at all. You're not like that. You're tough. Ever since you were born you've been tough and a survivor. I remember the midwife telling me that the first thing you did when you came into the world was to turn your eyes toward Anni, purse your lips, and whistle. You whistled, Karin. The midwife had never seen anything like it before.

Father and I sat down on a bench outside the National Theater; we didn't go anywhere to eat, we didn't take a walk, we didn't do any of the things we usually do after we've been to the movies. It was snowing. Father had to catch the subway to Tøyen soon. I had to take the bus home. But first we sat for a while on a bench; if anyone had looked at us they would have thought we were two snow-covered snowmen sitting side by side. Father with his strange dark-brown cowboy hat, Karin with a long red knitted scarf around her neck.

It was a few minutes before he asked: Why did she do it, do you think?

You mean Julie?

Of course.

She tried it several times, you know. Anni only knows about the one time. But it happened several times.

Really?

There are many ways to die, I say.

Don't get all melodramatic on me, says Father, just tell me the plain truth.

I'm not being melodramatic. Julie found out there are lots of ways to die, or lots of ways for a seventeen-year-old girl *not* to die. It's a matter of how you choose to look at it. First she jumped into a full bathtub with a buzzing electric hair dryer in her hands; the hair dryer must have had some kind of safety device that made it switch off as soon as it hit water. Nothing happened, except the hair dryer was ruined for good. Then she stole one of Anni's pillboxes—the red one that always has Valium in it—and she swallowed all the pills, there must have been thirty or forty of them. But it wasn't Valium in the red box. Anni has one pillbox with Valium, one pillbox with sleeping pills, one pillbox with Ibux painkillers, one pillbox with vitamin B tablets for beautiful hair, one pillbox with something to get her going in the morning, one pillbox with healing sugar pills that a green-eyed homeopath had given her, one pillbox with multivitamins. Julie stole the sugar pills and just got sick to her stomach and threw up all night and cried that it's so damned difficult to die! Then she tried to hang herself, she put a screw in the ceiling, bought a pitch-black rope at the hardware store, climbed up onto a chair, and fastened the noose around her neck. But the screw wasn't fastened to the ceiling properly, and when she kicked the chair out from under her, she dropped to the floor with the rope on top of her while pieces of white plaster rained down on her hair from the ceiling. Then she decided to jump out the window, but for some reason she didn't dare jump when she was standing with one leg dangling in midair and the other leg still planted inside the room. Right after that she got in Anni's car and drove like mad toward the city—she's never been a good driver, anyone who longs for death should take a ride in the car with Julie, and back then she didn't even have a license. Thank God the cops stopped her before anyone got hurt. So, finally, she slit her wrists in the shower, and that's when Anni found her. Luckily. Because this time she hadn't made a single mistake.

t's evening now and the guests sitting around the long, festively set table are shrouded in overripe sunlight. The platter of roast veal passes from hand to hand around the table for the third time, even though the custom on occasions like this is for each person to help himself twice from the main course, and there are still five different kinds of cheese to eat, a raspberry dessert with vanilla sauce, homemade lemon sorbet, Aunt Edel's wedding cake in eight layers, Ingeborg's marzipan cake, and Anni's cheesecake, mint chocolates with coffee, Italian beef soup with tiny spiced sausages for a midnight snack. The two red-clad serving girls are sitting shoulder to shoulder on the floor next to the wall in the kitchen, they're so full that they don't even have the energy to serve dessert. A single candle is lit on the kitchen table.

I sink down onto a chair next to Uncle Fritz, Aaron goes straight over to the blonde woman and cautiously kisses her on the top of the head, she turns around and gives him a questioning smile—where were you? where have you been?—he whispers something in her ear, let's say that he tells her how sick he suddenly felt, how he had to get some fresh air, but I'm better now, he assures her, I love you, he says, I love you and you're the most beautiful woman here.

Uncle Fritz looks around and belches, once, twice, and stares down at a tiny little lump of vomit on his plate.

Are you sick, Uncle Fritz, are you going to throw up for real?

I don't want to throw up, Karin, I don't want to, but sometimes I can't help it. He starts to cry. The tears pour out.

I give him my napkin.

It's not so terrible, Uncle Fritz. It's not so terrible.

But before all of this, before I seduce Aaron, before Aaron kisses his wife and tells her she's the most beautiful of all women, before Uncle Fritz throws up on his plate, Uncle Robert strikes his glass and says that now the bride's mother has the floor, and Anni stands up and says *dear Julie.*

Dear Julie, says Anni.

I want so much to promise you that everything will go well, that you and Aleksander will be happy and have lots of children and live a good, long life. But I can't promise you anything. Nobody can. You know that as well as I do. But when I saw your face in church today; when I saw Julie's face in church today, I thought: *Thank you, Aleksander, thanks for the trouble you took from her eyes. I thought it was there for good, so I never tried.*

I don't have any good advice for your marriage. I've thought about it: I don't know how it's done—and I don't think your father does either, Julie.

But if you'll permit me, I'd like to tell you a story.

The story is about Rikard Blom. Julie and Karin's grandfather. Else's and my father. If he was here tonight—and it could very well be that he is, I have a feeling that he's with us whenever we have some kind of family celebration, I know that he was a man who liked to celebrate—but if he was here tonight, *in real life,* then he probably would have said:

Julie! Aleksander! You love each other. Be brave and keep going!

Rikard Blom died when I was a little girl, and I don't remember much about him. I remember that one day he came home to our apartment in Brooklyn and shouted: Now, by gosh, this place is gonna swing! Now we're gonna have some fun! I remember that he dressed up like Santa Claus, stomped into the living room, and said HO HO HO, but he took off his mask and beard at once because Else and I didn't recognize him and started to cry. I remember that he hummed and sang at all hours of the day and night, except once when he read in a Norwegian newspaper that the boxer Pete Sanstøl had become a bitter man. Then he cried like a baby. But best of all I remember the time, just before the war broke out in Norway, when he took us to the World's Fair in New York.

It was only a short ride on the subway from Brooklyn to Flushing Meadows in Queens—but it felt like we'd been traveling a long, long way. To the castle of Soria Moria. Or some other enchanted place. I remember that the first thing we saw when we came out of the subway was a man selling oranges and lemons, and I expected to see tiny little princesses rise up out of the lemons, stretching out their arms to the sky—like in the fairy tale.

It was summer, the sun was shining, I was wearing a new yellow dress that didn't scratch or dig into my skin.

There was so much to see. We walked and walked and walked all day. I remember all the lights. And the music in the streets. After a while I was worn out and wanted to sit down.

And then I wanted to ride the merry-go-round. Rikard had promised Else and me that we could ride the merry-go-round when it got dark.

But before that, late in the afternoon, we went past a monument.

Rikard told us that at this spot some men had buried a

greeting to the future, a time capsule that nobody could touch for five thousand years.

Cupaloy, he said. This is the time capsule of Cupaloy.

I'll never forget the sight of Rikard—your grandfather— standing in front of the monument, a man beaming with joy who shouted: June! Selma! Else! Anni! Five thousand years! Can you believe it? Five thousand years!

Everyone is quiet, listening.

Dear Julie, Anni continues. When I saw you in church today, I happened to think about your grandfather on that day in Flushing Meadows. The man beaming with joy. The five thousand years. The sun shining. The enchanted lemons and oranges.

It was that kind of day. The summer light fell so soft and warm over all the faces, the ice cream tasted of real vanilla—I even remember the tiny little black specks of vanilla, like fleas, in all that white—and the lemonade was sour and sweet at the same time; the kind of day when everything was good and everything was possible. I remember that Rikard lifted me up, high up, and twirled me around in his outstretched arms, and said that things will always be the way they are today.

Things will always be the way they are today, repeated Anni, and Julie raised her eyes and looked at me, shifted her gaze and looked at Aleksander, the man she had married. And many hours later, in the gray light of the following day, the wedding celebration was over, and all the guests returned to their own homes.

# Days 1990–1997

A year after the wedding I meet Billy. We shop at the same supermarket.

He doesn't pay any attention to me at first, just walks restlessly up and down the narrow aisles between the stocked shelves, helping himself to corn flakes, milk, strawberry jam, rye bread, peanut butter, fish sticks, mashed potatoes, frozen spinach, light beer, cigarettes, and a copy of *Dagbladet*. Almost always same things. Sometimes he chooses regular beer instead of light beer, stew instead of fish sticks, *Arbeiderbladet* instead of *Dagbladet*.

We don't say anything to each other for the first few weeks. We don't even say hi, or rather he doesn't say hi, but I know he recognizes me. He can't help recognizing me. Sometimes I run into him, hard, from behind, with my shopping cart, smile and say sorry. He never looks at me when that happens, just mumbles that it's okay and keeps going. One time I try to talk to him in front of the frozen foods section. I ask him whether he's tried fish sticks with yogurt sauce. I've noticed that you like fish sticks. It's good, you know, the yogurt sauce, I mean. Listen to this: You mix yogurt with grated apples and a healthy dash of curry. That's it.

Uh huh, he says, thanks.

It's good with mashed potatoes, I offer. But by then he is already gone.

Another time I follow him over to the bread section and stand right next to him. We stare at the loaves of bread.

I think it's hard to choose bread, I say. Bread gets boring after a while. Morning, noon, and night: bread, bread, bread, the same eternal slice of bread every day. Even though, I add, even though it always surprises you. The slice of bread I mean. It tastes better than you thought beforehand. Have you ever had fresh rye bread with banana? My grandmother used to make it for me. She cut up the slices of bread into little triangles, didn't skimp on the butter, and put the banana slices on top. That's a good memory: It's winter outdoors, it's snowing outside the window. Grandma and I are sitting on either side of the kitchen table, she has turned off the ceiling light and lit a candle. She's reading a fairy tale. She's made hot chocolate with whipped cream. There aren't many people that I love, but I loved my grandmother. She reminded me of Marlon Brando in *The Godfather*—the way she was, I mean. She was tough you know, stern, calculating, a bit cool. But—and this is the point—she could suddenly, without realizing it herself, look so worn out and vulnerable. Vulnerable in a way that made me, even though I was only eight or nine years old, feel like leaning across the table to stroke her cheek. When she drank hot chocolate she always got whipped cream on her face, especially right under her nose. Here, I say, pointing at myself.

That sounds nice, Billy interrupts me. But I don't like cocoa, he says.

Hot chocolate, I say firmly.

What?

There's actually a difference between hot chocolate and cocoa, I say.

Billy shakes his head and takes off.

One afternoon he's standing behind me in the checkout line. I turn around to face him, stand on my toes, and whisper into his ear with as much urgency as I can muster: I can't stand it any longer. I have to say it. You're a totally irresistible man. I envy the woman who eats dinner with you every night.

Hey now, you've got to cut that out, he says, and his cheeks and forehead turn red.

It takes me four weeks to persuade Billy to sleep with me.

I never thought about giving up. I don't give up once I've made up my mind. That's the whole point. But Billy got on my nerves. Billy irritated me. I felt more like slapping him than sleeping with him.

Regardless, I finally talk him into it.

This is how it happens: I hang around the supermarket entrance and wait for him. It's Thursday night. He's always there on Thursdays, after seven. Billy comes in, gives me a nod, and hurries over toward the canned goods and spice shelves. I fill up my shopping cart with red, yellow, reddish-yellow, and green apples and follow him. I hide behind the taco and spaghetti shelves, I can see him clearly. He has ground beef and wild rice in his cart. That's not like him. The fish stick king himself. I crouch down. I take one apple after another out of the cart and roll them across the floor. Over to Billy. Lots of apples. I've taken all the apples in the fruit section. I like watching them roll across the floor.

Billy stands rooted to the spot and watches the apples come rolling toward him, first he looks at the floor and then up. I'm hiding behind the taco and spaghetti shelves. Billy stands there staring. The apples are rolling. Suddenly he lets go of his cart and comes toward me. I hide behind the shelves. He lets go of his cart and comes toward me. I hide behind the shelves. *I run away*. I hide behind the shelves. Billy comes toward me and finds me and grabs my arm and says, Let's go.

am Karin.

Julie is my sister, married to Aleksander.

If anyone should ask me how things are going with them, I could tell one of many stories.

This is one of them:

One night Julie is awakened by a voice that is trying to say something. It's Aleksander's voice. *Are you asleep, Julie? Do you hear me?*

Julie doesn't answer. She's lying on her back, her mouth half-open, her eyes closed. Aleksander is also lying on his back. His eyes are open. They're sharing a big, blue-flowered comforter.

There's a rock lying between them.

Aleksander doesn't know where the rock came from. It wasn't there when they went to bed. He doesn't discover it until he stretches out his arms to hold her. Then one of his arms scrapes against the rock. He doesn't notice the cut on his skin until the next day, but he can feel the sting.

The rock is dark gray although Aleksander can't be sure that it's dark gray because the room is dark, and he doesn't feel like turning on the light. The rock isn't big, no bigger than a liver, he thinks without really knowing exactly what a liver looks like. Or something that Julie spit out or threw up in her sleep, he thinks.

Aleksander shuts his eyes.

He feels sick to his stomach.

He doesn't want to have to wake up the next morning.

It's only three hours until the next morning.

Aleksander opens his eyes.

He picks up the rock. He lets his index finger glide over it, over the hollows, the grooves, the rough spots, and dents. It's cold.

Aleksander thinks that he'll be damned if he's going to have a rock in his bed. He sits up and looks around the dark bedroom. The hardwood floor is painted white, the radiator is yellow, the walls and window frames are blue. He painted them all himself.

Then Aleksander sees what he had hoped not to see, even though, strangely enough, it doesn't surprise him. He was expecting it.

In the corner, behind the bedroom door, there's a rock.

The rock in the corner is exactly like the rock in the bed, only much bigger, as big as the torso of an old man, thinks Aleksander.

He looks at Julie. He knows she's not asleep, she knows that he knows she's not asleep. She breathes. Sometimes he has the urge to crush her skull against the wall.

There's a rock on top of the wardrobe too.

He *hadn't* expected to see that one.

Aleksander stares at it. It's bigger than the rock in the bed, but smaller than the rock on the floor.

So what are you going to do about it? asks Julie suddenly. She turns over to face him, she has opened her eyes now.

He didn't realize that he was talking out loud.

I don't know, he says. I don't know.

Anni is my mother.

Once upon a time Anni was irresistible. In many ways she's still irresistible. Anni has always been two things. Irresistible and mad. In the past she was more irresistible and less mad; now she's unfortunately more mad and less irresistible.

When Anni turns fifty-six, shortly after the big wedding, Julie and I buy her a round-trip plane ticket from Oslo to New York, book her a room at the Hotel Excelsior on the corner of West 81st Street and Columbus Avenue, drive her to the airport, and wave goodbye. Ten days later we get in Julie's car and drive back to the airport to pick her up.

Julie insists on driving. It's my car, she says. That's what she says, even though we both know she can't drive. She just tricked the driving instructor when she got her license. Tricked him good. She can't drive a car. She's crazy. She drives way too fast and recklessly, and she doesn't pay any attention to road signs. Luckily today she has to stop the car several times and throw up at the side of the road. She's wearing a long yellow silk scarf around her neck. It's windy. Julie looks up from the curb and squeezes her eyes shut, her face looks bruised, but it's not.

———

Just back from the honeymoon in Italy, Julie reports that she's pregnant. Aleksander is so happy that he takes out his camera and snaps a picture of her.

I look at Julie.

Her eyes are big and dark. Her body is bony, thin, huddled up. I don't see how Julie's body is going to bear a child. I picture how the child will gnaw its way through her, through her womb, intestines, bones, skin. How the baby's head will stick out of her stomach when there's nothing left for it to gnaw through.

Hi, says the baby, here I am, God's little gift to the world.

Julie, I say, you can forget all that stuff about pregnant women having a glow. You don't have a glow.

We're getting close to Fornebu Airport. Julie wipes her mouth, smiles wanly. Then she stops the car again and throws up. Shit, she says. And then: I'm sorry I'm making us late. I think we'll still be on time for the plane.

She puts her foot on the gas pedal, Julie's big foot on the gas pedal, and we roar off.

Sometimes, when I least expect it, I imagine I'm hearing Julie's voice.

Julie says:

At first I don't feel anything. But I know. I lose interest in wine, I won't let Aleksander touch me. I remember the click-clacking of the nurse's footsteps on the linoleum. It's the same nurse who tells me to go to the bathroom and pee in a paper cup. She says I should take the cup along and give it back to her afterwards. It won't take more than fifteen minutes, she says.

The hallway between her and me is long and narrow. I sit on a faded yellow spindle-back chair and wait for the results. I look up when I hear her footsteps, she's coming toward me, she has nothing in her hands, she's in no rush. I wonder whether she walks just as casually, click-clacking, when she has other kinds of news: I'm sorry but the tests weren't what we had hoped, I'm sorry but you've tested positive, I'm sorry there's nothing we can do for you, there's absolutely no hope, not for you, no! And I don't care either, she whispers and comes so close that you can smell the peppermint candy in her mouth, because I myself am unreachable, immortal, white. The nurse smiles and I think that at least Aleksander will be happy if the test is positive, if the answer is yes.

The nausea comes later. It starts like a little murmuring in my stomach and spreads like liquid nettles through my body. Nausea, can you understand this? Soured school milk. Quivering aspic. Day-old bacon fat. Spoiled venison. I've moved onto a rocking boat, I'm full of sludge, and the deck is spinning, I've eaten contaminated mussels, I throw up. I don't want to keep anything down and so I throw up. Aleksander tries to feed me but the only thing I want to eat is a teaspoonful of cold water. I'm scared of killing the baby. These violent convulsions in my body. I'm scared the baby will fly out of my mouth and down into the toilet bowl, into the bucket, onto the floor with a smack. I'm sorry. I'm sorry. I won't think about that. I know that sometimes I think about your face. That at this very moment your face is being formed by invisible fingers inside me. Your forehead, nose, nostrils, cheekbones, chin. We can be friends, you and I. I will sing to you in the evenings, you will sleep next to me under my comforter, I will console you with kisses, I will nurse you when you want, because my breasts are big and heavy now, even though the rest of me is disappearing. This morning I weighed three kilos less than yesterday. I'm scared that I might belch you up, shove you out, I'm scared that I won't be able to keep you. I wonder whether you're a boy or a girl. Won't you tell me? Won't you? Just go ahead and sleep. I won't let anyone disturb you as long as you're inside me. Aleksander thinks you're a little girl and every time he sees a little girl on the street he tells me about it when he gets home, *the little girl was skipping across the street wearing a short apple-yellow dress and shouting Daddy, come on hurry up, Daddy, come and look*. Sometimes I dream about you. You're a big black spider that's creeping around inside me. Sometimes you're not a spider but a cockroach, a worm, a tumor, a fragrant orchid. Something that's eating me up from inside. Can't you leave me alone? Is it your nostrils that can't stand the smell of fresh-brewed coffee, fried fish, cigarette smoke, a strange woman's perfume, Aleksander's semen? I faint from the smells. Or I throw up. I faint and I throw up. I can't hold onto you much longer. Your body is transparent, your head is transparent, your fingers are transparent, but I can feel you grabbing at me, I want you to stop grabbing at me and I want Aleksander to stop. Is he supposed to be inside me too? This can't be true. Let me out, there's no room for me anymore. When he walks naked across the room, I look away. I'm like you. Trapped. Are you scared, little one? I wish I could promise you that I will take care of you always. I will take care of you. I put my hand on my big stomach and know that here you're safe. An old man gets up for me on the trolley and smiles at me and says: *You must need to sit down, little Mother.* Oh yes, I say. Thanks, I say. And the stranger puts his long thick index finger under my eye and shows me the tear. I want him to hold me until you're born, and long afterwards too. I want him to hold me because what if I die, what if? It's almost time, little one. I can feel that you're on the way. And I will sing to you. I will sing to you. Hush baby hush, for now you must sleep.

Billy wants to fuck me in public places, especially places in Oslo that he associates with something unpleasant.

We do it behind the most vulgar Vigeland sculptures in Frogner Park, in a bathroom at the Plaza Hotel, in the men's room of a café that he was once thrown out of; we do it against the palace wall without arousing the attention of the Royal Guard (Billy's a staunch antimonarchist), outside the main post office (because it's so ugly); he takes me over to the houses of famous politicians, politicians who in some way or other have annoyed Billy, and we do it in their gardens, basements, in the stairwells, one time we do it in an elevator. We do it on the Kolsås train late one night, but he doesn't want to touch me until we reach Smestad Station. Billy grew up in Smestad and his father—the supreme court prosecutor—used to like hounding his sons. Billy had two younger brothers and once, Billy tells me, the youngest brother was sitting on the toilet, my youngest brother was seven years old, he says, and Dad came into the bathroom and sneered and said: Goddamn, it smells fucking awful in here, can't you learn to lock the door and keep your shit to yourself, and my brother's eyes filled with tears and he said sorry, and Dad stood there in front of him and looked down at him and said: But you're still doing it, it stinks in here, and my brother cried and said sorry and couldn't get up from the toilet because he wasn't finished yet. I had just turned twelve and ran into the bathroom, straight at the shadow of Dad, straight at the shadow of Dad and punched him in the stomach with my fists and said: Now let him sit here in peace, and Dad laughed and laughed and assumed his usual stance, his knees bent, his fists in the air, ready to box. I didn't understand a thing. Dad wanted to box. Come on, he said, let's fight, come on, tough guy.

One day I suggest to Billy that we could do it someplace he associates with something good. We both know it's almost over between us.

All right, says Billy, I'll think about it.

Billy thinks for a couple of weeks.

In the meantime we do it in various places in Smestad. It's no longer good enough just to ride past Smestad Station on the subway. Now he wants to get out. And we do it outside the Smestad post office, the Smestad school, and on the stairs of an old eatery and bar near the Smestad crossroads. One night we walk past the house Billy lived in when he was a boy, it's a nice white house from the fifties. It's on the left side of a steep hill with attractive white, red, yellow, green, and brown houses on either side. The yards surrounding the houses are palely clad in the twilight.

Billy nods at the house and says that's where I lived. There's a yellow Mercedes parked in the driveway.

I'm afraid Billy will want us to do it again. I'm tired. I'm sore. I want to go home. I want to be alone. And besides, I don't want to do it in Smestad anymore, I've had enough of Smestad. Billy doesn't want to either. He keeps walking down the steep hill and gives his childhood home the finger.

Did you notice that the house was sneering at me? he says after a while.

I turn around and look at the white house.

No, I say, the house isn't sneering at you, Billy.

I've thought of a place that I associate with something good, Billy says one day.

Great, I say.

You want to go there now? says Billy.

Sure, I say.

We take the train to Drammen.

We walk for a while and reach a big, dilapidated yellow villa from the last century. The villa stands in the middle of an apple orchard, the grass is tall like reeds, the apple trees are wide and crooked with thick branches that stick out in all directions.

Billy and I stand outside the garden gate and look up at the yellow villa.

An old lady lived here, one of my mother's relatives; she used to come to Smestad sometimes for Sunday dinner, Billy says. After a while she didn't come to Sunday dinner anymore, but she told me that I was always welcome at her home. I could pick as many apples as I wanted and take a bath in her big tub and spin her globe, which was from a whole different era, with place names like Belgian Congo, Italian East Africa, Río de Oro, Cape Colony, Palestine, Baluchistan.

I built a tree house in that big pine over there. Billy points to a pine tree in the farthest corner of the yard, behind the house. I used to sit in that tree house and eat apples and no one in the whole world could see me, he says.

I'm sure the tree house is still there, he says. I thought we could do it there.

Billy opens the gate. We trudge through the grass. It slaps against our legs. The tree house is there. Billy picks up a few apples from the ground. He gives me one and it tastes like fresh squeezed juice, and we silently climb up into the tree.

But it's not a particularly good idea to do it in that tree house in the pine behind the yellow villa in Drammen. Some of the planks are rotten, and the weight of both of us is too much for

Billy's old hiding place. Billy suffers the brunt of it. When the planks shatter under us and the tree house collapses, I catch hold of a branch and dangle in midair. Then I wrap my legs around the trunk and gently slide down to the ground. A few scratches on the inside of my thighs and on my palms, that's all, but poor Billy. Billy drops right through the tree house to the ground and breaks two ribs and one of his legs. I have to ring the bell of the neighboring house and ask the sleepy man and woman who live there to call an ambulance. They're extremely helpful. They both put on their identical egg-yolk-colored terry-cloth bathrobes and follow me out to have a look at Billy. He's lying on the ground in the tall grass and crying. The man and woman look at him.

What's his name? asks the husband.

His name is Billy, I say.

He asks what we were doing.

I don't answer.

Billy's pants are down around his knees. I bend over him and try to pull his pants back up. Billy starts howling when I touch him. The helpful man and woman say that it's probably best you don't touch him, he must have broken something. They kneel down beside him and try to look him in the eye. The husband moves his hand from side to side and shouts: CAN YOU SEE MY HAND, BILLY? CAN YOU SEE THAT I'M MOVING MY HAND? Billy stares at him in terror through his tears. The wife pats him on the cheek and says you poor poor thing, it hurts so much, poor, poor Billy. When the ambulance arrives he's put on a stretcher and lifted into the vehicle.

Billy doesn't want me to go with him.

After the ambulance drives off the man and woman ask me if I'd like to have coffee with them, because even though it's the middle of the night, they say, it's still summer after all and quite light and warm and we can have coffee on the veranda and watch the sunrise and chat—because I should at least get something pleasant out of making the trip to Drammen, they say.

A few days later I visit Billy at the hospital. I take flowers. Yellow orchids. Things aren't so good. Billy doesn't like being in the hospital. He's never been in the hospital before, but when his father was dying he went to visit. Dad used to lie in bed and gasp for air and I would sit on a metal chair next to him, Billy tells me. Sometimes Dad would feel better, he wanted us to hold hands and talk about things.

What kind of things?

Things. I don't remember.

Billy stares at the ceiling.

When Dad finally died he grabbed my arm and refused to let go. But that's not what I remember most. His bony hand clutching my arm. No, that's not what I remember most. What I remember is the stink that came out of his mouth when he gasped for air.

What kind of stink?

Poop, Billy says. And the stink of poop has seeped into the walls, into the sheets, into the food, into my nose. Billy sits up in bed as best he can and shouts *I want to get out of here, I want to get the hell out of here*.

I visit Billy one more time. He's feeling a little better now. It won't be long before they let him out. We do it behind a folding screen. It's not easy because of his broken leg and his crushed ribs; but the hospital qualifies as a place that he associates with something unpleasant, he says, so it'd be crazy for us not to try.

Of course I don't know exactly what happened between Julie and Aleksander before it all went wrong. I'm not a stupid girl, I don't believe it's possible to understand other people's marriages. It's true, I know the basic facts, and I'll be sure to present them here, but what really happened, why a husband suddenly begins to hate his wife, why a woman fights for a man she secretly holds in contempt, I have no idea.

I don't know whether Julie found Aleksander contemptible. I *think* she did. *I* did, at any rate. I saw through him right away. That whole impeccable quality of his. It's all show. Nothing but show. But as I said, I'm not a stupid girl. I don't believe it's possible to know the truth about other people's marriages.

No, I'm not so stupid that I think I know the truth. I remember one time, several years after Julie and Aleksander were married. A summer excursion to Sweden to a red cabin they had rented in Värmland, Selma Lagerlöf country Julie said, close to a village called Koppom. There were quite a few of us—Julie, Aleksander, Arvid, Torild, Val Bryn, and me and Carl. And little Sander, four years old. Carl was my beloved. I'll talk more about him later.

In the car Arvid is already drinking hard. He's annoying and crude. He calls Torild a horse. We drive past Bjørkelangen, through Setskog, Rømskog—the scenery changes instantly as soon as we cross the Swedish border and drive into Värmland: little red cabins, open countryside, grazing animals; this is not my country but it's beautiful, and every time Arvid sees a horse walking around grazing he sticks his head out the car window and yells TOOORILD, COME HERE AND I'LL GIVE YOU A LUMP OF SUGAR.

Carl asks Arvid to take it easy. Torild is sitting in the back seat and feels like crying all day long, all night too, long after we've arrived, she's just waiting to go to bed so she can be by herself and not attract attention.

It's still early evening.

Arvid stays behind in the kitchen, which is painted blue, at the kitchen table where we ate dinner and drank wine.

Julie is upstairs, singing Sander to sleep, Carl and Aleksander are trying to light a fire in the fireplace, it's a cool summer evening, Val Bryn is reclining in a white wicker chair. Later that evening, after Sander is asleep and Julie has come back down to the living room, we hear Arvid howling to himself in the kitchen, for a moment it sounds like he's crying, a couple of times he shouts the word cunt and laughs real loud, suddenly he's standing in the doorway to the living room, big and fat and staggering and shadowy in the light from the fireplace and mumbling something incoherent. Everybody stops talking and looks up, spit is running out of his mouth, he tries to say something again . . . don't you understand a damn thing? he says . . . don't you have any damn sense of humor? Aleksander says: Go to bed, Arvid, you're drunk and disgusting and crude. Arvid raises his index finger and points at Aleksander. Let me tell you one thing, he says . . . you're my fucking little brother, he says . . . CRUDE, he says, I'LL BE DAMNED IF . . . let me tell you one thing . . . Arvid points at Aleksander. We sit in silence and wait for him to finish talking. But now he can't remember what he was going to say. He goes back out to the kitchen. An hour later we hear him trying to wake up Torild in their bedroom.

The following day, I wake up next to Carl with the usual nauseating morning headache. I wake up, staring right at the old rose-colored wallpaper with little flowers on it, and the little flowers are bedbugs on their way into my eyes, nostrils, mouth, armpits.

I get up and walk down the green stairs, which are steep.

The door to the kitchen is ajar. Through the crack I see Arvid and Torild. A band of green summer light falls in through one of the kitchen windows. Arvid and Torild are sitting in the light, on the hardwood floor, in their pajamas, each holding a big cup of coffee. Arvid strokes Torild's face. Torild smiles. They say something to each other, but I can't hear what. Forehead to forehead.

So I'm not going to claim that I know the truth about other people's marriages, everything that makes up a marriage, all the tiny little things, for example that Aleksander clears his throat so vigorously, seeming self-important every time he states his opinion about something and gets nervous, and the tenderness this arouses in Julie, all the tiny little things that no one else knows, and yet there they are, all of them, just sitting around passing judgment—*they have a good marriage, they have a bad marriage*—and the truth is, they know nothing at all.

The first few years after Julie's wedding I see a lot of Julie, Val Bryn, and Torild. We drink beer and wine and gin and tonics. Someone once wrote that the secret to a happy life is staying two drinks ahead of reality and three drinks behind inebriation. Let that be a motto.

We go to cafés.

We tell each other secrets.

Julie is sitting across from us at a table in a café in the city, she's running her hand through her hair which she has decided to grow long, and says that she has to go home, the baby-sitter who's watching Sander has an exam and can only stay until one, and then she says that she thinks Aleksander is cheating on her. Val Bryn looks at Julie, she seems surprised, she opens her mouth and closes it again, opens it and says I don't think that's true, Aleksander isn't the type. Torild shakes her head and says not on your life. She says: Arvid Lange Bakke is a stupid pig, but Aleksander Lange Bakke is an honorable man. If there's one thing I'm sure of, it's that.

That same evening, or maybe a different evening: Julie, Val Bryn, Torild, and I are walking up Bogstad Way, arm in arm the way schoolgirls do, we're walking like this to keep warm. Puffs of frost are coming out of our mouths. It's night. We're wearing heavy coats. Someone, I think it's Torild, not Julie, says that sometimes I think about what it would be like to catch my husband in the act, find some undeniable proof that he's unfaithful, finally be done with listening to all his lies, be in the right, know that now I'm free to hate him.

I know a woman who was married for ten years, says Val Bryn, to a man who told her every day that he loved her because she asked him to. This woman thought she was living in a good and, above all, secure marriage right up until she found a photograph of another woman's naked breasts in his jacket pocket, inside the torn lining. She hadn't intended to turn his seams inside out, so to speak, she didn't suspect her husband of anything, she was looking for a receipt from the cleaners, that was all, but then she found a picture of another woman's naked breasts instead. No face. No name. Nothing. Underneath the breasts it said in green ink: We miss you!

That's the kind of undeniable proof I'm talking about, mutters Torild, giving a little laugh.

You can take a picture of *my* breasts and put them in Arvid's jacket pocket, says Val Bryn.

What? says Torild, turning around to face Val Bryn.

You can take a picture of my breasts and put them in his jacket pocket, repeats Val Bryn. And then you find the picture while he's standing there watching, fish it out of his pocket, look at it with big horrified eyes, stick it under his nose, and ask him what the hell this is supposed to mean. Then you'll see that you have justice on your side. You see? It's absolutely perfect. No man would consider you crazy enough to plant the proof of infidelity yourself, just so that you could yell at him, throw him out, possibly torment him with a guilty conscience for the rest of his life.

That's right, because what's poor Arvid supposed to do, I say, when Torild stands there shaking, practically exploding with righteousness, with a picture of another woman's naked breasts in her hand, a picture she found in *his pocket?* What's he supposed to say? *I've never seen that picture before?* Is that what he should say? *That's not my picture?* Is that what he should say? *I don't recognize those breasts?* What an idiot. He'll keep on denying it to the very last second. You'd think he'd give up. Tell the truth for once. After all the years they've been together—Arvid and Torild—and then this. A painful little final scene, *I haven't been unfaithful to you, Torild, it's not what you think.*

Poor Arvid, says Torild.

Cut it out, you guys, says Julie.

Come on, says Val Bryn, we've all had our own experiences, you have to let us joke about it.

What happened to the woman who found the picture of the breasts in real life? I ask.

Oh her, says Val Bryn. The husband didn't deny a thing when she confronted him with the photograph, just said that the woman in the picture also had a face, a face that he couldn't live without, that her name was . . . well, that doesn't matter . . . that he thought about her every single minute of his life, even when he was making love to his wife, *especially then,* he said, and once he got started, once the unfaithful husband got started on his confessions, there was no stopping him, no stopping him at all, so he simply told her that he wanted to spend the rest of his life with the other woman. He had even packed his suitcase, he said. His wife cried and cried and all she could say, the only question she could think of, was: When on earth did you pack your suitcase?

Now was this a question she should have asked? Dear God in heaven, why do people want to hurt themselves so much? says Val Bryn, and continues her story:

*My suitcase,* said the unfaithful husband, and now I imagine that he might have given a little smile. *I packed my suitcase ten years ago, honey, exactly four months after we got married.* Or rather: I started packing it then. Little by little, you understand. Every time you spread out on the couch with that big ugly sweater that you liked so much and hardly bothered to open your mouth to order me around, practically burping out your commands, *could you please get me a glass of milk, could you please get me an apple, could you please get me a bowl of chips.* Or all those times you would put your arms around my neck when I was sitting in my own quiet world, reading a book, listening to music or just looking out the window, put your arms around my neck and whisper *what are you thinking, what are you thinking?* And all those times I forced myself to come up with an answer that would satisfy you, *I'm thinking about our summer vacation and what a good time we had at the movies last week or how pretty you look in that dress or maybe we should paint the kitchen yellow soon* because you were always redecorating, were never pleased; and every time you ate prunes; who the hell eats prunes, gobbles down prune after prune the way you do—smacking your lips! So you see, any little thing like that, some detail or other, I'd add another piece of clothing to my suitcase. A pair of boxer shorts, a shirt, a sock, another sock, a silk tie, an undershirt . . . The worse your . . . what shall I say? The worse your offense was . . . the bigger or finer the piece of clothing I packed. If you coughed all night long, the way you sometimes do, I packed a pullover sweater. For every "what are you thinking about" I packed a tie. For every prune a sock. If you forced me to fuck you, as you, in your own way of course, force me to fuck you, I packed linen shirts. And now and then, when I sensed the smell of you on my fingers, I might decide to pack a whole suit.

Ten years is a big suitcase, says Torild.

He must have needed a trunk after a while, I say.

A whole goddamn container, says Val Bryn.

Cut it out, says Julie.

What was it people used to say when men went off to get their kicks elsewhere? *You have to fight for him, Julie* if you really want to hold on to him, says Val Bryn.

*Staaand by your maaaan*, sings Torild, and keeps on humming the melody.

Then we all sing: *Staaaand by your maaaaan*.

Sky-high jubilation, deadly despair, Julie interrupts in a low voice and starts to weep.

Julie dear, says Val Bryn, lighting a cigarette. Thick smoke pours out of her nose and mouth; her face is hidden by the winter darkness, the black coat and the black hat.

Aleksander isn't unfaithful, Torild consoles her.

Aleksander isn't unfaithful, I console her.

Because who's he going to be unfaithful with? asks Val Bryn.

I have no idea, says Julie.

Then what makes you think he's unfaithful? I ask.

Trivial things, says Julie. He seems distracted when I try talking to him, he comes home late, often in the middle of the night, and then he doesn't sleep; he's got himself a cell phone so I never really know where he is, he switches between being way too tender and way too irritable, he takes a shower after work and before he comes to bed at night, he tells ridiculously detailed stories about where he's been and gives me answers to trick questions that I didn't even ask.

Nighttime. Julie should have been asleep long ago, and Aleksander has just come home. He's lying next to her in the double bed. He listens to her breathing, that regular deep breathing of hers. Her eyes are closed. What does she think? That he doesn't know she's awake, that he doesn't know she's awake and noticing every single movement he makes? She thinks that he thinks she's asleep. That's because she doesn't know how she looks, she doesn't know her own sounds at night. Her sleep isn't deep and regular like the sleep she's trying to feign right now. Her sleep is brittle and fragile like old newsprint, her breath barely audible. Now and then he bends over her to make sure she's still alive, the way they both used to bend over Sander's crib, put their ear to his mouth and nose, to make sure he was alive. Her sleep. A single abrupt movement on his part and her eyes fly open, *still asleep of course,* although he didn't know that when they first shared a bed, that she was still asleep when her eyes flew open and she even spoke, disjointed sentences, usually totally meaningless things *so what are you going to do about it . . . I want to hang my dresses there,* and things like that.

He has to wait until she's fast asleep so he can get rid of the rocks.

And first he will have to get rid of the rock lying between them in bed.

It doesn't make any sense to have a rock in bed, he thinks, pleased that he manages to have such a clear and precise thought in the middle of the night, and to top it all off, decide that it's that particular rock and not another rock he's going to get rid of first.

He looks around the room, dimly lit, gloomy with night, the window closed all the way again because it's so cold outside. She has even wrapped thread around the window hasps because she claims there's a draft.

He doesn't like that rock lying on top of the wardrobe.

He sees only its shadow, it's impossible to say anything about its size, shape, edges, will it be heavy to carry away? Does he need additional equipment?

There's also a little crablike rock under the chair, he hasn't noticed that one before.

Julie's breathing is heavy and regular. Isn't she going to fall asleep soon? Stop lying there pretending?

First the rock in the bed, he thinks, he's already made up his mind about that. Not the rock on the wardrobe. Not the rock under the chair. First the rock in the bed. That was the clearly formulated thought he was so pleased with just now. No time to get muddled right now. Isn't that typical? Here he has actually had a clear and sensible thought and then he starts getting it all muddled and confused. First the rock in the bed! He's going to have to make a list, a plan, it's important to have a plan, a procedural plan, he thinks, first that rock and then that rock and then that rock. It'll be fine, thinks Aleksander, giving himself a friendly pat on the shoulder.

The first time I see Carl is at the Theater Café in Oslo. He's waiting for the maître d' and letting his eyes slide around the room. He's tall, has shoulder-length dark curly hair and plum-red cowboy boots.

Father and I have been to the movies and Father is treating me to dinner and dessert. Steak with fried onions and potatoes au gratin, the house red wine, vanilla ice cream with hot fudge topping.

I catch sight of Carl before he catches sight of me.

I put my elbows on the table, rest my head in my hands, look at him. Look and look at him. Carl is leaning against the pastry case and lunch counter in his plum-red cowboy boots, waiting for the maître d' to give him a table. He's not paying any attention to me.

I look at him. Look and look at him, try to catch his eye, really fix my gaze on him—but it's no use. I blink and roll my eyes, I lick up the hot fudge topping, I roll my tongue around and around the dessert spoon, I twirl a lock of hair around my index finger and send little kisses into the air . . . nothing . . . and I take long slow sips from my glass, I slurp up the wine so my lips and cheeks turn red, hum a little refrain from Gershwin, put my hand to my forehead and sigh, blush and turn pale, fall off my chair with a crash and pretend to faint, lie exhausted and bruised on the floor, under the table, raise my head and look at him, *he's not paying any attention to me.*

What do you do with a man like that?

After a while he catches sight of a lovely young tan blonde with big breasts. The blonde and her girlfriend are sitting at a table near Father's and mine. The blonde waves to him. She points at an empty chair next to her own. You can sit with me and my girlfriend, she winks. I'm lying on my stomach under the table and watching the plum-red cowboy boots coming closer. They're coming closer. But they're not coming to me. They're coming to her.

*He's not paying any attention to me,* I snarl.

Who? says Father.

Father looks around and finally notices that I'm lying on the floor, floundering. He says he thinks I ought to sit on my chair. I agree with Father about that. When I'm back in my seat again, he asks me who isn't paying any attention to me.

The tall guy who's just sitting down over there, I say, at the table over there, with the blonde and her girlfriend, the guy with the dark curly hair.

That blonde is really stunning, says Father.

Why doesn't anyone ever look at me? I say.

You haven't found your own style yet, says Father.

I wish I was Catherine Deneuve, I say.

If I stretch my imagination a little I might agree that you look like Mary Pickford, says Father.

I look at the man with the dark curly hair.

But I can sing, I say. No man can resist me when I sing.

The man with the dark curly hair is laughing with the blonde.

You're quite a good dancer too, says Father. Better than Julie.

I turn to Father: I think Aleksander's cheating on her, I say.

Cheating on Julie? says Father.

Yes, I say.

With who? says Father.

I don't know.

I was hoping that Aleksander would make her happy, Father says in a low voice.

He's not making her happy.

But I suppose you could say it isn't his job to make her happy, says Father.

Then what's the point of marriage? I look at Father. Then what's the point?

I don't understand who told you that the point of anything is to be happy, says Father.


Sometimes I think about that summer excursion to the little cabin in Värmland. I think about a scene that seemed meaningless at the time but suddenly made sense when Julie said that Aleksander was cheating on her.

Val Bryn is sitting in the wicker chair next to the open window and enjoying the breeze. Or rather: She's practically lying in the chair, a big straw hat hiding her face, one thin arm hanging limply to the floor, the stub of a cigarette between her fingers.

Carl and Aleksander try to light a fire in the fireplace. Out in the kitchen Arvid is sitting around howling to himself.

Upstairs: In one room Torild is lying under the comforter, in the next room Julie is singing to Sander.

I don't remember what I was doing.

Maybe I took a walk in the garden and imagined I was listening to grasshoppers, pretended I was invisible among all the trees. Now and then I would peek in through the living room window. Peek at Carl in front of the fireplace and think that he was my beloved. Peek at Aleksander in front of the fireplace and think nothing. I picked some wildflowers and stuck them into the buttonholes of my blouse. I took off my shoes and socks. I chased a bumblebee down the slope to the outhouse. I went back up to the main cabin. I peeked in the living room window. Val Bryn is reclining in the wicker chair, the straw hat, the cigarette, the long thin arm. Val Bryn is barefoot. She's wiggling her toes to the rhythm of the music that someone has put on. Evert Taube, since we're in Sweden out in the country and it's summer, I think. Val Bryn has a pair of incredibly lovely little white feet. Her toes are as smooth as pearls. Her toenails are painted red like the wild strawberries we ate for dessert, with a little sugar on top. She's wiggling and wiggling. I suddenly have an urge to taste her toe. I've never felt any desire for a woman before and can't say that I feel a desire for Val Bryn right now. I just have an urge to taste a toe, it doesn't matter which one. They're so indescribably sweet. I'm sure they taste heavenly. And she's wiggling them in such an enticing way. I stand there and stare. Aleksander turns around, having finally started the fire in the fireplace. He and Val Bryn are alone in the room. Carl has gone out to the kitchen to get something. Aleksander turns around. He looks at Val Bryn. He looks at all of Val Bryn. And suddenly he's kneeling down in front of her with her whole foot in his mouth. She smiles, closes her eyes. He's practically slurping up her toes, one by one, like oysters. And then he licks his lips. Afterwards he stands up abruptly and leaves the room.

I didn't give much thought to what had happened. I naturally understood why Aleksander had done it. I don't care much for oysters myself. But if there's a bowl of strawberry pudding with whipped cream on the kitchen table, I can't help gobbling it all up, even if it was really intended for someone else. Because how often do you actually come across a bowl of genuine strawberry pudding with whipped cream nowadays? I haven't eaten strawberry pudding with whipped cream since I was little and Grandma used to sing that song: Strawberry pudding with whipped cream, it tastes like a dream, and makes children beam.

As I said: I didn't give it much thought. I forgave Aleksander his little—what shall I call it?—his little indiscretion, and of course I didn't say anything to Julie.

But I tell the story to Father. A year later. At a different restaurant, not the Theater Café.

Father scratches under his eye.

Takes a swallow of red wine.

Do you mean that Aleksander is cheating on Julie with Val Bryn, her maid of honor? he says.

I don't know, I'm just telling you the story.

Exactly how far into his mouth was her foot? asks Father.

I open my mouth as wide as I can and stick my hand inside.

Father nods.

That far—is that right?

About this far, yes.

We're both silent for a moment. Then I ask: Exactly what do you think the word infidelity implies, Father?

Intercourse, says Father.

That's obvious.

Everything that involves total nakedness on both sides, he says hesitantly.

Total nakedness as opposed to partial nakedness? I ask.

Something like that, he mutters.

What about deep kisses?

Nooo, says Father.

I disagree, I say. Think about everything you find out about another person from a kiss. I know *everything* about how a man—if you'll pardon me for being so direct, Father—I know everything I need to know about a man from the way he kisses me. If he's married and kisses me, I know things about him that only his former lovers and wife should know.

That's nonsense, says Father. You don't know a thing.

What about the eating, kissing, slurping, and licking of fingers and toes—is that infidelity?

Karin, I think that depends on how it's done, you should know that, says Father, resigned.

A whole foot in the mouth?

Father looks at the ceiling.

A whole foot in the mouth? I repeat.

A whole foot in the mouth is not good, says Father.

Exactly, I say, I've never trusted Val Bryn.

This isn't just about her, says Father.

The impeccable Aleksander Lange Bakke! I say. One day I'll shoot him.

Now now, says Father, reaching across the table to stroke my hair. Don't get so melodramatic. Leave Julie and Aleksander in peace with their marriage. You're no angel yourself, Karin.

Aleksander sits up in bed. Julie is breathing beside him. Breathing in. Breathing out. Breathing in. Breathing out. Breathing in. Breathing out.

Aleksander looks toward the window.

Can you strangle a person with sewing thread?

Will the thread snap if you pull it tight around the neck of the person in question?

It's definitely bound to snap.

The next day he would see a red line, like a necklace around her neck where the thread had cut into her skin.

But nothing more.

He would have to use rope. Maybe twine. Or his bare hands.

He thinks about the final scene in *One Flew Over the Cuckoo's Nest*, when the Indian puts the pillow over Jack Nicholson's face and then breaks through the bars, disappearing out the window toward the light.

But Julie. Aleksander looks down at her lying beside him. But Julie just keeps on breathing heavily.

Breathing in. Breathing out. Breathing in. I'm never going to get out of here. Aleksander sits up abruptly in bed. I'm never going to get out of here.

Sometimes when he comes home at night and she's asleep

or pretending to be asleep, he pulls the comforter away and looks at her body. So skinny. So skinny it is. She usually sleeps on her stomach, her blond hair down her back, a pillow between her thighs. Her thin neck, ribs, butt, calves, toes.

Everything on Julie is small and thin and breakable.

Except for her feet, of course.

The rock lying between them in bed is about the same size as one of Julie's feet.

She doesn't paint her toenails red.

Aleksander reaches out for the rock. Picks it up, lifts it up.

I'm going to get rid of this rock. It's totally unacceptable to have a rock lying between us in bed, he thinks.

He holds the rock up in front of him, it's a little heavier than he thought. But not so heavy that he can't put it on the windowsill, or on the floor next to the other, bigger rock, or on top of the wardrobe.

He lets his index finger glide over it, feeling it, the hollows, the nubs, and then he puts it back on the bed.

Eventually he'll have to get the rock out of the house. Not just out of the bed. But out of the house. All the rocks out of the house!

To put it on the windowsill or on the floor or on top of the wardrobe is just a temporary solution, thinks Aleksander.

f anyone asks how in the world I managed to seduce Carl, the tall man with the dark curly hair and the plum-red cowboy boots, I just tell them what happened that evening in April when I was having dinner with Father at the Theater Café. The truth is, everything begins and ends with Gershwin. There are lots of things I have doubts about, but never Gershwin. A girl who can sing Gershwin doesn't have to worry about anything in life.

Just listen!

> *There's a boat dat's leavin' soon for New York,*
> *Come wid me*
> *Dat's where we belong, sister.*
> *You an' me kin live dat high life in New York.*
> *Come wid me,*
> *Dere you can't go wrong, sister!*

But I'm going to tell the story from the beginning. Father and I have been to the movies and seen that sappy musical *High Society* with Frank Sinatra and Grace Kelly in the starring roles. In the middle of the film Frank Sinatra lays the charm on Grace Kelly—probably charming her into bed, for all I know—but they didn't show things like that in the movies in the old days, instead they danced; but as I said, he put the charm on her just by singing about her eyes.

I get up from my chair and say to Father: Give me your hat!
    What? says Father.
    Give me your hat.
    It's in the cloakroom, says Father.
    Then I'll go and get it, I say.
    Sit down, Karin, says Father.
    I kiss Father on the forehead and turn away.
    You're not in charge of me anymore, I laugh.
    I'm in charge of my hat, shouts Father.

I get Father's hat from the cloakroom, put it on my head, and look at myself in the big mirror near the entrance.
    That hat is a little too big for you, says the doorman.
    I look at him in the mirror, meet his eyes.
    But it looks fine, I say.

I go back into the restaurant, past Father, and climb up onto the balcony where the Theater Café's trio is sitting.
    Let me introduce them: the leader Sørensen on piano, Charley on cello, Wikstrøm on violin. They're all old, close to a hundred, I'm sure. And they look a little like puppets in an Ivo Caprino movie.

Sørensen, I say, can you play Gershwin?
    Hmm, says Sørensen, giving Charley and Wikstrøm a doubtful look. There's nothing I despise more than half-tipsy ladies who suddenly decide they're going to sing "Summertime" in the restaurant, says Sørensen.
    I'm *not* half-tipsy (I'm more than that, I'm never just half anything, but I don't tell Sørensen that) and I'm *not* going to sing "Summertime," I say.

Hmm, says Sørensen, squinting his eyes.

I don't mind helping her out, says Charley.

Sure, why not, says Wikstrøm.

Hmm, says Sørensen hesitantly, peering over the railing and down at the man with the dark curly hair and the plum-red cowboy boots. You're trying to seduce that man down there? he asks.

I nod.

You haven't had much luck tonight, have you?

No, I say.

Sørensen shakes his head and turns to his colleagues.

That fellow isn't going to pay any attention to her no matter what she does. We can't help her. He'd rather have the blonde.

What blonde? says Charley.

That one over there. See? The one with the girlfriend.

Charley and Wikstrøm lean over the railing.

Lovely, murmurs Charley.

Enchanting, says Wikstrøm.

Listen here, I say. Are you playing Gershwin or aren't you?

You don't have a chance, says Sørensen, shrugging his shoulders.

I can sing, I say.

She can sing, says Charley.

But can you dance? asks Sørensen.

I can dance, I say.

She can dance, says Charley.


Wikstrøm peers at me from behind his glasses.

What's your name? he asks and even goes so far as to touch my hair. His hands are big and old.

Karin Blom. My name is Karin Blom.

Are you related to Rikard Blom, the one who emigrated to America?

I'm his granddaughter.

I knew there was something, says Wikstrøm.

Of course I never met him, I say. He died during the war.

I know, I knew him, says Wikstrøm.

You did?

Yes, I did. We arrived in New York at about the same time, must have been in 1931, I remember because that was the year the cornet player Buddy Bolden died in the insane asylum in Louisiana. I remember we talked about it, Rikard and I, that we'd never get to hear Buddy Bolden play, that his music died with him, that the only thing we could do was to close our eyes and *imagine* how it sounded when, sometime at the beginning of the century—before he was imprisoned, before he drank himself senseless and hit his mother-in-law over the head with a pitcher—he lifted the cornet to his lips and began to play.

Come off it, Wikstrøm, interrupts Sørensen. Nobody knew who Buddy Bolden was back then.

Let him talk, mutters Charley. It's not doing any harm.

Rikard and I had only three things on our minds, continues Wikstrøm: boxing, jazz, and women. And it didn't take long before your grandfather fell in love with a Norwegian lady who lived in Brooklyn, in Bay Ridge, I think, yes that must have been just before he met the woman who was to be your grandmother.

Do you know what her name was? I ask. The Norwegian lady, I mean, that he fell in love with?

I don't remember, he replies. I'm getting old. All muddle-headed, you know. Wikstrøm points at his own head, sketches circles in the air. Besides, I lost touch with Rikard after a while. But I can still see that woman of his before my eyes, I could certainly understand why he fell in love with her, she was quite a lady. Just as shapely, long-limbed, sleek, and beautiful as the George Washington Bridge. I remember it well, the bridge, that is; it was finished the same year I arrived. There was a lot of talk about it back then, of course, and I liked to stand a little distance away and look at it in the afternoon light. I'm not in the habit of comparing women to bridges, but she was no less impressive.

But you don't remember what her name was, not even if you close your eyes and think real hard?

Could it have been Selma? asks Wikstrøm.

Yes, of course, I say.

Then let's say that. Her name was probably Selma.

And Grandfather, what was he like? What kind of man was he, anyway?

A bit of a dreamer. But then he was hooked on Gershwin, just like you. I remember he told me about his first days in New York, after the long ship voyage and the endless hours on Ellis Island, when he walked and walked and walked, up and down the streets, forgetting the time, forgetting to eat, just taking in the city. Bewitched by the smells, the sounds, the sights, convinced that Gershwin had composed *Rhapsody in Blue* just for him. But you're asking me what kind of man he was.

Wikstrøm takes a deep breath. I'm going to tell you. It was well known. Rikard Blom was like Little Frikk in the fairy tale; *nobody could say no to the very first thing he asked for.*

Sørensen, the leader of the trio, raises his hand in the air, squints his eyes.

We've been taking a break, but the break is over now, he says, resuming his position at the piano.

I think we should give her a chance, says Charley, pointing at me.

Are you sure you can sing? says Sørensen. I'm not going to play for you if you can't sing.

I can sing, I say.

And dance? says Sørensen.

I can dance, I say.

So if anyone asks how I seduced Carl, the tall man with the dark curly hair and the plum-red cowboy boots, I just tell them what happened on that evening in April when I was having dinner with Father at the Theater Café.

The leader Sørensen waits until I get down from the balcony and stroll over to the table where Carl is sitting with the blonde and her girlfriend.

The blonde looks up. The blonde looks at me. The blonde opens her mouth and yawns as if the mere sight of me is enough to put her to sleep. *Who are you? Like, who are you? And why are you standing there taking up space? Don't you know that I'm the one, not you, who's blonde and pretty and captivating and fascinating and lovely and beautiful?*

Excuse me, she chirps sweetly, *but do we know you?*

I grab the bottle of red wine from the table and pour what's left of the wine over her head.

*Now,* I say, *now you know me!*

The girlfriend gasps.

Forgive me, I say.

I look at the blonde. I feel a little sorry for her now.

Don't get hysterical, I say. I didn't really mean for you to get so wet. But you see I *have* to take this man home with me tonight (I point at Carl) and YOU (I point at the blonde) are in the way.

I turn to face Carl: Carl! That's your name, isn't it? (I give a deep, heartfelt sigh.) *Carl.* The name alone. I've been watching you all evening and even though you're angry with me right now because I poured wine on your girlfriend, I have to tell you that you're *extraordinary,* that I think you're extraordinary, that I swear on my grandfather's grave that if you get up now and leave this restaurant with me, you'll never ever look back.

The blonde cautiously gets up, a dripping red sea monster with claws.

Who the hell do you think you are? she whispers.

I am Karin, I say, Karin Blom!

I doff my hat and make a deep bow.

At the same time I give a little signal, a little wave, to Sørensen, Charley, and Wikstrøm up on the balcony. They nod and give me a thumbs-up. Then they start to play.

Oh, how they play, Julie. You should have been there.

They play like they've never played before. And I sing like I've never sung before. A gasp goes through the Theater Café. And everybody's there that night—I won't name names—but everybody's there: the actress, the author, the journalist, the newspaper editor, the theater director, the publisher, the film director. You know who they are, Julie. And everybody stops talking and simply listens. Father too.

That's Gershwin.

I sweep the glasses and plates and silverware and tablecloth off the table, grab Carl by the hand, pull him up to me, say now it's time to dance, Carl, and I dance Carl like Carl has never been danced before.

'm not going to ask you to believe that Carl had magic cowboy boots. I might have said something like that to Julie, Torild, and Val Bryn one evening when we were out on the town. There are lots of things I say after a few too many glasses of one thing or another.

(So if you happen to run into Torild or Val Bryn sometime, and they happen to mention that they once knew a girl named Karin Blom, and that she was Carl's beloved, the man with the magic cowboy boots—then take it all with a grain of salt.)

I don't mean to brag. Or make things up. Or bite off more than I can chew. But sometimes it's actually necessary—to tell it not just like it is—but to tell it a little more than it is.

When I was a child, Grandma and Anni worried that I didn't tell the truth. They said that liars would not be tolerated in a community. They said I exaggerated to make other people like me. They said I would end up a lonely person. Look at Julie, they said, look at Julie, she doesn't carry on that way. I didn't think that was a very good example, using Julie, because she was much lonelier than I was. You were much lonelier than me, Julie.

---

I remember when I told Anni that I'd killed Pete, the insufferable dachshund, and I found out the difference between a lie that paid and a lie that didn't pay. The point is that Anni was furious with me even when I told her that I hadn't really killed Pete. She was furious because I was walking around with those kinds of thoughts; you're a horrible little child, walking around with those thoughts in your head, said Anni and gave me a shake. It wasn't worth it: getting into so much trouble over a lie that didn't pay. That's why I decided to get better. I decided to lie better. Then I wouldn't get in so much trouble. I wouldn't wind up a lonely person rejected by the community, the way Anni and Grandma had predicted I would.

I remember once—this happened several years before the incident with the dachshund—when the teacher sent me to detention after school. I was maybe eight or nine and in the third grade, and the teacher's name was Strung. Not Mrs. Strung or Miss Strung or Cecilie Strung. Just Strung. She scared me a little, and that's not such a small matter, since I'm usually not scared of anything. But Strung was cold and stern and had no sense of humor if truth be told.

At any rate, here's the story: The summer I turned nine I wrote a letter to the circus director Arne Arnardo and asked if I could join his next circus tour. I wrote that he could decide what I should do, seeing as he had experience with new performers after all, but if I was going to choose for myself then I'd prefer to be: 1) a tightrope walker; 2) a lady with plumes on a white horse; 3) an acrobat.

Several weeks later, after Arnardo had answered my letter and welcomed me to his circus as an apprentice tightrope walker, I happened to tell this to a few select classmates of mine. I didn't want to show them the letter. Letters are personal things, I said. But I told them I was going to quit school after fall vacation and start practicing my balancing acts full time so I'd be ready before the big circus tour the following summer. I also mentioned this to Strung, who complained that I wasn't doing my homework and that I stared out the window during class. I told her I was Arne Arnardo's new apprentice tightrope walker and that it really wasn't necessary for me to do my homework. The first time I told her this she shook her head as if I'd said something stupid. *Pull yourself together, Karin Blom,* she said and walked back to her desk. The next time I mentioned it, she pounded her fist on my desk and said: Don't you see you're making a fool of yourself with all your stories, why do you always have to exaggerate like that, isn't it good enough just to go to the circus like other children, why do you have to . . . ? She couldn't even finish her sentence, she was so annoyed with me.

I didn't reply, just clamped my mouth shut and looked out the window.

I remember thinking: It's *one* thing for nobody to believe me when I lie, but when nobody believes me when I'm telling the truth. . . . And then I thought . . . and then I hoped that Strung would die a gruesome and ghastly death because she'd said those things to me in front of the other children in my class.

The third time I mentioned Arne Arnardo to Strung she marched right up to the blackboard and gave a lecture. She told us what happens to people who lie and exaggerate, she said those kinds of people get a hole inside them, that for every lie they tell the hole gets bigger, until finally they're no longer a person but just a hole that anyone can stick his hand through. I thought about my body with Strung's hand inside it; I thought about my body, a hoop with little tiny circus dogs leaping through it; I thought about my body, and at exactly that moment—at exactly that moment—there was a knock on the classroom door, and Arne Arnardo was standing in the doorway with all his glittering eminence and said I'm here.

Bless you, Mr. Circus Director, for coming. I'm here, he said. I'm here looking for Karin Blom.

Let me assure you: *Nobody* ever believes that story when I tell it. Not Julie, not Val Bryn, not Torild, not anybody else. (But that my beloved Carl had magic cowboy boots—that they believe.) Unlike lots of other things—for example that I killed Anni's dachshund with a rock—the circus story is actually true. I don't remember too well how it all came about. But there *is* a perfectly reasonable explanation for why Arne Arnardo showed up at our classroom on exactly that day and asked for me. Maybe he was giving out free circus tickets to good schoolchildren—I don't know. But there *is* an explanation. It happened. Arnardo came.

And I'll tell you something else: Strung died a gruesome and ghastly death right after that episode. You might have heard about it. It was a famous murder case in the seventies. There was a lot about it in the papers. *Schoolteacher murdered by unknown assailant.*

*Schoolteacher murdered in Oslo.*

*Schoolteacher brutally murdered in her own home.*

One night a murderer crept into Strung's apartment and drilled a hole, no bigger than a peephole, right through her body, right between her breasts—which always reminded me of Dumbo's ears.

It was a horrible case. I won't deny it. I didn't wish her dead, not like that. To this day I regret that I had such hideous and unforgivable thoughts about another human being just because she didn't like my stories.

One night many years later, I remember waking up with a vision of light flooding through Strung's body, at last.

But to claim that Carl had magic cowboy boots—never! On that very first evening, after I had sung and danced him at the Theater Café; after he had bent down and whispered in that lovely tanned blonde's lovely tanned ear: *I'm sorry, darling, I have to go, I have to go now;* after we had snagged a cab and driven to my apartment on Sorgenfri Street; after we had undressed but before we lay down—that's when he said it. He said: I'm not taking off my cowboy boots!

He's standing on the hardwood floor next to my bed, big and dark and utterly delicious, an honest-to-god sexual athlete, and he says: I'm not taking off my cowboy boots. Oh really, I say, why not? Because they're magic, he says. I see, I say. You've never experienced anything like it, he says. I don't doubt it, I say, and push him down onto the bed.

So *I'm* not the one going around bragging about my beloved's magic cowboy boots. They can handle that all on their own. Or at least Carl can. And with good reason, to tell the truth. The first time we go to bed together, it takes five days before he lets me go.

Every once in a while I get out of bed, sit down on the window ledge, light a cigarette, and pretend that I don't see us. Shadows embracing each other, shadows clinging to each other. I open the window and feel the night breeze against my face. It's warm outside at night. We listen to an old Mingus recording on the CD player; I've pressed the repeat button.

I think about many different things when I'm in bed with Carl. That's not so strange. Five days and nights. That's a long time. For instance, I wonder why he always locks the door when he takes a bath in my bathroom. He doesn't have his own bathtub, and when he saw that I had one he practically started crying with joy and hugged me and kissed me so I got all flustered.

And then I think about something I said once as we lay in bed in my apartment. I said that I liked it so much when he touched my belly button, I said that the belly button was a woman's most sensitive spot, I said that my belly button was the only place on my body that no man had discovered yet, I said that the belly button was every woman's Abracadabra. So now we're lying here, for five days or more, and Mingus is playing *don't drop that atomic bomb on me,* and Carl has practically moved into my belly button, he preens and showers in my belly button as if it was a big cool pool—and I don't know how to tell him that it was just something I said. It was all nonsense. That stuff about my belly button.

And I think about that time he went with us to the cabin in Värmland. It must have been four or five in the morning, we were about to go to bed, the bed was little and narrow and hard and I said: Can't you take off your cowboy boots tonight, Carl? And Carl said: No, I'm nothing without my cowboy boots. Of course you are, I said. You're still Carl. No, said Carl, I'm nothing. Come on, I said, be brave.

Carl is sitting naked on the edge of the bed, staring down at his cowboy boot feet that seem big and out of place in that flower-strewn Värmland bedroom.

I start tugging on one of his boots.

Oh come on, I say softly, take them off.

No, he says, and tugs the opposite direction.

Come on, I say, tugging harder.

No, he says and pushes me away.

Come on, I say.

Leave me alone, he says.

Come on, I say.

Didn't you hear what I said? he says.

Carl looks at me and shouts: Didn't you hear what I said? Can't you leave me alone?

That night I waited until he'd fallen asleep. His breathing was heavy and regular and calm, he slept like a child, on his back, his palms open on either side of his head. I crawled under the covers, crawled down to his feet—he's a big man, it was a long way down to his feet—I crawled past his chest with the seven dark strands of hair, his stomach, his thighs, his knees, his calves, his feet. I took up a good position at the foot of the bed, all of me under the covers. I wanted to get as good a grip on the cowboy boots as possible.

Then I started tugging.

First the right cowboy boot.

It was on tighter than I thought. I tugged and tugged, was almost about to give up because it was on so tight, sweating and snorting under the covers. But at last, with a plop, like when a wine bottle lets go of its cork, I was sitting with one of the cowboy boots in my hand.

The left cowboy boot was easier to get off. It only took a few minutes. Not even that.

I peeked out from under the covers. Carl was still sleeping. Everything was quiet. Everything was normal. Carl was breathing normally. I set the cowboy boots neatly side by side under the bed, crawled up to the pillow, kissed him on the ear, and lay down to sleep.

The next morning I woke up because my head hurt and I felt like throwing up.

Carl was asleep.

I got up, went out of the bedroom, down the green-painted stairs that were steep. Torild and Arvid were sitting on the kitchen floor and talking in low voices. I didn't say anything to them. No one else was up yet. I went out to the yard and drank cold water from the pump. The sun was shining. A gray-striped cat was sitting motionless in the grass and looking at me.

Afterwards I went back inside, up the green stairs, into the bedroom.

Carl was awake.

Carl was no longer Carl.

Carl was a mackerel.

Carl was a little green-and-blue fish desperately wriggling around on top of the covers and shouting *what have you done to me what have you done to me?*

I looked at him.

He had bulging pale blue eyes, two big fins and seven small ones.

Carl gasped: *I need water, hurry up or I'm going to die.*

I put my hand over my mouth.

I sat down on the edge of the bed.

Carl, I said . . . I'm so terribly sorry . . .

Hurry up, he screamed, I need water! He sounded exactly the same as before: a touch too whiny and nasal for a man.

I ran down the green-painted stairs, into the kitchen. Torild was sitting alone on the floor with her coffee cup, reading the paper.

What's the matter with you? she asked, looking up.

Why can't I EVER find a real man, I shouted.

Torild shrugged her shoulders and kept on reading.

I found a big, clear glass bowl in the cupboard, ran out to the well, and filled it with water. Then I ran up the stairs, running so fast that I spilled water all over the floor and steps.

Carl was lying on the bed and gasping for air. He could barely move anymore. I picked him up in my hands—he was really slippery—and carefully put him into the glass bowl. It didn't take long before he began to recover.

He swam cautiously back and forth, then a little faster, and after a while he was just as frisky as ever. But the whole time he stared at me reproachfully through the glass bowl.

Do you have anything you'd like to tell me? he said. His voice was unnaturally calm. The water bubbled when he spoke.

I looked at the floor.

I took off your cowboy boots while you were sleeping, I whispered.

I told you not to do it, he said. I remember saying quite clearly last night that I was nothing without my cowboy boots.

I didn't know you meant it so *literally,* I said. I closed my eyes. I opened my eyes.

Carl swam back and forth. He didn't stop. My eyes hurt from looking at him.

Can't you stop swimming all the time, can't you stand still a minute? I said. It's so hard to talk to you when you're swimming back and forth all the time.

I can't stand still, Karin. I don't have an air bladder. If I stand still, I can't breathe.

I shook my head.

Is there any way we can fix this? I asked.

I don't know, said Carl. Yesterday I was a man, today I'm a mackerel. It's your fault. You're the one who did this. What are you planning to do about it?

I'd really like to help you. I didn't mean to cause all these problems.

Then what are you planning to do about it?

I looked at him, back and forth in the glass bowl.

I said: I have a slight headache right now, I'm not thinking so good, but maybe we could have breakfast first—then we can sit down and talk about it afterwards.

I can't eat breakfast . . . *like this*! snarled Carl, causing the water to sputter. Look at me, Karin! Just look at me! His fins flapped back and forth. Your family is going to laugh at me.

I sighed. I said: Everybody was up late last night. Everybody drank a little too much wine. I think everybody's going to have enough to do today dealing with their own problems. We'll pretend like nothing's happened, Carl. If anyone asks, then we'll say that you're not feeling like yourself. I picked up the glass bowl, holding it carefully in my hands; I went out of the bedroom, down the green-painted stairs, and into the kitchen.

Carl didn't like having everybody stare at him. It was bad enough that he had to swim around in a glass bowl, but the worst thing was that Torild began to laugh. That was his greatest fear, that people would laugh at him.

I put the glass bowl on the kitchen table. Aleksander, Julie, Torild, and Arvid tried pretending not to notice, but it wasn't easy. Carl swam back and forth and glared furiously at them all, and it didn't help his mood any when Sander jumped up and down in his place and shouted: *Look! We've got a fish!*

Julie tried to hush him—but Sander ignored her.

*Look, Mom! Look! Karin has caught a really big fish.*

It was no surprise that Torild began to laugh. She wasn't to blame. It was really all Sander's fault—but you can't blame a child either. He just wanted to help me feed the fish.

Before anyone realized what was going on, he grabbed the tin of mackerel in tomato sauce, scraped out what was left with a spoon, and dipped the spoon in the glass bowl.

The water turned red and murky and Carl started to scream.

*No, not that,* he screamed, *not that!*

That's when Torild couldn't contain herself any longer. That's when she began to laugh. It started with a couple of whimpers. Then a shrill singing sound. Then a couple of desperate sniffs. Then a snort—an explosion—that she couldn't stop. Torild laughed and laughed and laughed so the buttons on her white blouse—already covered with spots of mackerel in tomato sauce—popped off, one by one.

Carl sulked for the rest of the day. He said it was my fault that he'd been made a laughingstock. He said he doubted whether he could love me after that. Then he demanded that I carry his glass bowl up to the bedroom, close the door, and let him swim in peace.

Sometimes I ask myself: When is a marriage over?

I'm sure it's long before the spouses agree that now it's over, now we have to split up—and then actually go through with a divorce.

So that's why I ask: When is a marriage over?

Is it when one of us thinks: I wish you were dead?

Is it when one of us says (for the very first time): I don't want to live with you anymore? You're ruining my life?

Is it when one of us stares at the ceiling, whispering: I'd do anything not to sleep with you tonight?

I think about Julie and Aleksander—not about the scene that unfolded between Aleksander and Val Bryn in the living room of the cabin in Värmland, when Aleksander in a moment of forgetful bliss devoured one of her feet; I think about the scene that unfolded several hours later, late that night, after everyone had gone to bed. It wasn't even a scene, it was really nothing, just an image. An image of Julie sitting alone on the green-painted stairs and crying.

I get out of bed and leave the bedroom, it's the middle of the night, actually closer to morning than night, because the sun is shining through all the windows. I see her as soon as I close the bedroom door. She's sitting there, little and hunched up on the bottom step. She's wearing white panties and a white T-shirt. The sun is shining on all that white. She has wrapped her arms around her legs and is resting her forehead on her knees. She doesn't say anything. She's crying.

Sometimes I hear Julie's voice as if it were my own.

Julie says: Come and sit down here next to me, Karin, and I walk down the stairs, sit down next to her on the step.

Julie says:
    Sometimes I wish I were you, but I'm not you, I'm not you.

Then she says:
    A few months ago, at the beginning of May, I wake Aleksander up in the middle of the night, closer to morning than night, stroke his face, shake his shoulder a little, careful movements so as not to annoy him, and I know he's awake even though he's pretending to be asleep. Finally he can't keep pretending anymore. He says: What time is it? I tell him what time it is. He says I'm trying to sleep. I say we have to talk. We can't keep going on like this. He sighs and says what do you mean *like this*, Julie, it's the middle of the night. And I say *like this*. I know that something's wrong but I don't know what it is. Like this. Nothing is wrong, he says. Nothing. Nothing, for God's sake. Then I say: I think you're being unfaithful. Are you being unfaithful? No, he says. Maybe not, I say. But can't you for once tell the truth? Just once? I have nothing to tell, he says. Do you want me to make something up just to satisfy you? No, I say, I just want you to tell the truth. And then I say: I've got an idea. I've got an idea, I say. First I'll tell you something . . . something I haven't dared tell you before . . . and then you'll tell me something . . . and then we'll be even. Don't you see?

Then we'll be even. I can't be mad at you and you can't be mad at me. I just want us to be back together the way we used to be.

If you think you have something to tell me, he says in a low voice.

I'm not saying I have anything to tell you, I say, I'm not saying I've done anything, I'm just saying, purely hypothetically . . .

Hypothetically? he says.

You know what I mean, I say.

And then Julie says:

We sat up in bed, Aleksander turned on the lamp on the nightstand. We didn't speak. After a little while Aleksander went out to the kitchen, came back with coffee, sat down on the bed, and said: So come on, tell me!

We looked at each other, and I swear I heard God say to the devil: Now you'd better take over here, old friend, I can't do anything more for these people, and I cried and said that I'd met a man one evening when I was out on the town with Val and Torild; I said the man's name was Daniel; I said that I went home with him and had gone to bed with him; that of course I regretted it; that I hadn't seen him again. *But I lied,* don't you see? Daniel was just a name I made up. I *had* to say something. If I had said: Aleksander, I haven't been unfaithful to you, ever; well, then he would have replied: And I haven't been unfaithful to you—and then we would have been right back where we started, right? So I had to make up a story, not too extreme, of course, not three or four lovers over a long period of time, etc., he would never forgive that; but not too innocent either. I knew that he would adapt his story to match mine—how much he dared tell me, I mean—he didn't want to be left sitting there holding the bag. The point was to be even, right? Being even is zero. Being even is a new beginning. Being even is good.

Being even has always played a big role in our marriage. Especially after Sander was born. Last night I got up when he was crying. Tonight it's your turn. Things like that. Last Sunday I took him out so you could sleep, this Sunday you'll have to think up something. We kept track of everything: who had done the shopping, made dinner, washed laundry, who had worked the longest, who was most tired, who had gone into town and had fun while the other one didn't have fun, who had gone off with friends for a few days while the other one stayed home to take care of things, who had sung the most lullabies to Sander, who had read the most stories, who had spent the most hours alone with him on Sundays so the other one could have some peace; yes, we even counted the hours, and who had slept the longest in the morning. That was the big one. Who had slept the longest in the morning. We kept track, with time and sleep as the currency. Especially sleep. I fantasized about sleep, I thought sleep, I talked sleep, I dreamt sleep, I cried sleep, I wanted to furnish the whole apartment with sleep, a double bed in the bedroom, a rollaway bed in the living room, a cot in the hallway, mattresses and pillows and blankets in the attic. I wanted to have secret little rooms all over town, with beds in them too, so I could sleep, sleep as long as I wanted to without it costing anything, sleep without paying the price, because the price was to be awake, present, alert, as wife, as mother. I couldn't handle it. I didn't want to. I didn't want to be there. I didn't want to be.

After I told Aleksander about Daniel he calmly went into the bathroom, and slammed his fist into the mirror over the sink so it shattered. He stood there looking at his own face in what was left of the mirror. His hand was bleeding. When he came back he stretched out his hand toward me and asked me without words if we could stop now, not say anything more, and I smiled and said, also without words of course, that that's not very fair, is it, a deal is a deal, and he said: I ran into a woman about a year ago, I'd had too much to drink, I went home with her, it didn't mean anything. I swear it. She asked if we could meet again and I said no.

So what was her name? I say.

Is that so important? he says.

Yes, I say.

It doesn't make any difference, he says.

Yes it does, I say.

Her name was Vera, he says.

Vera what? I say.

Vera Lund, he says. You don't know her. It meant nothing to me.

So then we made love—that was the first time since Sander was born that I wanted to, really *wanted* to; I was all knotted up inside and now it came unraveled. I reached out toward him, it spilled out of me, I didn't want to wait, I didn't want to wait anymore. I had been asleep so long, my body had been asleep so long—and suddenly this desire. This love, *at last*. This joy— like being set free, like deep sobbing.

I came almost at once, but Aleksander kept going, tender and considerate. He whispered loving words to me, he kissed me on the eyelids, the nose, the mouth, he caught my eye and smiled—but all of this just made me feel sick now. He repelled me. His body repelled me. His semen repelled me. My own lust repelled me. I remember thinking—as I smiled at him through my tears—can't you be done with it soon so I can sleep?

Afterwards we each lay on our own side of the bed. We reached for each other, my arms stretched out toward him, his arms stretched out toward me, but we couldn't reach each other. Aleksander sat up, turned off the light on the nightstand, lay back down. He says good night. I say good night. He says:

Do you think about him—about Daniel—when you're making love with me?

No, of course not.

I don't think we should talk about all this anymore, he says.

No, I say.

I think we should put it behind us.

Do you think we can?

Yes, I think so.

And then he stretched out his arms toward me again and I stretched out my arms toward him, and we stretched out toward each other.

I don't know, I say, I don't know if we can.


I'm awakened by Sander standing in the doorway and saying: Aren't you getting up soon? Aleksander doesn't move.

No, I say. Let me sleep some more. I prop myself up in bed. I see his shadow in the doorway. *Soon, sweetie* I say. Sander goes back to the living room and closes the door behind him.

No is the first word.

Every morning: *I can't, I don't know how, let me go.* Every morning, and I think about everything I could say so I don't have to get up. Not make breakfast, not take Sander to day care, not go to work, not meet any people. I can say I'm sick, I can get the doctor to write me an excuse, I can tell Aleksander I'm sick and call in to work and say I'm sick. Today is Sunday. I can tell Aleksander I'm sick. You have to get up, Aleksander. Sander's awake.

No is the first word. One time Sander came walking up the stairs alone with a much too big schoolbag on his back. We live on the fourth floor, Aleksander had let him out downstairs and driven off. He had to go somewhere else, I guess. I stood in the doorway and waited for him, for Sander. He came plodding up the stairs with that much too big schoolbag on his back. He hadn't even started school yet, but he wanted a bag like that anyway. He got it for his birthday. It's blue with pink squiggles of graffiti on the cover. It's big. It's almost bigger than he is. He can fill it up with all kinds of things. I stood in the doorway and a blue bag came plodding up the stairs and said: Hi, Mom.

Wait, Sander. Let me help you with that bag.

Up all those stairs with the bag on his back. He was out of breath. I could hear him panting. Light, quick, strained. But he wasn't worn out. I could have walked up ten thousand hundred more steps, Mom. Infinity is the biggest of all. Infinity is more than a million.

Once you were a tiny creature and lay close to me and slept. I remember your smooth head tucked against my armpit, my hand on your chest, your heart beating. How can I manage to protect you, Sander? This miracle that your heart is beating, that you're breathing, that you're alive—it makes me so afraid.

Afraid of losing you. Afraid that my hands will open and I'll drop you. Afraid that you might break.

You're too small and too much for me.

What about now? he says, standing in the doorway again. Are you done sleeping yet?

Aleksander? Aleksander? Can't you wake up?

No is the first word.

The problem with you, Julie, is that you're a zero. You're nothing. Sometimes it helps to throw up. Get it out, flush it away, get rid of it. After that, a tired, empty, numb feeling in your whole body that it's possible to live with. Butterflies in your stomach. I understand why they call it butterflies in your stomach. Every morning there's a crawling and creeping inside of me, I don't dare get up until it's gone, thousands of tiny wings flapping that aren't my own.

I like the thought of butterflies flying out of my mouth whenever I lean over the toilet to vomit.

The deal we made—first I tell you a secret, then you tell me a secret—was not a good idea. We didn't end up even. Once I was on my knees washing the floor with green soap. Sander was helping me. I had water on my dress, my hands, my elbows. It was dripping off me. Aleksander was leaning against the wall, looking at me. The sun was shining. He stood and looked at me. *Whore,* he whispered. All of a sudden. Very softly. But I couldn't help hearing it, the whispered word blew toward me, not just from his lips but from all corners of the room.

*What did you say?* I dropped the rag on the floor, turned to face him. *What did you say?*

Aleksander looked at me, looked at Sander. It didn't take long before Sander sensed danger, he didn't understand the words, but he understood danger, his body tensed like a little animal.

Aleksander smiled, winked at us, *you're doing such a good job washing the floor,* he said, *I'm going to make some juice for all of us and then I'll start on the windows.*

Sander smiled, relieved. We kept on washing. We each dipped our rag into the bucket of soapy water, and I showed Sander how to wring out the rag so he wouldn't leave water everywhere. I turned around again. Aleksander was still leaning against the wall and looking at me. *Whore,* he whispered again, without uttering a sound. Still with a smile on his lips, in case Sander happened to turn around too.

Sometimes, when Sander was around, we would speak English. We said things to each other, words in a foreign language, words we didn't yet dare say in our own.

What are you saying? Why are you talking that way? says Sander.

We're practicing speaking English, because someday we're going to go to America to see where your great-grandfather, your grandmother, and Aunt Selma lived.

I can't speak English. I don't want to go to America.

But you can learn, Sander. You can say:

Bike

House
Boy
Hello

And what about you, Julie, I say, where are you in all this?

Me? says Julie, I tried to find Vera Lund. I wanted to see the woman who slept with my husband, I didn't believe for a minute that it was only one night. There wasn't any Vera Lund in the phone book, so I called everybody named Lund in Oslo and Bærum and asked for Vera. I said my name was Karin.

Oh really?

I couldn't think of any other name.

I had a system. An X if the person on the other end of the line said I had the wrong number. A star if I got an answering machine. A squiggle if nobody answered the phone. There are lots of Lunds in Oslo and Bærum. One time I called a number and the woman who picked up the phone said: Yes, hello? Yes, hello, it's Karin, is Vera there? The woman got all quiet. Who's this? This is Karin, I said, is it possible to talk to Vera? The woman got quiet again. I think you already called here today, she said. Were you the one who called a few hours ago?

I slammed down the phone.

I didn't really know what to do with Vera if I ever found her. I imagined various scenarios with me playing different roles.

The understanding Julie: Hello, my name is Julie Blom. As I'm sure you know, I'm married to Aleksander. I just wanted to talk to you, maybe we could meet for coffee? I'm sure we're both feeling equally bad.

The sly Julie: Hi, this is Julie. Aleksander told me everything. How about meeting? I know you've been together for more than a year. . . . You haven't? Not even a year, you say . . . so how long?

The proud Julie: Hi, this is Julie. I hear you're fucking my husband. I think you should keep on doing it.

The terrorist Julie: Hello, my name is Karin Dalblom. I'm calling from the Medical Institute in Skillebekk. I don't want to alarm you but we have in our possession some disturbing information about a man you purportedly had sexual contact with. We're going to have to ask you to come in at once and have a blood test.

One night I wake up Aleksander. I turn on the light on the nightstand and sit up in bed.

Okay, I say. Now we're going to have a talk!

Aleksander opens his eyes, doesn't move.

Please, no, he says.

Oh yes, now we're going to talk. All night long if we have to.

I don't want to talk.

Of course you don't. You don't want to talk. You never want to talk. You lie awake next to me and pretend you're asleep and don't want to talk. *But I want to.* I want to talk. I want to know who she is. Do you understand?

I shake him.

Do you understand? Look at me, Aleksander! Look at me, I said!

I pull him by the hair and force him to look at me.

What the hell do you . . . he sits up and slaps me in the face.

Are you going to start hitting me now? I say.

You pulled my hair, he says. You're out of your mind. You're crazy.

I asked you a very simple question, and you can't even answer. I want to know who she is.

I said we should put it behind us.

He lies down again.

I can't put it behind me. I want to know who she is.

I said her name was Vera.

Vera Lund doesn't exist.

Lunde, Lundemo, Lunden . . . I don't remember. It was

only one night. It was a long time ago. I can't do this anymore, Julie.

What was she wearing?

What?

His voice is shrill. He covers his face with his hands.

What was she wearing that night? I said.

You're crazy.

Don't say that. You're not allowed to say that. I'm asking you a simple question. What was she wearing?

You're crazy.

Don't say that, I said.

Okay, okay, you want to know what she was wearing? She was wearing a dress.

What color?

Red.

Short or long?

Short.

So you think she was sexy, in that short red dress?

Yes, very.

And what kind of underwear was she wearing?

White panties.

Exactly. And where were you? Where did you do it?

We went to a hotel.

Which hotel?

The Plaza.

I see. The *Plaza*. Not bad. I guess you could afford that.

Shut up.

How long were you there?

A couple of hours, I think.

Two hours?

A couple of hours, I said.

A couple of hours is two hours—or do you mean something else? Do you mean something else when you say a couple of hours? Could you be a little more precise?

My God, you're crazy.

Was she lovely, Aleksander?

Yeah, not bad.

Did you hug her, did you kiss her?

Julie, stop it.

You want me to stop? You want *me* to stop? Did you come inside of her?

Yes, as a matter of fact.

Did she go down on you?

Yes.

And did you?

Yes.

How long were you there, in the hotel?

Until I had to leave.

And when did you have to leave?

Early in the morning.

That's when you had to come home to me, lie down next to me?

Exactly.

My God.

Julie puts her head in her hands. She's sitting huddled up on the green stairs. Crying quietly.

And then what? What happens next?

Do you remember when we were little and Father said there are certain things, certain words that fly out of your mouth that can never be taken back?

I don't remember . . . he probably said something like that.

Julie says:

We're trying. Now we're trying. We're trying to glue all the pieces back together. We wake up every morning and say good morning. We go to bed every night and say good night. We eat our meals together. Sometimes we make love. We play with Sander. But Sander isn't any dumber than we are.

Our words are in the walls, whispering to us when we least expect it.

And then she says:

I think about Sander. I think about how I've brought a child into the world and can't protect him from it. I can't protect him from us. I can't protect him from me. My anger, my contempt, my memories, my days, my sorrow that things didn't turn out the way I imagined. I think about our parents, Karin—about Father and Anni—all the things I've blamed them for. All the time I've wasted on blaming them. *Look at me! See what you've done to me! I don't want to live, because you didn't want me. So look at me, please, don't look away.* Someone is guilty of breaking a promise. That's how it seemed to me, that someone was guilty of breaking a promise. And now I'm the one who's breaking promises. Time after time. Every day. And Sander isn't big enough to blame me yet. He doesn't have the words. But I can see that he's withdrawing, getting quiet.

Quiet.

*Quiet,* I say, *quiet.*

My dear Sander:

I hold you in my arms, and you're only a few hours old. Your face and body are brown and sometimes they take you away from me and put you under a special lamp so you'll get strong enough to go home. I've never been anybody's home, I don't know how. They stick needles in your heels. They analyze your blood. They pinch my breasts to make the milk come and pinch your lips to teach you to eat. They wrap you in blankets and unwrap you again. They say goodbye and good luck. I hold you in my arms. We're ready now.

When the hospital door opens, the wind almost blows us over.

I promise to protect you. I can't protect you.

f I never get any more sleep, thinks Aleksander, maybe I'll die of sheer exhaustion.

But before I die I have to put my house in order. It's a man's duty to put his house in order.

If, for example, I gather up all the rocks and put them between us, here in the bed, I'll have a certain overview of their size. I can count them. I can touch them. I can better plan how I'm going to get rid of them for good.

It's no use having a lot of rocks lying all over the place when you're trying to sleep, he thinks. It's just no use.

'm walking up along Bogstad Road with Julie, Torild, and Val Bryn. We're on our way home. The first time I see Dag is through a restaurant window, he's sitting with his friends and drinking beer.

I stop.

I go right up to the window.

I wait for him to raise his head and catch sight of me.

I wait a long time.

Finally one of his buddies points out to him that I'm standing there, outside the window, and looking at him. He looks up. For a moment he's confused: *Do I know this girl?* He turns to his friends, says something—*do we know this girl?*—they shake their heads, shrug their shoulders. He looks at me again, makes a swift gesture with his hand: *Get out of here. I don't know who you are. Can't you see that I'm sitting here with my buddies and having a good time?*

Val Bryn watches the whole thing from a distance.

Don't take it too hard, she says softly, putting her arm around me. That man would much rather be with his drinking pals than with you.

———

The next night I go back to the restaurant alone. I put on my big black coat, my scarf, and my hat. Dag and his pals are sitting there that night too. I stand in front of the window. It's snowing hard. It doesn't matter. I just want Dag to notice me. I look at him. I look and look at him. Dag raises his head, catches sight of me. *What do you want?* his eyes say. *What do you want from me?*

What do you think, Dag? I raise my eyebrows. What do you think?

I'm not interested.

I can sing for you.

No.

I can dance with you.

No, I don't think so.

I can flatter you.

So what?

I can fuck you more tenderly than anyone has ever fucked you before.

On the third night I stand outside the restaurant window until it's past two in the morning. This time he doesn't pay any attention to me. He and his pals have gotten used to me standing there, outside the window, looking in.

They've gotten used to me!

Dag and I haven't even been introduced to each other, and that shithead is already taking me for granted.

No, Dag, this won't do! Somebody should have told you that I don't take no for an answer. I won't give up until I get what I want.

The next evening I go to the movies with Father and don't have time to hang around outside the restaurant window staring. But the night after that I decide the time is right. Dag is going to come home with me whether he wants to or not. I go up to the attic, to my attic storage room, and get out the old American trunk full of clothes, masks, glasses, and wigs. I find exactly what I'm looking for: a big black pair of pants, a pair of suspenders, a white shirt with a big droopy collar, a jacket, a bowler hat, and a big black mustache.

I change my clothes and look at myself in front of the mirror. Twist and turn in the mirror.

Still thin.

Still short.

But quite masculine even so.

I look a little like my grandfather.

I go into my living room, open the window. The cold winter air brushes against my face. I look up at the sky. I can count seven stars.

You and me, Grandfather, I say to the stars. You and me. No one can knock us out.

That night I don't stand outside the restaurant window, looking in. I go inside. I pull the pants up to my waist, refasten my suspenders, straighten my mustache, and walk in. The loud music blares at me. A waiter asks me whether I have a reservation. I say that I'll sit at the bar. I bow politely, smile at Dag and his buddies and everyone else who's looking at me. Then I hop up onto a bar stool; the stool is so high that my legs dangle in midair. I order a beer.

And one more thing, I say to the bartender. The bartender stops and looks at me.

I want to buy a round of pints for all those guys over there. I nod toward Dag and his pals.

Okay, man, says the bartender.

He fills the glasses while he dances around to the loud music, then, still dancing, he heads for Dag's table.

He sets the pints on the table.

Dag and his pals give the bartender a questioning look, and he nods at me.

Dag looks up. Dag sees me.

I chew on my mustache a bit, raise my glass, and toast them nonchalantly, as they say. Then I jump down from the bar stool and saunter over to his table.

Hi, says Dag with surprise.

HEY! I say. My voice is dark and hoarse.

Hi, say his pals.

HEY! HEY! I say.

I flop down into an empty chair, take out my cigars—a box of Monte Cristos from Havana—and pass them around.

No one says no.

So now four men—five if you include me—are sitting around drinking pints and smoking huge cigars. Several beautiful women with long hair and wearing tight-fitting purple outfits slink around our table, trying to catch our attention. One of them brushes against me, kisses my cheek, tries to sit on my lap. She's pretty, I can't deny it. But I've had enough when she grabs my hat and puts it on her own head.

HEY! I shout. THAT'S MY HAT, OKAY!

Dag and our pals and I order more rounds of pints. Then Dag suggests that we play poker—and of course I beat them all. Over and over again. Dag is good, but I'm better. I beat him at chess too, and backgammon, and a card game called *Høff*—which my grandmother once taught me a long time ago. I don't remember the rules anymore, it was so long ago—I just remember that it's important to say the word HØFF at the right moment. Late in the evening Dag tells a joke. It's not especially funny, but I pound him on the back and laugh so hard I fall off my chair.

They have to help me get up.

Finally we decide—I think I'm the one who comes up with

the idea—to have a drinking contest. That's when we switch to whisky. I wave to the bartender and the bartender comes dancing up to our table.

Yeah man, he nods.

All right, I nod.

Allrightallrightallright, he nods.

Oh yeah, I nod.

Did you want something? he asks.

Oh yeah, I say.

What'll it be? he nods, life is a dream.

Whisky all around, I say.

The thing is, I can drink anybody under the table. You wouldn't think it from looking at me, because as I said, I'm quite small and thin. But tonight I prove for the thousandth time that I can drink anybody under the table.

After seven shots of whisky the first pal drops out.

I pound the table, call for the bartender.

GIDDY UP! ANOTHER ROUND!

Yeah man, says the bartender.

After eight shots the second and third pals drop out. They slowly topple over and lie on the floor, unconscious.

Well, Dag, ready to give up? I say and fix my eyes on him.

No, he belches.

ANOTHER ROUND, I shriek.

After eleven shots Dag drops out.

He downs the eleventh glass of whisky, sets it down on the table, says: OH SHIT. His eyes roll, his mouth opens and shuts—and then he falls.

He falls and falls, on top of the heap of his buddies, and lies there—it's a *knockout!*

It's quiet in the restaurant now, almost nobody there.

I look around.

I chew on my mustache, take off my hat and put it on the table, wipe the sweat from my brow, and call for the bartender.

One more for the road, I nod.

Okay, man, he nods.

We look at the four men passed out on the floor, shrug our shoulders.

That's the way it goes, says the bartender.

That's the way it goes, I nod and drink the last shot of the night.

Then I stand up, give my body a little shake, look at the pile of buddies under the table.

Some men are such weaklings, no tolerance for anything, I say and stub out my cigar in the ashtray.

I bend down, lift Dag off the floor, sling him over my back, and take him home with me.

# America

ulie and I wait until the last passenger has tumbled red-
eyed and jet-lagged out of the arrival hall at Fornebu Airport. We're here to meet Anni, who's coming from America,
but Anni is missing. Anni is lost. Anni should have been out
long ago. The plane, SK911 nonstop from Newark Airport, has
landed and disgorged its passengers, and now the cleaning staff
has taken over.

The cleaning staff probably would have found Anni if, for
instance, she had had so much to drink from the tiny little
whisky and gin bottles that she fell asleep in one of the toilets;
or was roaming around confused and alone out on the tarmac.
Somebody would have found her.

Maybe the cleaning staff is already done. Maybe they've
left, vanished into the snowstorm just like the passengers, the
captain, the purser, the flight attendants, and all the others who
had anything to do with SK911 nonstop from Newark Airport.
Big empty planes in dimly lit hangars.

Where's Anni?

Julie, where's Anni?

I don't know, says Julie. I have to sit down over there for a
while. She points to a group of chairs near the tall windows. Go
to the information desk and have her paged.

Julie is pale. Julie looks like she's going to throw up again.

That's all I need right now, I say. Another relative who pukes under stress.

Julie looks at me. Resigned.

I go over to the information desk.

I ask them to page Anni Blom.

They page Anni Blom.

Anni doesn't hear a thing.

Anni is missing.

I go to the SAS office and ask if they can check the name Anni Blom on the passenger list. Anni Blom was supposed to be on SK911 nonstop from Newark Airport. Today. Anni Blom has been in New York for ten days, I know that, my sister and I were the ones who bought the ticket, we were the ones who drove her to the airport, we were the ones who made her hotel reservation.

We're not allowed to give out any information about the passenger list, says the bouffant airline woman behind the counter. Unfortunately.

Those dry pink lips of hers smile. That trembling gaze of hers is not fixed on me but on the businessman way in the back of the line.

This is about my mother, I say, my voice friendly. My mother isn't always quite right in the head. It is very, *with emphasis on very,* important for me to locate her as soon as possible.

I'm sorry, says Pink Lips. I can't give you the information you want. This rule is for the security of our passengers.

The woman behind the counter runs her tongue over her lips, opens her eyes wide so her false eyelashes brush against her forehead. First she winks at the businessman in line, then she looks at me. Aren't you going to leave now, says her glance, I don't want to talk to you anymore, I don't care about your problem, I'm busy.

Now I have no other choice.

I take my Smith & Wesson out of my belt, grab the bitch

by the throat, and press the gun to her forehead. The woman screams, the people behind me in line scatter; off in the distance I see Julie's pale face. I tighten my grip around the woman's neck and throat and whisper that if you don't give me the passenger list this very instant I'm going to blow your head off and that cute businessman who's standing back there and shaking won't have anything left to lick up but the contents of your brain—which I'm afraid are nothing to brag about. I bite the woman's ear, *yum yum businessman,* I whisper.

Let me tell you, that made an impression.

Pink Lips is suddenly very helpful. She cautiously straightens her hair, punches a few buttons on the computer, and tells me that Anni Blom never checked in at Newark Airport, Anni Blom never set foot on board SK911. Anni Blom, she says and smiles cautiously, is probably still in New York.

Many years later I think that what happened with Anni could by all accounts only have happened in New York, or to be more specific, in Manhattan, to be more specific on Lexington Avenue, to be more specific outside a Korean nail salon on the corner of Lexington Avenue and 79th Street. It's here, outside this nail salon, that Anni turns up five days before the planned return trip to Oslo.

But to tell the story I have to tell another story first. This story took place a long time ago, before I was born, before Julie was born.

It's a story that begins with my grandfather, Rikard Blom, stepping ashore in New York in 1931 but in a way it ends right here, outside what is now a Korean nail salon on the corner of 79th and Lexington.

Anni is standing motionless.

I can see her before me. She's making that typical gesture of hers: lifting her hand up and fiddling a little with one eyebrow.

She's probably thinking something like: Nothing ever looks like it used to look back in . . . well . . . time flies . . . how many years ago was it actually? Forty-five years ago that we went back home to Norway . . . forty-five years since I stood on this *exact* same spot for the last time. Anni shifts her feet a little and keeps on staring at the building in front of her. Back then there wasn't a nail salon here, no, just a filthy nicotine-yellow apartment building . . . the eternal sound of the plink-plunking piano exercises from that window, the rush of cars, honking horns, sirens—cars had an entirely different sound back then—children laughing, a dog barking, a woman's voice shouting something. . . . Anni turns around and looks down Lexington Avenue. And *that* was where I used to ride my bike, she thinks, a borrowed bicycle of course, a yellow bike. Ooh, it went so fast. Down Lexington Avenue, farther and farther, 79th Street, 78th Street, 77th Street, 76th Street, 75th Street, and I could stand on the seat with one hand on the handlebars and one leg in the air, I could turn around and shout: hey look at me hey look at me hey look at me everybody . . . and Anni turns around and looks straight at a stranger, a distinguished-looking man who's coming toward her on the sidewalk.

Anni looks at the man. Looks and looks at the man. I wish she would stop. I wish she would stop looking at him. I wish she would walk away. Let man be man, memories be memories, the past be the past. But Anni doesn't stop. Anni keeps standing there. The man is a little older than she is, maybe sixty, tall, vigorous, wrinkles around his eyes, his coat from Burberry, his shoes polished, shiny, hand-stitched, Italian.

Excuse me, says the man, he's quite close to her now. Are you looking for something? Can I help you?

No no, says Anni, but thanks anyway.

I hope you won't mind me saying this, says the man. You don't know me, I know that, but I've been standing over there watching you for a while now. You have exceptional bone structure, *stunning*.

Thank you, says Anni.

You're not American, says the man, I can hear that from your accent. Are you Swedish? Maybe Norwegian?

Now I think you're starting to get a little too personal, Anni interrupts him. I think you'd better leave me alone.

My name is Dr. Preston, says the man. I'm a medical doctor. My office is right near here, on Park Avenue. I didn't mean to frighten you, it wasn't my intention to be forward. I'm sorry if I've offended you. I don't usually talk to strangers like this. I'll go now. Goodbye.

Goodbye, says Anni.

For a moment she feels puzzled.

Where am I? she thinks.

Lexington Avenue?

Yes . . . and then there were all those years in Brooklyn, she thinks, the years *before* we moved to Lexington Avenue. Those happy years when Father was still alive.

Anni smiles, tilts her head.

I see her before me and think now she's smiling.

Anni smiles because she's thinking about Grandfather.

Grandfather and Grandma.

Rikard and June.

Anni looks at the building again.

The stranger, Dr. Preston, is still standing some distance away and looking at her. Then he turns and walks away.

Anni turns around and stares after him.

Dr. Preston turns around too and smiles.

It's a good smile, thinks Anni. An open smile.

Hanging on the wall back home on Jacob Aall Street there's an old photograph in a silver frame. The photograph shows a young man wearing a new and ill-fitting suit. It's not a clear photograph. The man in the picture could be anybody. But I know quite well who he is. The man in the picture is Rikard Blom.

Rikard Blom.
What can I say about him?
My grandfather, Anni's father, Grandma's husband.
What else can I say?
He was more believable as an American than as a Norwegian, and in New York he became the man he always wanted to be, which is something that doesn't happen to many people. What I mean is that there aren't many men who are allowed to become exactly the men they wanted to be. But Rikard did. Rikard did.

Rikard Blom loved expensive tailor-made suits. He loved eggs and onions, bagels, lox and tomatoes for breakfast, spaghetti carbonara for lunch, and a big tender bloody American T-bone steak for dinner. He loved walking around in the streets and the fact that he never got lost because uptown was up and downtown was down, and as long as he knew the order of the avenues everything was okay. He loved the flickering lights on Broadway, the smell of sweat in the audience after ten rounds in the boxing ring, children playing around a gushing fire hydrant, chorus line girls with legs as sleek as the Empire State Building, street vendors who sold fruit, vegetables, roasted chestnuts, candy, hot dogs, and lemonade, and all this in sharp black-and-white photographs. He loved the sound of tap dancers on the stage, police sirens at night, the gong at Madison Square Garden, Duke Ellington, and the light in Central Park on a hot summer morning in June. He loved the Statue of Liberty. And this is what he told Grandma, and Grandma told it to Anni, and Anni told it to us: that when the ship glided toward land in a sea of whistles, small boats, flags, and voices in thousands of different languages, the Statue of Liberty lifted her green skirts ever so slightly and showed Rikard a glimpse of her ankle.

There was no doubt about it.

Rikard loved America.

When Rikard was younger he sometimes went skiing from Mysysæter across the mountain plateau toward Rondvassbu. On these outings he was often overcome by the feeling that something was missing, he didn't know what, it was a feeling of emptiness, maybe indifference, a feeling that made him sad. He would put on his skis and head across the mountain plateau toward Rondvassbu and the magnificent Norwegian landscape would open before him *but it didn't touch anything inside him.* He was quite simply *not overwhelmed.* Or *shaken.* Or *moved.* Or *spellbound.* He truly wanted to be. Now and then he would stop and look out over the Ronde Mountains—Rondeslottet, Storronden, Smiubelgen—bathed in the evening light and shed a tear because this was Norway, after all. This was *his* Norway. But deep in his heart he felt nothing. Deep in his heart he knew that he was standing there all alone, utterly alone on his skis, surrounded by the Norwegian mountains, and acting the hypocrite.

But when he wandered around in New York on those first days, from early in the morning until late at night, from the Bowery to the Bronx, dazzled by lights and impressions, overwhelmed by sounds which, when he thought back on it, reminded him of champagne corks hitting the ceiling every day; the big city, he thought, the bridges, the parks, the traffic, the El, the avenues, and the buildings that towered above him—the Waldorf-Astoria, the Chrysler Building, the Flatiron Building, Alwyn Court, the Woolworth Building—and the whole city, he thought, this whole vast city, is manmade. It was then, as he wandered around in New York on those first days after stepping ashore, it was then he felt what he was *supposed* to have felt, what every good Norwegian *should* feel, what it's our *damned national duty* to feel when encountering the Norwegian mountains. He was *spellbound.*

Ever since he was a little boy Rikard had loved America, but it was never the sun-yellow fields of Minnesota or the Dakotas that he longed for. It was the big cities. New York. Chicago. Philadelphia. Boston. The newspapers often ran stories from the big cities which he cut out and pasted into a yellow notebook. I found the notebook a while ago, packed away in a cardboard box up in Grandma's attic. The newspaper headlines must have leaped out at him every time he paged through it and made him even more impatient to get out of there.

Let me tell you something about my grandfather. The thing was, that whenever Rikard was flooded with joy—and he must be the only person in this whole family who had the capacity to let himself be flooded with joy—he would feel almost faint. He'd be so overcome with happiness that he had to stop whatever he was doing, sit down calmly, and close his eyes—as if to regain consciousness. And then, while he was sitting like that, very very calm and with his eyes closed, he would become aware of a distant green light flashing inside of him—and the green light told him that he was invincible.

What kind of articles did he cut out and paste in his notebook?

Mostly articles about gangsters—they might be a series of news reports running over several days—with lurid headlines like THE SHOT FROM THE LEFT-HANDED BLOND MAN or AUDIENCE WITH AL CAPONE AT ALL HOURS OF THE DAY AND NIGHT.

He cut out articles about eccentric multimillionaires, scandal-shrouded nightclub queens, suicide clubs, and society murders. Rikard was obsessed with jazz, movies, boxing, and he paid particular attention to the progress of the Norwegian professional boxers abroad, especially in America.

An odd little article, actually no more than a paragraph, which must have made an impression on him has been given an entire page in the notebook: EDITOR OF HUMOR MAGA-ZINE COMMITS SUICIDE.

The article reports that the illustrator Ralph Barton, employed by America's best and most widely read humor magazine *Life* (later a photo magazine), had taken his own life. Ralph Barton's suicide letter is quoted:

"I've had all the health and fame, earned all the money, and received all the love I could ever have wished for; there is no longer any reason for me to go on living."

I know these lines must have made an impression on Rikard because he has drawn a lot of exclamation marks in the margin and scribbled the words *Just wait, America! Here I come!* in green ink across the whole page.

Like most boys, he knew that one day he would have to leave. This is something every boy knows: One day he just has to get up and leave. In Rikard's case, the final decision was made on

Friday, April 24, 1931. This is the day when Rikard decided to stop being a Norwegian. Yes, that's it! He decided to stop being a Norwegian and re-create himself as an American—as only a true Norwegian can.

I know this because Friday, April 24, 1931, was the first time the newspaper *Dagbladet* wrote about the third big travel lottery under the headline TO THE WEST INDIES FOR ONE KRONE.

Rikard cut out the article and pasted it into his notebook.

The lottery was for "100 regular prizes of big and small trips, both domestic and foreign."

And furthermore:

"As for the grand prizes we can today report the following: A round-trip voyage to the West Indies on one of Wilhelmsen's great ships; a trip to England on the Bergen Line's new *Venus*, combined with a round-trip voyage to the Mediterranean with the same company's magnificent *Stella Polaris*; an aeroplane trip to Paris, returning home via the North Sea; *a trip to New York on the America Line*.

"Along with all of these grand prizes there is an extraordinary additional prize: 'Around Norway in your own car,' to which all lottery ticket purchasers will be eligible *gratis*, namely a 5-seater Graham Paige valued at 7,500 kroner, and free lodgings at a number of Norway's most luxurious hotels."

A trip to New York on the America Line.

The words glittered at him.

A trip to New York on the America Line.

Hadn't he always been waiting for this chance?

Hadn't he always known that one day the opportunity would present itself and he would have to seize it?

Now it was just a matter of winning, and winning properly. (He didn't want to end up with the prize "Around Norway in your own car"; it might be enticing enough for someone else but was of no value to him.)

I don't know exactly when Rikard packed his bag and left. What I do know is that he actually, as if by a miracle, *won* the trip to New York on the America Line, and that he left before the year was out. At any rate that's the story Julie and I heard over and over again at home on Jacob Aall Street, that our grandfather won a trip to America and left before the end of 1931. Anni told us the story, Else told us the story, and Grandma did too. *(A bit of an adventurer, that boy, and a ladies' man like you've never seen, it was unbelievable, the girls would go crazy if he so much as smiled at them.)* It's also the story that seems the most plausible from the newspaper clippings and notes in his notebook. Although Aunt Selma did say once that it was all a bunch of hooey, the part about Rikard winning a travel lottery. Rikard Blom came to America several months earlier than he claimed, in April 1931, the very month that *Dagbladet* wrote about the travel lottery for the first time, and he didn't arrive on the America Line; he came with the Norwegian steamer *Munorway*, which allegedly was mixed up in a nasty smuggling affair. I've read that the American customs authorities confiscated 512 gallons of liquor stowed away in the bunkers.

*(Aunt Selma: I knew that boy long before June got her claws on him, I was the one who took him in when he was just a poor scoundrel who had finagled his way past the immigration police on Ellis Island.)*

No matter how. No matter what time of the year. Rikard Blom stepped ashore in the land of his dreams, and the year was, and has always been, 1931.

It was the year that *Frankenstein, Dr. Jekyll and Mr. Hyde, The Champ,* and *City Lights* had their premieres, Orson Welles made his debut on Broadway, the poet García Lorca left the city after a year's stay without learning a single word of English. Fats Waller, who had been sentenced to prison in 1929 for nonpayment of alimony, recorded the tune "I'm Crazy 'bout My Baby," half the theaters on Broadway were closed, and the breadlines on Times Square were growing.

The year was 1931 and the boxer Pete Sanstøl from Stavanger won the world bantamweight championship against Archie Bell in a technical knockout in the tenth round. The same year he fought for the official title of World Champion in the bantamweight division against the legendary Al Brown but lost after fifteen rounds.

Rikard Blom attended the match, not in New York but in Montreal. Rikard Blom cried when Pete Sanstøl lost. Although, and this is no small point, *Pete Sanstøl was never knocked out*. Not even by Al Brown. Not even after fifteen rounds. Pete Sanstøl is the best boxer Norway has ever had, period.

The year was 1931 and Rikard Blom stepped ashore in the city of his dreams. If he had had even a scrap of Pete Sanstøl's magic—his elegant command of the ring, his fancy footwork, his sense of timing, his perfect jabs—he too would have become a boxer. But Rikard's talents lay in a whole different area.

Rikard could sew.

Rikard could sew, sketch, design, paint. He wanted, of course, to find a job in which he could use this part of himself, this talent which he had never actually asked for but which God had given him nevertheless. After giving it some thought, he decided that he would set himself up as a purveyor of costumes, masks, and fancy-dress attire for use at children's parties, family gatherings, masquerade balls, and amateur plays.

It started with Santa Claus costumes—suits, beards, wigs, masks, glasses, etc.—which seemed to give people an extraordinary sense of self-confidence. The rumors spread quickly. It was said that if you wore one of Rikard Blom's Santa Claus costumes, you *became* Santa Claus!

Rikard also knew how to promote himself, women couldn't

resist him, and he made much of the fact that he had come all the way from Norway: because you couldn't get any farther north or any closer to the North Pole than that.

After he made it through his first Christmas in New York with a tidy profit, Rikard began creating all kinds of costumes and the one thing that all the costumes had in common was the word joy. That's what we need in these times of crisis, Rikard exclaimed. *Joy!* And his customers continued to say that if you dressed up in one of Rikard's costumes you would *become* whoever or whatever you were dressed up as. Into his shop (yes, he had opened a shop by now) came Tom, Dick, and Harry and out of it walked Robert Montgomery, Clark Gable, or James Cagney. Into the shop came little Plain Jane whom no one had ever noticed, and out went Carole Lombard, Gloria Swanson, Claudette Colbert, Myrna Loy, Marlene Dietrich, or Greta Garbo.

The shop was called Cinderella Scissors and it was located between Seventh Avenue and Broadway, in the theater district, of course, which seemed deserted because of the Depression. On the door, which said *pling* every time anyone came in or went out, hung a drawing in a wooden frame that Rikard had made himself. I know what it looked like because, other than the blurry photograph of the young man in the suit and hat that's hanging in Jacob Aall Street and the signed photograph of Pete Sanstøl, the drawing is the most tangible memory of Grandfather that Grandma brought with her when she came back home to Norway.

The drawing shows a vamplike Cinderella figure who frankly looks more like Mae West than Cinderella, wearing a tight-fitting bottle-green evening gown slit up to the thigh; in one hand she's holding a cigarette, in the other a golden slipper, and under the picture it says: *You can be anyone you want to be tonight!* And underneath that it says in smaller type: *Ritzy Rich can make your dreams come true: Give me a pumpkin and I'll give you the world.*

The radio was always on in the shop; the first thing Rikard bought with the money he earned was a radio, and he hummed along with the big band music while he helped his customers try on costumes. Rudy Vallee sang *drink to all the happy hours, drink to the careless days;* the vocalist Fred Astaire made his breakthrough with the Cole Porter tune "Night and Day" with the Leo Reisman Orchestra; and Duke Ellington's "Mood Indigo" was a sure winner.

Rikard was as much an artist as a tailor, there was no doubt about that; I don't know how else I can explain the remarkable success he enjoyed with his costume shop. There was nothing he couldn't make, there was no dream he couldn't fulfill. He made a Roosevelt costume for the person who wanted to be a statesman (a popular costume in 1932 and 1933, when Governor Roosevelt was elected president of the country, defeating dry-as-a-stick Hoover, who didn't know what the American people needed to hear, which was that the only thing they had to fear was fear itself), a pope costume for the person who wanted to be pope, a Napoleon costume for the one who wanted to be emperor, and for everyone who wanted to be even more than that: splendid copies of Babe Ruth's and Lou Gehrig's striped New York Yankees uniforms, not to mention some very special cotton shorts and boxing gloves that allowed any man, cool as a cucumber, to call himself Gene Tunney, Mickey "Toy Bulldog" Walker, Jack Sharkey, King Lewinsky, Max Schmeling, or Joe Louis. The heavyweights, of course. (Here Grandfather would probably want me to point out to the reader the following: Rikard Blom was *not* someone who thought the heavyweights deserved more attention than the boys who fought in the lower weight classes. On the contrary! Technical brilliance is, in spite of everything, more important than sheer physical weight. Boxing isn't just about knocking out your opponent in the shortest possible time, boxing is about *how* you knock out your opponent. It's the same with boxing as with everything else, Rikard would have said: It's not a man's size that's important, it's his *style*. Unfortunately there weren't very many who shared this opinion, and Rikard quickly realized that most men who came into his shop would rather dress up as a heavyweight boxer than a lightweight boxer. That's just how the world is, and business is business.)

Now and then Rikard would think about Norway and then he would feel wistful. Wistful is the proper word here. Not sad. Not dejected. Not despairing. He didn't long for home in such a way that he actually wanted to *go* home. He longed for home because it felt good and proper to do so. It made him a better person. And whenever Rikard felt wistful he would think about the emigrant Ole Knudsen Trovatten from Telemark.

When Rikard stepped ashore in New York it didn't take long for him to find his way to the sailor's church in Brooklyn, not so much because of the services—Rikard was not a religious man, although it's difficult to say this with certainty. God exists, God doesn't exist, God is the only one who can exist and not exist at the same time, he once wrote in a letter to Aunt Selma. He met Selma right after he stepped ashore, and they spent a lot of time together for a while (I've sneaked a look at some of the letters he sent her.)

I don't know whether Rikard himself made up all that stuff about God; it's doubtful. He was profound when he talked about boxing but not particularly profound when he talked about anything else. Anyway, the point is that Rikard visited the sailor's church in Brooklyn, not so much because of the services but because of the good coffee and the pleasant company afterwards. To speak Norwegian with other Norwegians in America gives a person an especially good feeling of solidarity, even if that person, as mentioned, has stopped being a Norwegian.

At the sailor's church he once met a sailor named Palmer

Stotensveisen. The two of them became good friends. Palmer Stotensveisen was a well-read and interesting man who told Rikard about his travels both at sea and through literature. Stotensveisen also knew how to sing and he entertained the Norwegians of Brooklyn with old emigrant ballads. There was one song in particular he liked to sing, the song that Ole Knudsen Trovatten from Telemark had written sometime in the 1880s.

The year was 1841 when Ole Knudsen Trovatten from Telemark emigrated to America, Stotensveisen would tell everybody. He first settled in Muskego and later in the famed Koshkonong colony in Wisconsin. Like many men of the time, Ole Knudsen Trovatten wrote letters to his relatives back home in Norway and told them about the good life and the fertile fields of America. And whenever anyone asked him: Do you regret leaving your homeland? he would always reply no; and whenever they asked him: Do you think the path to heaven is shorter from America than from Norway? he always replied yes. And Ole Knudsen Trovatten prospered in life, earned a great deal of money, and lived happily all his days.

But was he really happy? asked Stotensveisen quietly.

In the 1880s he wrote a song—and the tone of the song was quite different from the tone of the letters to his relatives in Norway. More sorrowful. Disappointed maybe. A yearning for I don't know what. Perhaps a bit disillusioned. That's the way things turn out sometimes. You can never be totally sure when it comes to people. They say one thing and mean both that and something else at the same time—and that's all I know about Ole Knudsen Trovatten, Palmer Stotensveisen would conclude and then start to sing so poignantly that even the church walls in Brooklyn shed tears.

*Pockets full of money are not enough*
*To ease regrets or smooth the rough.*

*What good are heaps of money and gold*
*If your heart is sad and unconsoled?*

*Over here they feast and dance*
*But true contentment has little chance.*
*And the gibberish that people speak*
*Makes Olav feel both dizzy and weak.*

*Olav has learned to sing a refrain*
*To sing it everywhere, again and again.*
*It breaks my heart to hear his song:*
*Back to Norway is where I long.*

*Work is ample and easy to find,*
*Life is good and people are kind.*
*And money in America breeds like flies.*
*Those who deny this are telling lies.*

*But fine wheat bread is not enough*
*To ease regrets or smooth the rough.*
*What good are butter and fine wheat bread*
*When every bite is eaten with dread?*

The winter of '32 was cold and long and the wind in New York was just as bitter as the economy. The breadlines, the soup lines, the unemployment lines made men lose heart. The suicide figures were high. But Prohibition was coming to an end, and it was still possible to go to the theater and the movies. The ticket sellers on Broadway accepted checks as willingly as cash from the audience. Most often the checks bounced, but sometimes they cleared—and it was worth taking the chance.

Rikard and Selma were inseparable. Night and day, Rikard's arm was almost always around Selma's shoulders, not exactly tenderly or protectively, but in a companionable way. They often put their heads together and laughed, especially when no one else was laughing or even understood what was so funny. No wonder that many in their circle of friends—young Norwegians and Italians living in Brooklyn—speculated that they were secretly engaged. But both Rikard and Selma denied it.

Rumors of their amorous adventures were reinforced when Selma, for the first and last time in her life, stopped smoking cigarettes. She didn't touch liquor either. When her friends asked her what was wrong, she just said: Haven't you heard? There's a prohibition against booze in America. Then she smiled.

It was the gleam in her eyes, the roses in her cheeks, and the little too rounded shape of her body that gave her away, some thought. Was it possible that the scandalous girl from Norway was in the family way?

The fact that Rikard also recited poetry in the evenings, in a loud resounding voice for anyone who cared to listen, didn't exactly put a stop to the gossip. He was not a well-read man. Poetry and other such things he could do without. His only literary connection was, as mentioned, the sailor Palmer Stotensveisen.

I once asked Aunt Selma straight out: Were you and Grandfather sweethearts in New York?

Selma raised her eyebrows: Sometimes there's a limit to what you're allowed to ask me about, her expression said. As expected, she didn't bother to give me an answer, just blew cigarette smoke in my face and laughed when I coughed.

I also asked Grandma: Were Selma and Grandfather sweethearts in New York, before he met you?

Grandma looked out the window and said—in a voice I didn't recognize, it wasn't Grandma's deep calm cool voice that replied, it was a high-pitched stubborn young girl's voice—do you really think your grandfather would have fallen for someone like her? Do you even know what kind of girl she was?

The official story about Grandfather, Grandma, and Aunt Selma is this:

In June 1932 Selma's big sister June comes to New York to see whether everything is all right with the younger daughter. The Family in Trondheim has not been entirely happy with Selma's correspondence during the past six months, just a few trivial letters about the weather, a long, disjointed letter about the kidnapping of the Lindbergh baby and then another letter about the weather. It was the Lindbergh letter, dated Bay Ridge, March 5, 1932, that made the Family in Trondheim start to worry in earnest. It was the tone of the letter that made them uneasy. Of course it was a tragedy that Colonel Lindbergh's little boy was kidnapped, and so brutally too! But this despair! No, it wasn't like Selma.

> . . . and I'm quite sure the baby is dead, that the kidnappers have killed him, that Lindbergh and his wife have been tricked into paying a lot of money, tricked into going around with false hopes; meaning <u>that they'll see their baby alive again</u>. And I can't help wondering what they did with him. What kind of people have we become anyway? Can you tell me that? Or do you think things like this only happen here? Don't you think evil things happen all over the world, in secret, every single day?
>
> <u>Little children know nothing about evil and dishonesty—oh, it is so terribly cold out there!</u>
>
> I think about his face, Mamma, the little boy's face, I can't help it. His face keeps me awake at night. I dream that I'm looking for him, but something always gets in the way and I don't manage to find him in time. A stranger climbs in through the bedroom window, strange hands rip him out of my body, he wakes up and cries. He calls for his mother.

*His face, Mamma. Why did they leave the window open?*
*Why is there blood on my sheet?*

The Family in Trondheim decides that Grandma should go and see to her little sister, no matter what it might cost; Selma has been alone among the American madmen for long enough (the Family thinks). And of course Grandma doesn't object to staying in New York for a few months if Selma is having a difficult time, that is, and needs her help.

It is Selma who introduces June to Rikard.

The two sisters are on their way up the street in Brooklyn and happen to run into Rikard on the sidewalk. Grandma is smoking Alibaba cigarettes which she brought from Norway, she pulls a little picture out of the cigarette pack and gives it to Rikard. The picture is of Pete Sanstøl. Grandma laughs as if her mouth is full—not of smoke, but of gold coins. She is—how would Grandfather have said it?—Grandma is devastating in a yellow tight-fitting dress and a crocheted rose-colored straw cloche with a big old-fashioned rose at the nape.

Rikard looks at June.

Rikard looks at June and becomes aware of the flashing green light inside himself—that everything *in* him and *around* him is indescribably and irresistibly and joyously green.

They shake hands. She's wearing gloves.

They shake hands and Rikard asks, flustered, if he might show her Central Park the next day.

June replies eagerly that of course he may.

She turns to her sister: Provided you don't need me for anything, Selma. You don't need me for anything tomorrow, do you?

And back to Rikard: Thank you, I'd really love to see Central Park. Maybe you could show me the Empire State Building too? And I'd love to go to the movies.

———

That evening Rikard Blom went back to his workshop in his store and made a costume inspired by this first meeting with June. A green dress, a green cloche made of straw, a pair of green gloves, and a big old-fashioned rose made of silk which he decided should be red.

The costume was given the name "Hjemme."

It's true that none of his customers could pronounce such a difficult foreign word, but that didn't matter. When "Hjemme" was hung up in the display window people stopped to stare. Some wept. All the women wanted to buy it. All of them wanted to wear it. All of them wanted to be admired by their sweethearts—wearing just that dress.

No one could explain what exactly it was that made this particular costume so desirable. Maybe it was something about the transparency of the green fabric, the way the skirts swung around a woman's hips and legs, the way the straw cloche emphasized the enticing glint in the eyes, the way the cut of the bodice revealed just enough of the back of the neck to make any man jealous with desire.

But success cannot always be explained, Rikard pointed out, and after sewing fifty costumes he had to sew fifty more, and fifty more after that.

It became a fever. Everyone wanted to have "Hjemme"— whether they pronounced it "jam" or "gem" or "jume" which is the name of a South African plant, or "hem."

Even the kind little rabbi who occasionally, in all secrecy, slipped into the shop to buy a modest gift for his wife, wanted to have the new costume.

But tell me, said the rabbi, as he stood there with the beautiful green garments and straw cloche in his hands. How do you actually pronounce this odd word H-J-E-M-M-E?

Rikard smiled, bared his teeth, and pointed to his tongue to show the rabbi how he pronounced the "hj" sound. The rabbi shaped his lips in the same way and made a sound.

Listen to me, said Rikard. *Hjemme,* he said slowly.

*Yammi,* said the rabbi.

*Hjemme,* said Rikard.

*Yemmei,* said the rabbi.

Almost, said Rikard. Try again.

*Yammeii,* said the rabbi.

*Hjemme,* said Rikard.

*Yummy,* said the rabbi, bewildered.

*Hjemme,* said Rikard.

The rabbi shook his head. It is the same way with God, he smiled. In prayer and in speech we give Him all kinds of different names—for His true name no one can, or should, pronounce.

Rikard and June were married and had two daughters—Else and Anni—one right after the other. Rikard's business flourished. He had a beautiful wife. Two lovely healthy daughters. An excellent circle of friends. And almost no enemies. As mentioned: Rikard, or Richard, or simply Rich as he had started calling himself, never wanted to go back to Norway. America was everything he had dreamed of, everything he had striven for; this was exactly the life he had imagined when he sat bent over his scrapbook back home in Norway. And time passed.

1932 became 1933 and 1933 became 1934 and 1934 became 1935 and 1935 became 1936 and so on: Everything was truly fine and good. June, as opposed to Rikard, was interested in everything happening around her; she feared the advance of the Nazis in Germany, she worried about friends and acquaintances who were unemployed and came to Rikard to borrow money.

(And Rikard never said no to anyone who wanted to borrow money from him; you have to be loyal to your friends, he pointed out, and then your friends will be loyal to you.)

But when Rikard noticed that June grew sad and silent, when her longing for home grew too great, when Roosevelt's voice on the radio was no longer as reassuring as it had been before, and the threat of war in Europe was no longer possible to ignore, then he took her out to Brighton Beach, sat down close to her, and looked out at the sea. Yes, he took her to Brighton Beach, sat down close to her, looked out at the sea, and sang his song, the only song he knew, the song of the Norwegian Ole Knudsen Trovatten, who emigrated to America in 1841.

> *But fine wheat bread is not enough*
> *To ease regrets or smooth the rough.*
> *What good are butter and fine wheat bread*
> *When every bite is eaten with dread?*
>
> *Low in spirit and sad of heart*
> *I sit here yearning to depart.*
> *America is no place for songs of joy*
> *And no place for this Norwegian boy.*

Then he would put his arm around her shoulders, turn, and say: *Shhh,* June, *shhh,* don't be so sad; I imagine him placing his long index finger under her eye and showing her the tear; and he moved even closer to her, as if he could possibly sit any closer to her than he already was, and then he whispered the last verse of the song so softly that no one else could hear it, only her.

> *My homeland I thought I might forget*
> *And old memories would be buried yet.*
> *My mind still echoes with the song*
> *Back to Norway is where I long.*

Something like that. Yes, that's probably how it all happened.

can't really think of Grandma as *June*. It's the name, I think. Grandma's name tastes of summer, charm, youth. It's hard to think of Grandma as anyone but the calculating old woman who for a time ruled our home on Jacob Aall Street; the same old woman with whipped cream under her nose who sat across the kitchen table and told stories from the old days. Grandma told me about all kinds of things, about her own childhood in Trondheim, about her sister Selma's scandalous behavior even as a young girl, about the difficult return home to Norway in '45, about her daughters Anni and Else.

But Grandma rarely talked about the years spent in New York.

Anni has told me a lot, Else has told me a little the few times I've seen her, Selma has told me some, but the rest I've had to piece together myself.

I have a black-and-white photograph of Grandma—taken sometime around 1934–35—wearing a tight-fitting light-colored dress, sitting on a stone stairway outside the apartment building in Bay Ridge. The sun is shining on her face, she's squinting at the camera and smiling because the photographer has told her to smile. She has one hand raised to shade her eyes from the sun.

I also have another photograph that I found in a book at

the library in Oslo. The picture was taken by the newspaper photographer Arthur Fellig, known as Weegee, on a cool sunny day in March 1941, at Coney Island. Hundreds of people in thin coats and fancy hats have poured in to enjoy the first real spring day of the year. The first thing I notice is the dark swarm of people, then the bright warm sunlight and the long shadows of men and women on the boardwalk. I can feel the warmth of the sun that day, a kind of early-spring warmth when you still have to wear a thin coat or maybe just a sweater outside. Several dark-clad figures have ventured down to the sandy beach itself and are strolling along. The long narrow piers stretch out into the cold white sea.

On the surface a sunshine picture, a mood picture, a crowd picture, a memory. But if you look closer—beyond the clusters of men, women, and children who are smiling at the photographer because they know he's there, to the left of the picture—then you see a black-clad woman with a light-colored hat and light silk stockings. Although I'm not all that sure about the silk stockings. They weren't easy to come by in 1941; most likely the woman in the picture—like other women who came to Coney Island on this particular day to enjoy the first spring day of the year—has applied makeup to her legs and drawn a thin black line up the back to mark the place where the seam should have been.

The black-clad woman, who you wouldn't have noticed if I hadn't pointed her out to you, is covering her face with her hands. Her shoulders are hunched. A man and woman glance at her as they walk by. It's impossible to see what kind of look they give her—inquisitive, sympathetic, comforting, indifferent, maybe they want to help her?

The black-clad woman is Grandma.

Grandma is in despair because her younger daughter Anni has gotten lost in the crowd. Grandma can't find her. Anni is lost. Grandma can't even find her under the familiar Coney Island LOST CHILDREN sign.

Anni is the one who told me about that day at Coney Island when she was little and her mother suddenly disappeared. She said the women's backs I encountered were either too narrow or too wide and not Mother's back; that the strange, wrongly constructed women's faces that peered down at me were not Mother's face.

In the photograph you can actually see, with a little effort, the slender coat-clad back belonging to Anni. It looks as if she's trying to force her way through the crowd, but she's heading away, in the opposite direction from Grandma.

I bend over the photograph in the book.

If both of them, Grandma and Anni, had turned around at the same instant that Weegee snapped the picture, they would have caught sight of each other. I'm sure of it.

Grandma never talked about that spring day at Coney Island, never talked very much about Cinderella Scissors, never talked about when Rikard sang for her. But I remember once when she sat down and started telling me her story. I remember it well because something happened to her face that day. I was over at her apartment helping her clean up, there were boxes and bags and drawers everywhere. She wanted the contents to be sorted and organized: letters, photographs, newspaper clippings, costumes, hats, records. Some of the things she gave to me. Other things were supposed to be carried up to the attic and forgotten. It was then, while we were cleaning up, that she came across a newspaper clipping: an article about Rikard and his shop; a photograph of Rikard, Grandma, and the two little girls Anni and Else. She quickly scanned the article and then put it back where she had found it—in an old shoebox. *Have you ever seen such nonsense,* she said and stayed sitting motionless on the floor.

That was when I saw it: The old woman on the floor was no longer an old woman. It was something about the way she was sitting, her legs sticking out in front of her, her back straight—and on the floor. It was the way she ran a hand impatiently through her hair when she said the words *Have you ever seen such nonsense*. It was the soft but at the same time stubborn expression in her eyes and around her mouth.

I remember it so well.

Something happened to me too.

Because at the same time Grandma ran her hand impatiently through her hair (which was not long and blond and shiny anymore), my eyes stroked the years away from her face. Suddenly I saw Grandma the way she had looked back then, so long ago.

I sat down on the floor, very close to her, and said: Won't you tell me about it, Grandma? Won't you tell me about the time you lived in America with Rikard?

I had just turned eighteen, it was two years before Julie got married, one year before Grandma died.

I remember it well.

I remember well the day Grandma started telling me her story.

The year was 1938, Grandma said, it was an October evening, just a few years before your grandfather died. It must have been around Halloween because there was a pumpkin in the living room. The children and I had all used knives to carve out eyes, a nose, and a jagged mouth so the pumpkin would have a face. Inside the face a candle was shining.

I was sitting listening to Edgar Bergen and Charlie McCarthy—it was a crazy program, a ventriloquist and his dummy—a ventriloquist on the radio, have you ever heard anything so silly? Usually I enjoyed the program, but that evening they had a guest in the studio I didn't care for, so I switched to a different station where they were playing music.

I sat there for a while, thinking.

I remember thinking that I was homesick. I was homesick but couldn't tell Rikard about it—no, no, I could never tell him that—Rikard had planned out this whole incomparable life of ours in America and there was just no room for me in that life.

On the other hand, I was indispensable, I knew that, but always as part of Rikard's stage set. I was June, his wife; and the children were children, his children. One day the newspaper *Nordisk Tidende* arrived to take a picture of us outside the shop on Broadway, the woman reporter interviewed both Rikard and me. I also worked in the shop occasionally, you know, as a seamstress. In the article it told all about the adventurous boy from Norway who had defied homesickness, the immigration police on Ellis Island, the Depression, the gossip, and had even run off a few gangsters; and by the way, the reporter wrote, the rumor that Rikard Blom started his career in New York by selling illegal liquor was debunked long ago. "Woe unto him who, driven by his own envy, spreads mean-spirited gossip about others!" she wrote.

I myself never touch liquor, the article reported Rikard as saying, not during Prohibition and not today. Life has enough to offer all by itself.

But he never defied love, the article said, and in the spring of 1932 he met his dear wife June in Brooklyn.

And the reporter wondered how he had managed it all. How had he managed to create all this (a loving family, a happy home, a flourishing business) in these difficult times?

With Joy, replied Rikard Blom. I wanted to create Joy.


The newspaper article with the photograph was hung up for general viewing both in the shop and at home in Brooklyn, Grandma continued.

For me it was just a reminder that there was no room for me in this life.

I closed my eyes and thought: Then who am I, this person

there's no room for? I saw before me a stunted windblown tree with branches trying to reach out in all directions. I've seen trees like that; they need air, wind, solitude, silence; a desolate landscape surrounding them.

Later on I've thought that Rikard's and my wonderful love story—that's how Rikard liked to describe our life together, as our wonderful love story—that this story became a burden for both of us; we couldn't live up to it, I couldn't live up to it.

But what would he have said if all of a sudden one day I came to him with these words: Listen to me, Rikard: My love for you is not perfect, don't *dilute* it, don't demand too much of it; don't give me the role of *your* happiness, *your* dream, *your* home, because I can't be any of those things.

Who knows what he would have said?

He probably would have been offended.

He would say that I was complicating things.

And then he would have explained to me how everything actually works. He was fond of complex metaphors, sometimes he was the only one who understood what he was talking about. He was also convinced that life's big questions could be resolved as long as you knew a little about boxing.

June, said Rikard, our love story—if I think about it—can only be compared to a title match at Madison Square Garden—or in Montreal.

THE WORLD CHAMPIONSHIP, do you see?

You can't get any further than that in life . . . Edgar Christensen didn't make it . . . Otto von Porat went far, but not that far . . . first-class Norwegian boxers, both of them, I don't deny it. . . . But you and I, June, *you and me baby*, we're going to do for love what Pete Sanstøl did for Norwegian boxing: We're going to fight for the title, do you hear me? And even if we lose in the last round, we'll still be on our feet, June, you and me, nobody can knock *us* out.

After a speech like that there wasn't much I could say, Grandma went on. I didn't have the words. I was in my early thirties and I didn't have the words. I think you find the words after it's too late, and for me it's been too late for almost fifty years now. She laughs. To be honest: I don't know myself what I did or didn't understand back then.

I remember that I sat there on the chair, listening to the radio and thinking that I wanted to get out.

That's the feeling I remember most from my time in New York. I wanted to get out out out.

And I have such terrible regrets about it; it was as if God heard my thoughts and said to Himself that of course she'll have her wish granted—and then she can blame herself later.

Sitting there, I remember that the music on the radio suddenly stopped.

I remember looking up.

I remember that a dark voice started talking, that the voice was somber *("Citizens of the nation: I shall not try to conceal the gravity of the situation that confronts the people").* The voice said that America had been attacked by Martians.

The Orson Welles broadcast, I interrupted, when Orson Welles fooled all the radio listeners. Did you hear it? Did you really hear it? You didn't really think . . .

I didn't know what to think, said Grandma. Everybody was talking about what was going on in Europe, the feeling of impending danger wasn't foreign to anyone. That bitter cold winter of '33 when it seemed like everyone, no matter what kind of work they did, had lost their job and only the luckiest found temporary work as door-to-door salesmen or shoveling snow—that winter left its mark on people. And the following winter was just as bad, and the winter after that. Only Rikard kept on going like before, year after year, as if nothing was wrong. The shop was doing well, we lacked for nothing.

He used to sing. Hum to himself. He was actually never completely quiet. Maybe because there were always women around. *Wrap your troubles in dreams, and dream your troubles away,* he would hum as he sat behind his counter and waited for the customers to step out of the dressing room, one after another, woman after woman, day after day, wearing a new costume.

But the point is, continued Grandma. The point is that even Rikard must have felt uneasy from time to time. Even though he never said anything. All of us, in our own way, were probably going around waiting for the big *catastrophe.*

And so then the Martians attacked America? I interrupted.

Mm-hmm, said Grandma. The voice on the radio said that New Jersey had already surrendered in spite of valiant efforts by the police, that they were on their way to New York, that we should keep up our courage and have faith in God.

A moment later the light went out in the entryway.

I heard footsteps running up the stairs.

Miss Iversen—the neighbor—began screaming.

Help! she screamed. We're all going to die!

Rikard had taken the children somewhere. Maybe they were all with Selma, who was in New York, visiting from Minnesota. I thought now I'm never going to see Rikard and the children again, I have to do something, I can't just sit here while the nation, my family, I myself, everything disappears. But I couldn't make myself stand up, I couldn't do it. I just kept sitting there in the dim light, staring at the face of the jack-o'-lantern shining orange-yellow on the windowsill.

The voice on the radio said that the Martians had obliterated all opposition in New York, that they were in the process of slaughtering the population with poison gas, that the last radio announcer, his name was Collins, had died bravely at the top of the CBS Building.

Gradually I realized that the whole thing was made up. I

guess I knew it the whole time. But I still felt something like disappointment when I heard the voice of Orson Welles assuring the listeners that they weren't being threatened by Martians after all. Panic had broken out all over the country and Orson Welles had to step forward and explain. Don't you see? It was all theater, but the nation believed it, the nation came unglued, the nation. . . . *If your doorbell is ringing right at this moment and no one is standing outside, let me assure you: It is not a Martian. It's Halloween.*

That's what he said. Orson Welles.

But the disappointment? Disappointment, I thought. The fact that I was disappointed. Relieved too, of course. *That* I could understand. But I didn't understand the disappointment. There must have been part of me that hoped it was over then; that something was finally about to end.

Later in life, said Grandma, I've often caught myself longing for the great, all-encompassing, unavoidable, and irrevocable catastrophe. An undertow that leaves nothing behind; no remains, no memories, no sorrows. Just_____. And then: peace. And then: the end.

What actually happened when Grandfather died, nobody in the family knows. I've heard a few stories here, a few stories there, and have come to the conclusion that it must have gone something like this:

After having eaten his daily serving of spaghetti carbonara at Tony's, his favorite restaurant, Rikard opened his mouth to say something to Tony the café owner, most likely something about the Japanese bombing of Pearl Harbor because it was right around Christmas in 1941, and as always around Christmastime, Rikard was busy making his Santa Claus costumes.

But when he opened his mouth to speak, he couldn't get a single word out. His tongue simply tumbled out of his mouth—and in the next instant he fell off his chair and died.

We all gotta go sometime, baby, said Tony.

Tony was one of many who tried to console Grandma when she stormed into the café and collapsed in tears next to her husband's body.

Grandfather's funeral took place on the East Side in a chapel not far from Central Park. Anni and Else wore white dresses, black coats, black shoes, black bows in their hair, and black silk sashes around their waists.

Anni is the one who told me this:

I was six years old and Else and I had never felt so dressed up before. Mother thought we should be spared from all the horror that had happened: Death is not something for children, she said.

Aunt Selma disagreed, of course. She came from Minnesota to attend the funeral. She said that children are hurt more by life than by death.

They're my children, not yours, Mother then said.

Thank God for that, said Aunt Selma.

(Aunt Selma moved to Minnesota right after June and Rikard got engaged. In 1934 she married a Norwegian-American, who unfortunately died in 1935. The Norwegian-American had told Selma that he was very rich, something that turned out not to be true when she read his will. Selma stayed on in Minnesota but often came to New York to visit. She and Rikard were good friends for the rest of his life, but her relationship with her sister was strained.)

Mother and Aunt Selma reached a kind of compromise when it came to the funeral, Anni explained. Else and I went along *to* the chapel, but not *into* the chapel. Tony the café owner stayed with us outside. Tony didn't like the three cops who had come to pay their respects to Rikard. Tony didn't say why. We didn't ask. The important thing for us was that *Father* had never had any trouble with the police. He was a friend of the police—that's what he'd been ever since he made the costumes for the annual policemen's ball in 1936.

For some reason we stayed right there on the street, continued Anni, I don't know why we didn't go and buy some nuts or something; Tony stood leaning against a stone wall, smoking one cigarette after another. Lots of people walked past. It must have been the middle of the day because the winter sun was shining on the shopwindows, there were Christmas decorations and Christmas carols everywhere, and light snow flurries were falling from the sky.

People were in a hurry, everybody must be out buying presents for their children, I remember thinking, and then I started counting the daddies walking past me on the street. A middle-aged man with a nice face, Christmas packages and bags from Macy's in his hands, qualified as a daddy.

It was just a game, said Anni, like counting cars, it wasn't even especially sad.

Lots of people stopped when they saw us standing there outside the chapel. Oh, how pretty you look, what pretty dresses you're wearing, beautiful little girls, they said.

Tony shook his head and said: Oh yeah, they just lost their daddy and are utterly grief-struck. Then he nodded toward the chapel and said: Their daddy is right inside there, it's an awful shame you know, he's gonna be cremated soon, poor bastard. And the people would squat down, look at us with tears in their eyes, pat us on the cheek, and give us candy, some even gave us money.

I remember the whole thing as a very peculiar day, said Anni. All those nice people and that lovely white dress, the black coat, the black silk sash—and Father who was dead. But that part I didn't really understand.

Later I realized that nothing would ever be the same as before.

Things went downhill fast with Cinderella Scissors. Mother couldn't keep the shop afloat after Father's death. She was a good seamstress, that wasn't the problem—but there was no joy in it and the customers came to find joy. She spent a long time recreating a costume Rikard had had great success with two years earlier, a costume depicting Vivien Leigh as Scarlett O'Hara, but Mother's dresses tugged or drooped in all the wrong places. The women didn't look even close to beautiful when they came out of the dressing room and posed in front of the mirror, their faces just as worn out and drawn as ever; and she didn't even consider making a new Clark Gable costume.

Her grief at Rikard's death took far too much time, the tear streaks on her face were noticed by the regulars, and no one came to Cinderella Scissors to see tears. The shop went bankrupt in the spring of 1942, and we had to look around for a new place to live.

The Family in Trondheim wrote to America and suggested that Aunt Selma should stay in New York and help her sister with the children. Usually things turned out the way the Family in Trondheim wanted. This time was no exception.

And so it was that June, Selma, Else, and Anni moved together in to the dark little one-bedroom apartment on the corner of 79th and Lexington.

It's true that Selma was the younger of the two widows, but

by the first week she had already appointed herself the new head of the family. Every day she yelled at June, telling her to pull herself together, that the mourning period was over, that she should put the past behind her—and if she absolutely had to cry, then she should be crying over the Norwegian boys back home who were risking their lives every day in order to free their homeland from the Germans; *so that you and I and your children can go home to a free Norway someday!*

Anni continues the story:

Every Sunday evening before Aunt Selma lay down to sleep, she would set the mousetraps in the apartment, and every Monday morning, before anyone else got up, she would inspect the two rooms and the kitchen and tally up the night's bounty. She would place the mouse corpses on the windowsill in the living room, lining them up, side by side—and then they would lie there in a kind of funeral procession for the rest of the day.

We had a neighbor. Her name was Mrs. Paley. An older woman, tall and gaunt, with long flowing gray hair. She was a lonely woman—a widow. Unfortunately, Mr. Paley jumped out the window in 1930, they had no children.

Every time anyone went past her apartment, Mrs. Paley would stand behind her partially open door with big black eyes that begged *talk to me, sit with me, don't go into your own place right away.*

One day Else and I came home from school . . . we had both started school, Else was in the third grade, I was in the second . . . and when Mrs. Paley heard us come in, she opened her door a crack and beckoned to us.

*Pssst,* she hissed. Do you want some chocolate? I've got chocolate. I have a whole cupboard full of chocolate.

Sweets were not exactly an everyday item back then. I even remember that Mother, as a kind of compensation for everything we were lacking at home, used to tell us about what awaited us when we went back to Norway one day.

In Norway, Mother would whisper, children eat napoleons and drink red soda.

What's a napoleon? asked Else.

A napoleon is a cake made from pastry dough, vanilla cream, and frosting with essence of rum, replied Mother, enunciating each word carefully.

We had no idea what she was talking about, but the words pastry dough, vanilla cream, and essence of rum were said in such a way that we thought they had something to do with God.

But anyway: One day Else and I came home from school, and Mrs. Paley popped out of her door and asked us if we wanted to come inside and have some chocolate.

We said yes, we guessed we could do that, and followed her into the dark, damp apartment.

We realized at once that it had been a mistake to say yes.

Both Aunt Selma and Mother had said that we weren't allowed to have anything to do with Mrs. Paley, that Mrs. Paley wasn't quite right in the head, that something in her head had exploded after Mr. Paley . . . well, you know . . . flew out the window.

The next thing that happened was that Mrs. Paley seated us on the sofa—and I remember so clearly that I felt something move underneath me, something that might eventually crawl up under my skirt. I thought of Aunt Selma's mouse corpses on the windowsill and leaped up, shook out my skirt, and stared at the spot where I'd been sitting—but there was nothing there, just an old spotted sofa cushion.

You have to sit still, said Else, otherwise she might not give us any chocolate.

I sat down, but couldn't get rid of the feeling that something was moving underneath me.

Mrs. Paley was gone for a minute and came back with a china dish full of candy in pink wrappers. At the same moment the door to the bedroom swung open—there was a cold draft from the walls, just like in our apartment—and I remember catching a glimpse of a big, unmade double bed with a dark wooden frame and a lighted kerosene lamp. Mrs. Paley shut the door, set the dish with the pink candy on the table, and sat down in the brown chair right across from us.

Have some! she said.

Else and I each took a piece of candy. I stared at Mrs. Paley, at her long flowing hair that was so utterly gray. I thought about what Mother and Aunt Selma had said, that something in Mrs. Paley's head had exploded when her husband jumped out the window. I saw before me a sprinkling of shredded skin, hair tufts, and pieces of brain, how everything swirled around and around in the apartment, like the snow outside her window at that very moment.

She was wearing a loose, low-cut yellow dress. I looked at her heavy breasts, the deep dark crack between her breasts. I leaned forward. Something was moving. There was something moving in the crack between her breasts.

A bedbug came crawling out of the crack between Mrs. Paley's breasts.

The bedbug was long and yellow and about the size of an earthworm. I poked Else in the side and whispered in Norwegian *Look at that! Look at that bug crawling out of the crack between her breasts!*

Have some! said Mrs. Paley again, a little less friendly this time. This isn't just ordinary chocolate, this here, she said. . . . What spoiled brats, she snarled to herself, spoiled, spoiled brats. . . . I was given this chocolate as a present from one of the richest men in America, she said, Mr. James Gatz, at a party on Long Island in 1928—back when people still knew how to throw a party, she added.

Else and I each bent over our piece of chocolate and tried to remove the wrapper. It wasn't easy. The paper was stuck on good.

I gave Mrs. Paley a desperate look—couldn't she just let us go?

The bedbug crept upward, over her neck, over her face, and finally settled on her cheek, under her right eye.

It didn't seem to matter much.

Rikard Blom was dead, but not buried. June refused to be parted from him and took him along to the apartment on Lexington Avenue, in an urn. June also refused to put him away. Instead she placed him in the cupboard with the good china. Now and then she would take him out and dust him off. I can just imagine the conversations that went on between the two sisters when the children were asleep.

When we leave for Norway someday, Rikard is coming with us, said June.

Rikard didn't want to go back to Norway, said Aunt Selma.

And you think you knew him! shrieked June.

Maybe I did, yes, snarled Aunt Selma. Maybe I even knew him better than you did. At any rate I know he never wanted to go back to Norway.

Their voices are getting louder and louder. Rikard's urn is standing on a little table in the middle of the living room. The two sisters are standing on either side of the table.

I'm going to take him with me to Trondheim, said June, there's nothing more to say about it.

That's not what he wanted, said Aunt Selma.

Both of them look at the urn as if expecting it to settle the argument in some way—and tell them who was in the right.

For a moment there's complete silence in the room.

He doesn't want to go to Trondheim, said Aunt Selma, resigned.

June ran a hand through her hair. He's going to Trondheim whether he wants to or not, she said. She lit a cigarette and pointed at the urn. He doesn't have much to say about it anymore, anyway.

The sisters June and Selma lived in the dark apartment on Lexington Avenue for three more years—together with the little girls Anni and Else. Everything was dark, not just the apartment; no bright memories. Else has told me that it rained for three years. I know that's not true, I've seen the sunny picture from Coney Island. Anni has told me that when she fell off the borrowed yellow bicycle she had to spend several months in the hospital. That's not true either. Grandma said a week. Else said ten days. Selma said a few hours.

*(Aunt Selma: a little scrape here and there, a little cut on her head, nothing to make a fuss about. All children fall off their bikes, it wasn't any worse for Anni than for anyone else. Get up! Don't just lie there crying! That's what I say.)*

Everyone was waiting for the war to be over so they could go home. To Norway. To Trondheim. To napoleons. To peace and quiet.

In the spring of 1942 I know that they all made a trip to Times Square. It was a dark evening, it was cold, an icy wind was blowing right through their coats and capes. A huge crowd had gathered to mark Hitler's birthday. Anni and Else didn't understand what was going on, didn't understand the fury. A kind of execution took place that evening: A Hitler dummy that was the size of a real person was hanged—to the unanimous applause of the spectators.

Anni told me that she remembers people bumping into her, that she was scared of letting go of June's hand, of falling down and being trampled in the dark by the crowd.

In early June of 1945 Aunt Selma told everyone that she had made arrangements for the whole family to obtain passage on a steamer back to Norway. The apartment on Lexington Avenue was packed up as quickly as possible, and it wasn't long before they were all ready to go and be installed on board.

Anni told me that the word she heard most during the last days they lived in New York was the word SHUSH.

But how long is the trip, Mother?

Shush!

What are we going to do when we get to Norway?

Shush!

Aren't we ever coming back to America?

No! Shush! I don't think so.

Never?

You should just be glad that we can finally go home!

Yes, but I've never been there before, so how can it be called home?

Shush!

As the steamer neared Newfoundland, Anni asked: Is that Norway?

No no. It's still a long way from here. A long way!

They anchored in Bergen and had to stay on board for more than twenty-four hours. Anni told me that she and Else stood on deck and threw oranges down to the little boys who had rowed out to have a look at the boat from America.

The journey continued to Oslo by train. June had promised the little girls they would go to a pastry shop, a proper Norwegian pastry shop, and drink sodas and eat napoleons.

Then we'll celebrate, said June.

*Pastry dough. Vanilla cream. And frosting with essence of rum.*

Napoleons weren't exactly what we ended up with, smiled Anni. We got wartime cakes made with margarine—and malt beer.

Finally they were all sitting in the night train to Trondheim. Nobody slept. Selma read a book. Else and Anni stared out the window. June sat holding on to Rikard's urn, crying. The whole way home—on board ship, on the train to Oslo, at the pastry shop, and now—she had sat, mute holding Rikard's urn.

Anni told me that once Selma got so furious at June—at that poor young widow holding an urn in her hands—that she tried to take the urn away from her.

This happened while they were still on board the steamer.

Selma had sneaked up behind June, snatched the urn out of her hands, and run across the deck. June ran after her and caught up with her—in the nick of time, you might say.

Because Selma was just about to pour Rikard's ashes into the sea. That's when June came running up behind her and hit her in the face so they both fell on all fours. The urn, which luckily wasn't open yet, rolled across the deck and stopped right at the feet of little Anni, who picked it up.

(Anni: *I'll take care of you, Daddy. So you won't fall and hurt yourself again!*)

The scene led to a terrible fight on deck between the two sisters. No one had ever seen anything like it. It took several strong men to separate them.

After that they stopped speaking to each other.

When they were safely back home in Trondheim, all

contact between them ceased. Not a word. Not a glance. If they ran into each other downtown—for example on a Sunday afternoon in May of 1957—they didn't even say hello.

Grandma and Aunt Selma were active enemies for forty-four years, meaning right up until Grandma died in 1989, one year before I turned twenty, Julie got married to Aleksander, and Anni went back to America.

And all of this, all of this, thinks Anni, happened so many years ago. She turns around again and notices that he's still standing there and smiling that nice smile of his. The man who introduced himself as Dr. Preston. He's still standing there. As I said before: Keep going, Anni! Don't just stand there. Let man be man, memories be memories, the past be the past.

Now it's too late.

Now he notices that she's looking at him. Now he thinks that he should try to talk to her again. Now he's walking toward her. Now he stops in front of her, giving her his hand, greeting her. And she doesn't turn away. She wants him to talk to her. She doesn't know who he is, but he has a nice smile, she thinks, and it's been such a long time since anyone smiled at her that way.

What can I do?

I can't stop this. I'm in Oslo thinking that Anni's in New York and behaving like an ordinary mother on vacation. Maybe she's at the Guggenheim or on Broadway or taking the elevator to the top of the Empire State Building and looking at the view. I forget that she's not an ordinary mother on vacation. She's Anni and not quite right in the head. Just listen! Now he's asking her if he could take her to lunch, maybe a little French bistro on Madison Avenue, not far from where they're standing right now.

No, she doesn't know who he is. And it won't make any difference if I tell her. Tell her everything about Dr. Preston. It won't change a thing. She won't listen to me anyway. And very soon it will be too late.

# Faces

Dr. Mort Andrew Preston was born in Washington, D.C., in 1931, the same year Rikard Blom traveled to America. I've done a little investigating and found out quite a lot about that man. Excellent education, good taste, fabulous address. 666 Park Avenue, New York. No wonder Anni was impressed.

In the 1960s, having finished his training as a surgeon, the young Dr. Preston went to Tokyo and specialized in one of the most lucrative fields of plastic surgery: eyelid operations—the so-called reshaping of the Asian eye—performed primarily on women, but also on men, who wanted a more Western-looking face. As far as that goes, there was nothing Dr. Preston couldn't fix, embellish, alter, normalize, or correct. He cut you up and sewed you back together: Dr. Preston could do anything to anybody, as long as he wore his white doctor's coat.

In the 1970s he went to the Philippines and was admitted to the large circle of friends surrounding President Marcos and the president's wife Imelda—the former beauty queen and then mayor of Manila. Dr. Preston was—and it took me some time to find this out—Dr. Preston was actually the *very first* plastic surgeon to operate on Imelda's world-famous face.

---

When he removed the bandages from her face, he stood before the mirror as if bewitched. You're no longer a *former* beauty queen, Madame President, he gasped, with emphasis on the word former.

Imelda sat on a chair, Dr. Preston stood behind her.

You are eternally beautiful and eternally a queen! he murmured.

When the queen's newly operated face appeared in the mirror, both of them were so moved that they started to cry. They simply had to lie down next to each other on Imelda's silk bed. And there they lay, day after day, staring at each other in the mirrored ceiling. Occasionally they would hug each other, then they would sleep, then they would lie totally still and simply look at each other. Look and look.

It was in this way that one night Dr. Preston caught sight of Imelda's naked feet. Usually she wore silk slippers—even when she was sleeping. She never took them off in public. Even when Dr. Preston asked her to, never, she said, no one must see the queen's feet.

But one night Imelda was plagued by frightening dreams and sounds coming from outside. Not even the thick walls of the president's palace could protect her from these sounds. She tossed and turned in bed so much that one of her silk slippers slid off her foot and landed on the floor.

Then he saw it.

He saw her foot.

He saw her naked foot.

It was completely black, as if it had been baking in the oven for several days. A heavy, foul stench rose up from the sole of her foot, an odor so strong that he had to put his hand to his mouth. She also had several shrimp-like toes sticking out between the five normal ones.

At first he was so startled that he leaped out of bed.

But then he lay back down, reassuring himself.

I'm a doctor. I'm a doctor, he thought. I can do something about this.

Gently he woke her up.

Imelda, he whispered.

She opened her eyes, and he pointed at the mirror on the ceiling.

Look, he said, you've lost one of your slippers. I've seen it now. I've seen your foot. I can do something about this, he said and pointed.

And it was true: He *could* do something. Nothing was too difficult for Dr. Preston.

After the operation Imelda could finally walk barefoot in the grass, whenever she felt like it. And her need for new shoes was no longer as overwhelming. Several hundred boxes of shoes—shoes that had been ordered from the finest designers in Paris and Milan—remained unopened and untouched in her closet.

And as for Dr. Preston: The president's wife was so pleased with his work that she offered him the honorable position of chief of staff of the maternity ward at the biggest hospital in Manila. (A bit outside Dr. Preston's medical specialty perhaps, but "I travel widely in my quest for beauty," he said in an interview with the daily *Manila Times*—pictured in a dazzling white lab coat with a dazzling white infant in his arms.) And Dr. Preston impressed everyone, especially Imelda, with his tireless, heartfelt, and hands-on medical practice. The stately, white-clad figure was seen wherever women gathered or gave birth: in the hospital corridors, in clinics, in slum districts, on garbage dumps behind the presidential palace. Rumors circulated about his big white well-manicured hands; about his ability to touch a newborn so that it would stop crying and fall asleep.

Dr. Preston's knowledge about the vulnerability of the body was put to good use in his new position as chief of staff: In confidence he would advise new mothers about how they could preserve their breasts, and the suppleness of their stomach and skin after childbirth.

*To let a newborn infant suckle mucus from the mother's breast, to deny a baby the best, most nourishing, highly developed milk products that science has to offer, that . . . Dr. Preston has to search for the right word—that is primitive! A woman who chooses to breast-feed malnourishes her child, forsakes her own beautiful body, and ignores the rights of the husband who once desired her.*

In the maternity ward and in the birthing rooms hung framed, signed photographs of Dr. Preston's American patients, lovely women holding lovely children in their arms, *and there's no reason why you and your child can't look as healthy and lovely as women and children in America,* he used to say, presenting the young Filipino mothers with American women's magazines, chocolate, vitamins, and powdered milk.

(And the young Filipino mothers would scrimp and save to buy the expensive white powdered milk and mix it with polluted water, not understanding why their infants withered like sunflowers in the spring; because no one ever talked about it.)

(Nor did they talk about Dr. Preston's bank account in Geneva—an expression of gratitude from the multinational Swiss corporation that supplies baby food and chocolate milk every morning to children all over the world.)

Dr. Preston had a good rapport with children, that's no secret; children trusted him, leaned on him, loved him, there was no reason to cry as long as he placed his hand on you, nothing bad or dangerous could happen when he was near. Dr. Preston returned the children's love, took time to play with them, console and hug them, listen and read to them. He returned the children's love because children were so *pure,* I think that's the word he would have used, children were so *pure.*

I think he thought that children, the way God has created them, represented everything that he, as a doctor, valued most in a person. With age came illness and bad smells and obesity and death.

We've reached the end of the 1980s: I don't think Dr. Preston saw anything blatantly wrong about *taking* what a child had and *giving* it to paying patients who needed it. I think he saw it as a way of ennobling humanity. A way of combining the best with the best, pure child's blood on the one hand, with money, power, and status on the other; because it was only people with money, power, and status who could afford to buy pure child's blood; commonly called *Preston blood,* guaranteed free of infection because it came from the very youngest.

*Like everything else in medicine, it's all a matter of demand,* he used to say. *How many stories have you heard about people who are diagnosed with HIV after a single blood transfusion in the hospital? You can't trust hospitals anymore. You don't know what kind of blood they're pumping into your veins. And you can't live with doubts like that.*

Here he lowers his voice.

*You have to have your own blood with you—always!*

Yes, the stately white-clad figure was seen everywhere in the world where little children gathered and played: in big cities, on the streets, outside the schools, in the slum districts, on the garbage dumps.

*Pure uninfected blood,* said Dr. Preston: *They have it, we need it. They aren't harmed by it. Just a little light-headed and pale after we've drained them. Some are afraid it will hurt. Some call for their mothers. Some wonder why the light shines so brightly in their eyes. But I hold them the whole time. I hold them.*

You're not listening, Anni. He's coming toward you. He's the devil, Anni. He's Satan himself.

And rumors circulated about his big white well-manicured hands, his ability to touch a newborn in such a way that it would stop crying and fall asleep.

Julie and I receive two telegrams from Anni after she disappeared in America.

The first telegram arrives the same day we find out that Anni is still in New York, that she never set foot on board SK911 from Newark Airport to Oslo.

Julie's phone rings, we hear it out on the stairs as we're on our way up to her apartment, we run, we're both out of breath, we're just back from the airport.

Julie picks up the phone.

The woman on the other end of the line asks for Julie Blom.

Speaking, says Julie.

The woman says that she has a telegram for Julie from Anni Blom in New York. Do you want me to read it to you? says the woman.

Yes, please, says Julie.

Can you hear me? says the woman.

Yes, says Julie.

Okay, says the woman, I'll read the telegram now.

All right, says Julie.

"Anni is staying here," says the woman.

It that all? asks Julie.

Yes, says the woman.

———

The next day the telegram arrives in the mail. "Anni is staying here," it says.

Well, says Julie, she can do what she wants, she's a grown woman.

And not quite right in the head, I say.

We can't force her to come home from New York if she doesn't want to, says Julie. We can't force Anni to do anything. She's a grown woman.

And not quite right in the head, I repeat.

That may be, says Julie.

Four weeks later Julie's phone rings. It's another telegram. In the old days telegrams used to be delivered to the door, but now they arrive by phone—it's not quite the same. I don't think there are many people who send telegrams anymore, the telegram woman probably doesn't have a lot to do. But anyway, the phone rings and a voice says: Is this Julie Blom?

Yes, says Julie.

I have a telegram for you from Anni Blom in New York, says the woman.

Yes, says Julie.

I'm the one who read the telegram to you four weeks ago, says the woman.

I see, says Julie.

Should I read it now? says the woman.

Yes, please, says Julie.

"Anni wants to come home," says the woman.

Is that all? says Julie.

Yes, says the woman.

Thank you, says Julie.

Who is Anni? asks the woman.

What? says Julie. Surprised.

Who is this Anni who wants to come home? asks the woman.

My mother, says Julie.

I see, says the woman.

Goodbye, says Julie, and thanks.

Well well, says the woman, I hope everything turns out all right.

Telegram number two is lying in the mailbox the next day. I place the two telegrams side by side.

"Anni is staying here."

"Anni wants to come home."

I look at Julie, shake my head.

I don't know, Julie, I say. I don't like it.

We figure that Anni will arrive sometime during the next few days, and take turns standing out at Fornebu Airport every morning to wait.

Anni doesn't come on the first day, or the second day, or the third day, but on the fourth day she arrives. On SK911 from Newark Airport. Four weeks and four days late, of course. But on the fourth day she arrives.

At first I don't recognize her. No, I don't recognize her.

What should I tell you about Anni's face? At first I think it's me, that I've gotten something in my eyes, dust or dirt, but it just gets worse the longer I look at her, it starts to sting, like when you open both eyes underwater or stare too long at a film that's out of focus. Everything is liquid.

Anni is standing in the middle of the arrival hall with two suitcases, one on each side of her, and looking around. She's looking for Julie or me. I've been to the refreshment stand to buy a hot dog. I turn around, the hot dog in my hand, my mouth open and about to take a bite, and then I see her. What a peculiar face on that woman, I think. Her nose looks like a bow. I turn around and look at that face and think what a peculiar face on that woman.

———

Once a long time ago when I was little, I broke a mirror. I didn't do it on purpose. I was playing with a ball in Anni's room, and the ball hit the mirror over the mahogany dresser, the mirror shattered, not in a thousand pieces as the saying goes, but in exactly thirty-seven different pieces which I proceeded to glue back together before anyone came home. I was so scared that Anni and Grandma (who was living with us) would be angry. But no one was angry. Everybody thought the mirror was much prettier that way. We looked at ourselves in the mirror, one after the other, Grandma, Anni, Julie, and I, and our faces were so strange.

Oh no, I don't like looking at myself like this, said Julie when she saw her face, all broken up, in the new mirror.

But Grandma and Anni and I just laughed and made faces.

Now the woman in the airport makes a gesture that I recognize: She raises her right hand and fiddles a bit with one eyebrow—that's when I realize that it's Anni. Maybe I knew it all along, but I didn't want it to be true, I didn't want the woman with the peculiar liquid face to be Anni. And at the very moment I realize it's Anni, my eyes start to sting. I look and look at her face, trying to find some point where I can fix my gaze, but everything is all liquid, and it stings to look at her.

I look away. I let my eyes flit from face to face in the airport and everything is normal. There's nothing wrong with my eyes. I think that maybe I should run away, maybe I should just run away and let the strange woman with the liquid face who is my mother manage on her own, but then Anni catches sight of me and it's too late. She raises her hand and waves. I try to look at her, but my eyes instantly start stinging. We walk toward each other. She's smiling. At least I think that's what she's doing. I hope she never smiles again. I can't take it. It hurts so much. I look down.

Anni comes right up to me.

Karin, she says. Home at last.

Anni, I say. But I don't raise my head to look at her. I stare at a fixed point on the floor, a light-brown piece of gum that somebody spit out.

Karin, says Anni, what's the matter with you?

I raise my head cautiously. She's real close to me now, she's hugging me, she's much taller than I am.

I raise my head cautiously, and now she looks exactly the way she looked when I was a little girl and could wrap myself up in her thick reddish-blonde hair and smell her breasts and her throat and it was so good, even though I was never allowed to stand there like that for very long, and I just want to keep standing that way and then I notice that I've started to cry. I want to stand close to Anni and cry. I look up at her. But now her face has escaped me again, and my eyes start to sting. I don't understand it. My eyes can't hold onto anything about her. One minute she looks like a one-eyed queen, and that's beautiful even though she has two noses and only one eye, as I said; but then that image falls apart too, and Anni says: Aren't you going to help me with my suitcases, Karin? I want to go home, I'm so tired, I've had a hard time, I've been robbed, I thought New York was my second home, but I guess it's not my home after all.

Then she starts crying.

Cautiously I look up at her, and it's as if all of Anni is dissolving and running across the floor. If she cries for much longer, I think, I'm going to have to find a rag and wipe her up.

I was robbed in New York, she cries, I was robbed.

We'll talk about it when we get home, I mumble. I'll call Julie, then we'll talk about it. Right now I'm going to drive you home to Jacob Aall Street.

I get the car, gather up Anni and her suitcases outside the arrival hall, and drive to Majorstua. Anni sits in the back seat. She's scared to ride in cars and always sits in the back seat. I can't help looking at her face in the mirror. I think about all the weird things I made out of clay when I was little—three-headed trolls, witches with crooked noses, faces with way too many eyes—how I squished the clay together and made something new every time I wasn't satisfied. I don't understand what has happened.

Dr. Preston, says Anni, Dr. Preston has robbed me.

I don't want to hear about it.

I look at her in the rearview mirror. Now her face is swollen and ready to burst, like a soap bubble, and then it changes again right before my eyes, shrivels up, gets small and prune-like. I don't like her staring, she's staring at me without knowing that she's staring.

But look how white the landscape's gotten since I've been gone, she says in a low voice.

She thinks she's looking out the car window.

But she's not looking out the car window, she's staring at me in the mirror, staring and staring, eyes wide open, terrified.

After carrying her suitcases up the stairs to her apartment on Jacob Aall Street I tell Anni that I'm going to run her a hot bubble bath and call Julie. She nods. I look at her, cautiously, with one eye open and one eye closed, but I have to turn away quickly. I can't stand it, I quite simply can't stand looking at her face. Anni notices. I know she notices. The one eye open and the one eye closed. The fact that I have to turn away every time I look at her. I know she thinks I'm acting strange. But she doesn't say a thing.

And Julie asks: What do you mean her face is liquid?

Julie comes over as soon as I call. She's standing in the doorway. You can't yet tell that she's pregnant, except that she's so pale, I think. And then she asks: What do you mean her face is liquid?

She's taking a bath, I say. Just go and see. I don't think she realizes it herself, she knows something's wrong, but I don't think she knows what it is. I have no idea what she sees when she looks at herself in the mirror. She cries and says that she's been robbed in New York, but she doesn't say anything about her face. It stings to look at her, Julie, it stings your eyes. At Fornebu Airport. At first I didn't recognize her and when I looked at her closer, it started to sting.

You're always exaggerating, Karin, says Julie.

Go and see for yourself, I say.

Julie goes into the kitchen first, takes a bottle of Farris mineral water out of the fridge, opens it, and takes a swallow. She leans against the wall, shuts her eyes, rubs her hand over her forehead. She puts the bottle down on the kitchen counter, calmly goes into the bathroom.

After a moment I hear Julie's voice, loud, shrill.

My God! she shouts. My God, Anni!

Then there's silence.

I hear only a low whispering from the bathroom. I don't want to go in. A little later I hear crying. Anni's crying. No, I'm not going in there. I go into the living room instead and take a little whisky from Anni's liquor cabinet, fill up the bottle with water so she won't notice. After a moment I take some more whisky. I sit down on the floor. I see that it's starting to get dark outside. I lie down on the floor, I pretend not to hear when Julie calls me. Pretty soon I have no idea how long they've been in there, in the bathroom, or how long I've been lying here on the floor. Long enough, I think. Because I don't want to do this anymore. No, I don't want to do this anymore. I refuse. I get up, go out to the hallway. I hear their voices in the bathroom; *Karin?* Julie calls. *Karin? Are you there?*

I take my jacket, open the front door, run down the stairs and the short way home to my own apartment so I can lock the door behind me.

Your face, Anni. It's somewhere else. It's somewhere else now.

've never found out exactly what happened between Anni and Dr. Preston in New York. But I imagine that it went something like this:

Dr. Preston invites Anni to lunch and to dinner on the day they meet at the corner of 79th and Lexington. It was here, on exactly this spot, that Anni many years before climbed up onto the seat of a borrowed yellow bicycle—one leg in the air and one hand on the handlebars—and raced off.

The following day he calls her again at the hotel and invites her out. Dr. Preston says he knows a place where they serve oysters, in fact the best oysters in New York—would she honor him with her company for another evening?

Of course she will.

He picks her up at seven o'clock and drives to Grand Central Station. That's where they're going, first down one stairway and then down another. Anni stops in the main concourse, a short distance from the restaurant—staring up at the high ceiling shaped like a vault and painted blue so it looks like a starry sky. She stares up at the ceiling and thinks that this vault, in Grand Central Station, reminds her of the vault at Ellis Island, in the registration room. She thinks that Rikard Blom must have stood like this, just like she's standing, with his head tilted back looking at a similar vaulted ceiling as he waited to slip past the American immigration officers.

Dr. Preston takes her hand and says in a low voice: Let's go eat now. We can't stand here all day looking at the stars.

No, of course not, says Anni, of course not.

They're given a table at once and sit down. The room is big and dimly lit. Anni notices a woman on the other side of the restaurant. The woman's face is powdered white, her lips are constantly in motion and Anni can hear bits and pieces of what she's saying quite clearly. The woman is talking to the man sitting across from her. She's talking about a child that's missing, says that the child went out to buy some milk at the store and simply disappeared along the way. The man nods and says something. The woman keeps on talking, says that the mother has been walking up and down the streets for several days now, calling her child, calling and crying, and the neighbors stand in their windows and watch, just watch, the desperate woman down below.

Dr. Preston taps Anni on the arm and asks whether she'd like something to drink.

Anni turns, sees that a waiter is standing there to take her order.

Excuse me, I didn't see you, she says to the waiter. I didn't hear you.

Would you like something to drink? repeats Dr. Preston.

Excuse me, she says again, and orders a glass of wine.

This room has strange acoustics, says Dr. Preston. You don't always necessarily hear what you're supposed to hear.

I can hear what that woman is saying, says Anni, I can hear what she's saying, the woman sitting over there. I can hear what she's saying even though she's talking softly, having an intimate conversation with her companion.

It's true what Dr. Preston says: The acoustics are strange in there. That's why that part of Grand Central Station is sometimes called *the whispering room*. The sound of strange whispered voices rises up along the walls, and nobody knows for sure who is hearing what. Anni, for example, hears not only the woman's story about the child who disappeared on the way to the corner grocery, she also hears a man say that he woke up one morning with a peeping sound in his ear that's getting louder and louder and now he starts off each day by screaming in an attempt to drown out the sound; she hears a couple arguing about which of them should eat the last oyster, she hears a little girl crying. But she doesn't hear everything that Dr. Preston is saying, even though he's sitting quite close to her. He talks the whole time, telling her about his work, how he can shape a face, complete the real potential of a face. He says that the faces we're born with don't have anything to do with us. People look at themselves in the mirror and think *Is this me? Is this me?* and grow dizzy and delirious—not because they recognize themselves, but because they don't. *No, this is not me!* He tells Anni that she's a beautiful woman, but that her face is in the process of betraying her, and why let that happen? Those who don't know any better—cowardly people—talk about aging with grace, but they won't say what's so graceful about it. They won't say because deep inside they know the truth. What's so charming? A face that reminds others that death is approaching?

Dr. Preston sighs, reaches across the table, and strokes Anni's hair, touches her eyes, her cheeks, her lips.

I can do something about this, he says.

I think that Dr. Preston's touch did something to Anni—it had been so long since anyone had touched her that way. I think that several days later she steps into his office on Park Avenue, he shows her pictures on his computer, pictures of her, pictures of a possible Anni.

This is you, he says. Can you see it?

He gets his scalpel.

Then he says:

Before you sleep, I want you to think about who you are. You have to help me. You know better than I do. We'll do this together. I don't cover up. I open up. I open you up. And when you wake up you will thank me—because then I will have found you. Then I will have found you at last.

Julie and I are standing outside Anni's door on Jacob Aall Street. I haven't been back to Anni's apartment since the day I met her at the airport. Julie hasn't either. But Julie has called, asked her if she needed anything, if she felt like taking a walk, felt like having dinner or coffee.

Julie is still newly married and pregnant with Sander. Of course we don't know that it's *Sander* who's inside her stomach and waiting to come into the light.

I remember hands stroking Julie's stomach.

I think it's an Andrina inside your stomach, I say.

Aleksander thinks it's a Ruth.

Julie doesn't think anything.

Father thinks it's a Gabriel, Aunt Edel and Uncle Fritz think it's a Lotte, Aunt Selma thinks it's a Selma, Hannah and Harald think it's an Ole-Petter, Arvid thinks it's a Karoline, Torild thinks it's a Synnøve, Anni thinks it's a teapot.

Anni looks at Julie's stomach, bends down, puts her ear against it:

A teapot, she says.

Other times she says:

A ball.

A candle.

A barrel organ.
Sometimes she says:
A little boy.
A little boy in Julie's stomach that I can hold and protect.

Julie and I are standing outside her apartment. We ring the bell.
Once, twice, three times. I dread seeing Anni again.

I've tried to prepare myself.

Julie looks at me.

You're exaggerating, Julie says, wagging her index finger.
Take off those sunglasses before she opens the door.

No, I say. I'm protecting myself.

Suit yourself, says Julie.

We hear her footsteps. The door opens. Anni is standing in the
doorway. She smiles. I look at her. She has three noses and a
bow in her hair. And then my eyes start to sting. They sting
and run. Julie doesn't seem to notice a thing.

I pretend not to notice either, I'm wearing sunglasses, that
helps.

*So nice to see you*, says Anni.

Julie gets a hug.

Anni reaches for me to give me a hug too.

I look at her cautiously, one eye open and one eye closed.
Now she only has two noses, but her eyes are rolling around
like the wheels in a slot machine.

She gives me a hug.

Why are you wearing sunglasses? she asks and touches my
cheek. It's raining outside.

Oh, you know . . . I say lightly and make a dismissive gesture with my hand.

Julie and Anni sit down at the kitchen table to talk. I walk
around the apartment. I forget that I'm wearing sunglasses,
and all the rooms are darker than usual. Cold. Otherwise

everything is the same as before. Except the pictures on the walls.

There are new pictures hanging on the walls.

Photographs.

In the living room, in Anni's bedroom, in Julie's and my old bedrooms, in the hallway.

I lean closer to get a better look.

Photographs of children.

I count thirty-seven photographs of children on Anni's walls. Unknown children, smiling and crying children, children from all over the world. I don't know who the children are, I've never seen them before.

They're professional photographs, 8 by 10's, impersonal, probably reproduced a thousand times, glossy finish.

The children don't know they're being photographed. They stare into the camera lens with big wide eyes. They have different expressions. It's not important to the photographer whether the children are happy or sad. The point is that they look like children, that they play the role of children, manifest the very idea of what children are. The photographer understands that far far away someone's eyeballs will hurt from looking at the children, because they're suffering, because they need you.

I go into the kitchen. Anni looks up. I squint my eyes. I ask: Who are all the children? There are pictures of children on your walls. Who are they?

My children, says Anni.

She looks away.

I gesture with my arms, catch her attention, my hands ask: What do you mean, *your children?*

I adopted as many as I could afford, whispers Anni. They're going to send me pictures of themselves. The ones who can write will write me letters. I'm helping them.

Anni is a long-distance foster parent, says Julie.

Yes, says Anni and nods.

Why? I ask.

Because they need me, says Anni.

Why? I ask.

Because they're suffering, says Anni, weeping softly.

It's not like swimming underwater. Gradually I learned to swim underwater with my eyes open. That's not how it is with Anni. I can never learn to look at that face.

The next time I visit her I'm alone. I stand outside the door. I ring the bell. I hear her footsteps inside. For a moment I hope that everything will be back to normal, that she'll open the door and look like herself, that I've made it all up, dreamed it in the night.

She opens the door, stands on the threshold. I can't even say that we stare at each other. One glance and we both give a start.

What on earth . . . she says. What's the matter with you, Karin? Why are you dressed like that?

I'm freezing, I say.

Are you sick?

No, no.

Take off your scarf and sunglasses and let me have a look at you.

No, absolutely not.

Anni puts her hands on her hips and studies me.

Cap, sunglasses, scarf, coat, boots. It's not even freezing outside, Karin. You look like you're taking a trip to the North Pole.

Anni, I can wear whatever I like. I'm a big girl now.

She shakes her head and lets me in.

Do you want some tea? she says.

No thanks.

Don't you want to take off your things?

No!

You're going to get awfully hot.

I'm not staying long.

All right then.

I can only stay five minutes.

Of course. Do you want a cookie?

Yes thanks. I'd like a cookie.

It's no use. I can't take this. It stings no matter what.

Anni goes out to the kitchen to find a cookie. I don't go with her. My eyes are running. I don't want her to see it. I go into the living room, sit down on a chair. Wipe my eyes. It doesn't help. They just keep running and running. If I stay here one minute longer I'll be punctured and everything is going to gush out. I look around, sniff, there are more pictures on the walls. More pictures of children. Not just on the walls but on the windowsills too, framed photographs of unknown children; and on the table a little stack of pictures that have just arrived in the mail. Anni hasn't taken them out of the envelopes yet. I get up from my chair, take a look at a few of the pictures. My eye catches on the photograph of a smiling little boy wearing ragged green pants. Bare torso, a tiny little chest, shaggy black hair, and a heavy rifle on his shoulder. *They promised him a place in God's kingdom, all we can promise him is a place in your heart.*

I don't hear Anni. She tiptoes across the floor. Suddenly she's standing right behind me. Taps me on the back. I jump. My sunglasses fall to the floor. I turn around. I turn around, raise my hand, about to strike. Nobody is allowed to sneak up behind me that way.

No, Karin, don't! Anni puts her hands up in front of her face.

I lower my hand. Look at the floor. Pick up my sunglasses, put them back on.

You scared me, I say. I didn't mean to . . .

I was scared too, says Anni in a low voice.

She looks at me. She looks at me and I feel like hitting her again, hitting that liquid face of hers, hitting it back into something I can hold onto.

I've found the cookies, she says. I made a little tea anyway, set the kitchen table. I thought maybe . . .

I stare at the floor. My heavy coat is hot. I'm almost dissolving. The cap, the scarf, all the sweaters under my coat. My sunglasses. I have to get out of there. I can't take it.

No tea today, Anni. I have to go now. Some other time maybe.

call him Edwin. It's possible his name is something else. But that's not really the point here—because if I say his name is Edwin, then his name is Edwin.

It's summer, I'm walking through the Palace Park.

I've been to see Anni. I try to avoid visiting her. Especially in the summer. It's much too hot. Four wool sweaters, a down jacket, camouflage pants, an old helmet I found up in the attic, mirrored sunglasses, my scarf. It's no use. It stings just the same every time.

But anyway: I'm walking through Palace Park, in a hurry to get home, so I can take a cold bath and forget—and that's when I see him. Edwin.

He's sitting on the grass under a tree and playing with a little girl, three or four years old. They're rolling a white ball back and forth between them. The little girl has dark curls, a short white dress, and I can hear her bright laughter from far away. They're in their own world, those two, Edwin and the child.

They pay no attention to anyone.

They roll the ball back and forth between them.

They pay no attention to anyone, not even to me.

I stand there a short distance away, behind a tree, and watch them. Now and then he stretches out his arms to her and then she lets go of the ball, lies down in the grass, and rolls over to him, into his arms—as if she was the ball.

Edwin has big arms. They look like branches.

I would like to take Edwin and the little girl home with me.

Hey. Hey there. Here I am.

But they pay no attention to me. They're too involved in their game.

Now it's Edwin's turn to be the ball. He lies down in the grass and rolls around while the little girl laughs and laughs and laughs—exactly as if someone were tickling her stomach.

After a while it's too hot to stand there like that, behind the tree, in my heavy clothes. So I take off my helmet and scarf and sunglasses.

I peek out from behind the tree.

Hello. Do you see me?

But Edwin and the girl pay attention only to each other.

Then I take off my down jacket, wool sweaters, camouflage pants.

Hello there, you two, do you see me now?

But no. They pay no attention to me.

I take off my winter shoes.

Now I'm wearing only a thin transparent white summer dress. I'm no longer hiding behind the tree.

I sit down on the grass and look at them.

I lie down.

I roll down the hill and pretend that I'm a ball too.

It's no use. They pay no attention to me.

Hello there, do you want to come home with me?

I don't know exactly when Edwin catches sight of me. I'm so involved in rolling around on the grass that I actually forget about him for a moment. But when I'm done rolling and sit up again, I notice that something is different.

He's seen me, but pretends that nothing's going on.

He keeps on playing with the little girl. They're rolling the ball back and forth between them. Yes, he keeps on playing with the little girl. But not in the same way as before.

He's noticed me, but pretends he hasn't.

Come on, Edwin! *Don't bullshit a bullshitter.* Why are you putting on this act? Don't you think I can see right through you? *Pretending that you haven't noticed me.* I can see through all bad actors, so don't try me.

I know he's noticed me—noticed me as I sit totally motionless under the tree in my pretty white summer dress.

I know he's noticed me because he's playing with the little girl in a different way now.

His movements are bigger. His laughter is louder. His words aren't meant for her but for me. As if he's saying: See how great I am, see what fun I am, see how beautifully I play with the child?

The little girl notices it too. He's no longer with her.

She turns around and sees me.

*I don't want to go home with you, do you understand?* her eyes say.

That's fine. I understand.

Could you leave now so my father can be my father again?

Yes, I'll go.

Edwin laughs louder and louder, throws the ball high up in the air and says OH BOY, DID YOU SEE THAT? in a contrived tone. Then he claps his hands and falls backward onto the grass.

The little girl turns around and looks at me again, meets my eye, very quietly.

I nod.

I'm going now, I whisper. I'm going now.

I stand up, gather up my clothes that are strewn all over the grass, and start to leave. Edwin sits up, blades of grass in his hair, the ball in his hands.

I don't turn around, but I know he's watching me.

I'm going now.

I'm going now.

Okay, Edwin?

I don't want you after all.

I don't want you.

Out of consideration for the family I had to see Anni again. I'd decided not to visit her for a while. I don't know whether faces like hers ever settle down, but until it did, there was nothing I could do except stay away. But it so happened, around Christmastime, that the whole family got together again. Officially we met in mourning, as they say, but no one was particularly grief-stricken. If the truth be told, some were even relieved and joyful.

Hysterical might be exaggerating a bit.

Aunt Selma was dead at the age of eighty-three.

To her credit it has to be said that she was surly and angry and furious to the very end. The day before she died she yelled at a young female bookseller who didn't know that Karen Blixen and Isak Dinesen were one and the same person. She yelled at a boorish cabdriver who didn't want to help her up the stairs with her grocery bags. She yelled at her beau, a certain Mr. Berg, for drinking up all her cognac. *Dashing, it's true, but a scoundrel and a rogue and a good-for-nothing all the same.* She yelled at the editor-in-chief of one of Norway's major newspapers for not taking his readers seriously. *After forty-six years as a faithful reader I refuse to spend another cent on your rag, enough is enough.* She yelled at a prominent political figure in the government, went to her private residence and waved her cane in the air, *you'd have to search long and hard to find another woman as arrogant as you are.* She yelled at the whole family, called us each up in turn, in the middle of the night, and said: *I don't have much time left,* but before I die I want to tell you exactly what I think of all of you. Finally, bright and early the next day, she yelled at her neighbors, a young couple, because of their extraordinary poor taste in everything.

When all of this was taken care of, she washed her coffee cup and breakfast plate, straightened up the living room, washed the floor in the hallway and bedroom, put the mop and bucket back in the closet, glanced at several old letters and photographs that were lying in a box on the nightstand, lay down on the bed with a plaid wool blanket over her feet, and died.

The funeral took place five days later, followed by coffee and pastry at Ingeborg's house, which she once again loaned out. It was a brief gathering. The family sat quietly around the dining room table. The red velvet drapes were drawn, but the winter darkness seeped into the room just the same and enshrouded us. Ingeborg tried to say that *she lived an adventurous life anyway, that Selma.* Someone mumbled *yes, yes she did, no doubt about it.* After that nobody talked about the deceased. The pastries were eaten and praised. The weather was discussed. Aunt Edel's cream cake with four layers and eighty-three lit black birthday candles was admired. The cake platter was passed from hand to hand and everyone tried to blow out the candles, but they were the kind that flare up again as soon as you blow them out. But everybody tried even so. First Julie, then Ingeborg, then Fritz, then Aleksander, then me, then Anni.

Everyone looked at Anni.

The candles shone on her face, it was white as snow, almost transparent.

When she blew, her cheeks turned into big water bubbles. I

felt like getting up from the table and popping them. Pop! Pop! Away with that face.

Father looked at me. Father whispered: Why are you wearing sunglasses indoors, Karin?

Because I'm in mourning.

Yes, I see, said Father. Yes, of course.

t wasn't really a lie that I was in mourning. I missed Aunt Selma.

In church, during the funeral service, we all sat separately. Even though the whole family was there, the church seemed almost empty. A single wreath on the casket. No tears. She was not loved.

I sit way up front. The bells toll. We sing "Lovely Is the Earth." After a few minutes of silence the minister steps forward and says: May the grace and peace of God our Father and the Lord Jesus Christ be upon you.

He says:

We are gathered here at Selma's bier. God comforts all those who turn to Him. Therefore we shall consecrate this moment to God's words and prayers. Let us pray.

The minister bows his head. The congregation again falls silent.

It is very quiet, and I look around me. Anni, Father, Ingeborg, Julie, Aleksander, Aunt Edel, Uncle Fritz, Else, and her husband. A faint winter light shines through the stained glass windows. I sit there looking at that light.

A figure slips in beside me. Pokes me hard in the side.

Are you sitting here daydreaming again?

I'm sitting here waiting for this day to be over. I don't like funerals. I haven't been to very many. But I don't like them.

You can say that again! I don't like funerals either. At least not this one.

I can understand that.

It was the cigarettes that did it! Damn those cigarettes! I should have stopped smoking a long time ago.

Yes, well, I suppose you could say that. But you were quite old, you know. It's not so uncommon to die at your age.

Ha! I could have lived for years. I had things to do. But a greenhorn like you wouldn't understand that.

How . . . I say. How are things, actually . . . where you are?

Let me tell you, Karin. Things aren't very good. No! Things aren't very good at all! It's very depressing. All those words they say . . . promises of an afterlife and all that . . . I was hoping, of course . . . I was hoping he'd be waiting for me with a smile on his lips.

Who? God?

No, Rikard.

Of course.

You see, Karin, Rikard had a special kind of smile. A smile that promised you'd get to take part in exciting and wonderful things—as long as you did what he said.

I don't answer, just shift my glance to look at the minister who's folding his hands, I don't say a word.

The figure next to me pokes me in the side again.

I'm talking to you, Karin. Don't look away when I'm talking to you. It's not polite.

Shhhh, I whisper. The minister is praying for you. Listen!

> *Lord, Thou hast been a home for us*
> *from generation to generation.*
> *Before the mountains were born,*

*before the earth and the world were created,*
*yes, from eternity to eternity Thou art God.*

*Thou makest man to become dust again*
*and sayest: "Turn back, child."*
*For thousands of years are in Thine eyes*
*like unto yesterday as it raceth past,*
*like unto a watchman in the night.*

*Teach us, O Lord, to count our days,*
*that we may find wisdom in our hearts!*

Eager young lips against my ear:

Do you know what Rikard said to me once when we were lying side by side in bed? He said: When I lie next to your body, like now, before you sleep, I feel like I'm home.

That's the most beautiful thing anyone has ever said to me. This old old body—imagine that.

The figure beside me falls silent for a moment—and then gives a sigh:

But he's not here, do you understand? No one's here. I'm waiting and waiting for something to happen, but nothing happens. Do you understand? All my life I've been waiting for something to happen, and if not during my lifetime, then at least now. WHERE IS EVERYBODY?

I'm here, I whisper.

Yes, but soon you'll leave the church, you and everyone else, and I'll shout: *Don't leave yet.* But don't turn around, Karin. There's nothing you can do now. I'm dead and you're alive. But I'm still going to shout *Don't go.* But you shouldn't listen to me! Just keep walking. And one more thing: Don't worry so much about what's happened to your mother's face. It's not as bad as you think. You're a smart girl, Karin, but sometimes you exaggerate a little too much for your own good. One day something might happen in your life that is a lot more serious than what's come before. One day something might break inside you, and you won't be able to play as carefree as you have. One day life will demand that you take responsibility. Be brave, little Karin.

# Sander, December 1998

ulie is standing outside my door holding Sander's hand. They're each carrying a suitcase. Julie is carrying a big blue suitcase with straps across the top, Sander is carrying a little green suitcase.

Ready to travel.

That's the best term I can come up with.

Hand in hand outside my door. Somber faces. Almost formal. They've already said goodbye back at Julie's apartment. They both know that. No more tears now. Sander doesn't cry. Sander has packed his own suitcase. Inside his suitcase there are six pairs of long underwear, nine pairs of underpants, five T-shirts, two wool sweaters that Aunt Edel knit, three pairs of pants, and four turtlenecks.

Julie is standing outside my door, making a brisk gesture with her hand. She says thanks so much for agreeing to do this. Has Aleksander been over with the backpack? She looks around. Everything okay?

I nod. We'll call from Italy, she says. It won't be until late tonight. We arrive this afternoon and then we have to drive four or five hours to get there. We'll call before eleven, I promise. I think it's going to be fine. I think it'll work out.

Aleksander came by earlier to drop off a backpack. Then he drove off to his office to take care of a few last things before the trip. He had already said goodbye to Sander early in the morning. In the backpack Julie has put a down jacket, a parka, an extra wool sweater that he got for Christmas from Ingeborg last year (before she left Father), four videos, three books, a detective set with fingerprint powder, magic detective glasses and invisible ink, a soccer ball, a teddy bear named Pu, and another teddy bear that doesn't have a name.

Unlike Pu, the nameless teddy bear is used only as an indoor soccer ball.

Julie has a new coat. Yesterday she went to the hairdresser and had her long hair cut off. She's put on a little makeup.

I'm starting a new life, Aleksander and I are starting a new life, a new year and a new life, she says and gives a little laugh, raising one hand to smooth out her new haircut.

I say: Everything's going to be fine. Sander and I will be just fine. I say: You'd better hurry now, say hi to Aleksander, we'll see you after New Year's.

Julie stretches out her arms toward Sander, he turns away, but she pulls him close all the same and whispers something in his ear. He shrugs his shoulders, steps across the threshold and stands next to me. He has his knapsack on his back. When it's not vacation time, like now, he has schoolbooks in his knapsack: a reader, an arithmetic book, a composition book, and a drawing book.

Today he was allowed to put whatever he wanted in his knapsack. In his knapsack there's a cork, a sports Thermos, a bag of candy, a teddy bear named Bjørn, a thick book about Norwegian soccer over the years, a photo of Ole Gunnar Solskjær, a Manchester United scarf, a framed photo of himself with Julie and Aleksander on the stairs outside the red cabin in Värmland taken one summer afternoon several years ago, a green binder with plastic pockets, and a hundred and thirteen British soccer cards.

Ready to travel.

Well, I guess it's time, says Julie uncertainly and looks at

Sander. He's no longer standing next to me. He has gone into the living room, sat down on the floor, and started to unpack the things from his bag.

Yes, I say. It'll be fine, you know. We'll have a good time. You'd better hurry if you want to make the plane.

I'll call tonight. I'll call even if it's late, says Julie.

You'd better run now, I say.

Do you know what the difference is between a hotshot and a superstar?

I'm lying on the couch sleeping. The winter light falls through the living room windows. I like to sleep in this light.

Sander is standing there looking at me, talking to me.

At first he sighs heavily a couple of times. Then he rustles some papers on the table. After that he dribbles his soccer teddy bear with his foot for a while. Then he comes back and looks at me again.

Do you know what the difference is between a hotshot and a superstar?

Not really, I yawn.

Would you rather be a hotshot or a superstar?

I open my eyes. Look at the clock. Eight hours until he goes to bed.

I'd rather be a superstar.

That's dumb.

Why do you say that?

It's better to be a hotshot.

Huh. I thought it was better to be a superstar.

No, he says. Do you want to be a hotshot instead?

Sure.

Peter Schmeichel is a hotshot.

Mmmm.

And Ole Gunnar Solskjær.

Really.

And Ronaldo, Ryan Giggs, David Beckham.

Of course.

Dennis Bergkamp is only a superstar, but I like him best.

Are you sure you're right: that a hotshot is better than a superstar? I'd think a superstar would be better.

Do you even know anything about soccer? it's Sander's turn to ask, doubtfully.

No, I don't, Sander.

You can look at my soccer cards.

I stroke his hair. He doesn't pull away.

Maybe you could sit here on the couch and we could look at them together.

Sander goes to get his green binder. He says he has more soccer cards at home, in a tin box, he'll let me see them some other time. Then he sits down on the couch, opens the binder.

When are Mom and Dad going to call?

Tonight. After they get there. Before eleven. But after you go to bed.

Can I stay up till they call?

I don't know. I don't think so.

Please.

No, it'll be really late.

At home I'm allowed to stay up as long as I want to when there's no school.

No, you're not. I've been over at your place plenty of times. I know exactly what you're allowed and not allowed to do.

The day before the day before yesterday I was allowed to stay up until quarter after twelve at night.

That was because it was Christmas Eve.

Please?

We'll see.

Can't you say right now so I won't have to go and wonder if you're going to say yes or no?

I want to watch a movie on TV that starts at ten.

We can watch it together.

It's a movie for grown-ups.

I've seen grown-up movies before.

Oh all right!

I throw out my arms. Oh all right! You can stay up until they call. But after that it's straight to bed. And you have to put on your pajamas and brush your teeth before the movie.

What time is it now?

Five past one.

So how many hours before I have to go to bed?

I don't know. A lot.

Yeah! says Sander and claps his hands.

We sit on the couch and look at soccer cards.

You can learn a lot from looking at soccer cards, he says in a serious voice.

You don't always have to *learn* something, I say.

Nooo . . . But Mom thinks it's good if I learn something, about different countries and stuff like that.

Yes. I guess so. I'm not going to argue with your mom.

Are you going to argue with Mom?

No, Sander. I'm not going to argue with your mom.

Do you know how many soccer cards I have?

I shake my head.

A hundred and thirteen! But that's just in this binder. I have more at home, in a tin box.

Sander has fine, dark-blond hair like his father. His bangs are long. He has blue eyes and a sturdy little nose, the baby cleft between his nose and mouth is still deep. His lips are always slightly moist. His cheeks are round, with dry red patches. The same red patches have flared up on the back of his hands and wrists. He doesn't want me to rub cream on his skin.

He can do a lot of things with his hands. He can tie five different knots, draw practically every single flag in the world, pour juice into a glass, cut up slices of bread and butter them, and sew patches on his pants. Julie has told me that sometimes he rubs her stomach when she's feeling tired or sick. He likes to have his back rubbed. Then he moves real close to the other person's body and gets quiet and warm and heavy.

Sander is thin and lanky, born with big clunky feet like his mother. He plays soccer in a soccer league. His soccer uniform is blue and white.

*Winning isn't the most important thing,* says Sander, rolling his eyes (can I see how stupid this statement is?) *but last season I scored eight goals.*

He gets up from the couch and shows me how he scored one of the goals, how he just rolled the ball in past the goalie. It was easy as pie.

At two o'clock we eat lunch. Sander asks me what I have in the cupboard. I say I have whole-grain bread, bananas, jam, liverwurst, yellow cheese, brown cheese, and milk.

Do you have chocolate milk?

No.

Can we buy some chocolate milk?

Not right now, because we're going to eat now.

Can we buy some later, after we eat?

Sure.

Can you make hot chocolate milk?

Yes, I can.

You're really pretty nice.

Thanks.

Before she left Julie said:

I don't know whether this is going to work out. Starting over, as they say. Crossing out everything that's happened, everything we've said to each other—forgive. Aleksander was the one who decided we should go to Italy. I don't really know what he has in mind, but I said yes, that's a good idea. We've been to Italy before, on our honeymoon. This isn't a honeymoon. I'm afraid our expectations will be too high. I'm afraid it won't work out. Catch a plane, drive a car, check into a hotel in beautiful foreign surroundings, and wait for love to appear.

I can see the whole thing before me:

We're sitting in the same café we sat in almost nine years ago, waiting. Waiting for one of us to say something, for the wine to taste the way it tasted back then, for the evening light to have the same warmth, for a hand gesture to be just as uninhibited. I imagine that's almost how it'll be. Almost, you understand? If it weren't for that tiny fraction of a second when we both remember that it's not that way anymore. It's not that way. It's all just an act. That tiny fraction of a second it takes us to step out of ourselves and register that the words we say have no meaning, that the wine tastes bland, tepid; that the light is cooler; that the hand gesture is merely a resigned handshake: two defeated soldiers who shake hands and say: Had enough death yet?

Maybe it would have been easier if love hadn't been part of the plan.


Father once said that a marriage that lasts must consist of two things: *a good friendship and ardent lovemaking.*

Julie laughs.

But what does Father know about a marriage that lasts? First there's some woman we've never heard of who gives birth to his son, then our own mother who gives birth to us, then Ingeborg. All of them fell apart.

Besides: Aleksander and I have never been friends. We've loved each other. We've shared a kind of intimacy. But friends?

Not long ago I read a novel, it's called *The Private History of Loneliness*. I take it with me everywhere these days. I'm going to take it with me to Italy and read it to Aleksander—and most likely get annoyed when he falls asleep before I'm done, just like he gets annoyed because I always interrupt him in the middle of a sentence and tell him what he's really trying to say. All the time, do you understand? All the time: *Can't you be somebody else! Can't you be the way I want you to be?*

That day. Do you remember? I called you up and said that now it's over. Now I don't want to do it anymore. This marriage is over. I walked around town, browsed through a bookshop, but didn't really find anything. I was looking for something or other, solace maybe, and then on the way out I saw this book on the shelf. It was probably the title that made me stop. *The Private History of Loneliness.*

This is what I wanted to say about friendship.

Somewhere in the book the author talks about a grotto on the south side of Capri where Emperor Tiberius used to swim.

The grotto is completely dark. It seems scary because your eyes have gotten used to the sharp light outside. But it's not the dark that scares you the most. What scares you are the strange acoustics inside the grotto. You can scream as much as you like, and instinctively that's what you do in order to be heard, but your voice is drowned out by the roar of the waves.

No one can hear you.

But if you put your lips all the way up against the wall of the grotto and speak softly, every word you say will be heard.

Julie reads from the book:

*You have no idea where you should stand or go, or who is standing and listening at the other end. You can't be sure of being heard. Someone has to tell you that—someone has to say: "I'm listening to what you're saying, here—at the other end of the grotto. You're not alone. If you talk in a normal voice I can hear everything you say." But they don't always tell you this, and then you might end up shouting in vain.*

That day I called you up. I thought I wanted to leave, and if I just left then everything would be fine.

It's been hell.

Sheer hell.

But we still keep repeating these words: *for Sander's sake.* We have to stay together for Sander's sake.

Once Sander said: Why don't you get a divorce so you don't have to fight anymore?

His friends at school. I know that lots of them are children of divorced parents—that phrase: "children of divorced parents"—tiny little packs and bags that are sent back and forth every other week. And these enlightened, brave, liberated parents. I don't know. Maybe it would have been easier if love hadn't been part of the plan.

Sometimes when we fight—even though we think we're talking quietly—Sander comes in to us crying and holding his ears. His hands are shaking like an old man's.

Stop it!
Stop it!
Stop it!

For Sander's sake we're going to Italy. Can you hear how cowardly that sounds? Can you? Should we put that burden on him too—along with all the others?

For our sake we're going to Italy. Because we're scared. Because nothing is more painful or nastier or uglier than a divorce. But that love should be part of the plan?

That love somehow will reappear there, in that café, so many years later?

Maybe reconciliation is the word? Maybe a handshake is all we can hope for now? Maybe a handshake shouldn't be sneered at?

I think about another word. It came to me one day. The word armistice.

I think: Maybe not love. Maybe not forgiveness. At least not the way we're used to understanding those words. But maybe an armistice.

An armistice?

Can we start there? For **Sander's sake?**

Aleksander! Listen to me!

I read a book once. I only remember one sentence.

*Even hell has to be furnished.*

That's all we can promise each other right now.

Sander and I are sitting at the kitchen table eating lunch. My walls are yellow. I've set the table nicely, with a red Christmas tablecloth and candles. A clock is ticking on the kitchen wall. It's almost two-thirty.

Sander says: My dad is omniscient.

He's chewing his piece of bread. Talking with his mouth full. Do you know what omniscient is? It means he knows everything. Mom once said that she was omniscient too, but then she said she wasn't really. She said nobody can know everything.

She's probably right about that.

Are you omniscient?

Yes. Now that you mention it: As a matter of fact I am.

Do you know what I'm thinking right now?

Yes.

So what am I thinking?

People who are omniscient aren't supposed to tell what they know, that's part of the point of being omniscient.

What do you mean?

Sander stops chewing, squints his eyes. He gives me a suspicious look. Why can't you tell what you know?

Then I'd lose my omniscient powers.

I think you're lying. I don't think you're omniscient.

Do you think your dad is lying too?

No. Dad *is* omniscient. He knew who was going to win the World Cup. Nobody else knew that for sure.

We each butter a slice of bread. I get up to get some more milk from the fridge. As I pass his chair I try to stroke his hair but this time he pulls away.

After we're done eating and clear the table I say let's go out and buy some instant chocolate so we can make hot chocolate milk. Sander asks if we can take the soccer ball along. I say he can take it along but that it's too cold to kick the ball around outside.

We can kick it around a little, says Sander, in your back yard.

No, I say, it's too cold.

Just a little, he says.

Okay, a little, I say.

But we have to be back before Mom and Dad call, he says suddenly.

I turn around and look at him.

It's hours before they're going to call, Sander. They won't call until tonight.

A gray-and-black cat is sitting outside the building where I live. When it sees us, it hisses. It has white paws. A skinny body. Shaggy fur. It has a white patch over one eye. It follows along behind us.

Look, the cat's following us.

*Go on, kitty. Go home.*

We buy milk, instant chocolate, meat patties, lingonberry jam, potatoes, flatbread, and orange juice. It's a big bright super-market. I've been shopping here for years. Occasionally I nod to some of the people who walk by. They nod back.

Maybe they think the boy walking next to me is mine, I think.

Sander says: I usually get soccer cards when I go grocery shopping.

Always?

Not always, but when Mom and Dad have been fighting I get a whole lot.

But they're not fighting now.

No.

Now they're on their way to Italy to have a good time.

Uh-huh.

Do you think they fight a lot?

Of course not.

He looks around the store.

Can I buy some soccer cards with my own money? I have twenty-two kroner in my pocket, a hundred and eleven kroner at home, and seven hundred and seventy-eight kroner in the bank.

So how much do these soccer cards cost?

Seven kroner a pack.

Save your money, Sander. I'll get you two packs.

Thanks a lot.

The cat is waiting for us outside the store. When it sees us coming, it gets up, stretches out its white paws, and hisses. Then it cautiously rubs up against Sander. Sander bends down, lets the cat sniff his hand before he pets it.

Come on, Sander. Let's go home.

Don't forget that we're going to play soccer in your back yard.

Sander looks up at me. He's still squatting down and petting the cat.

Okay. But then we'd better get going. I don't want to play after it gets dark.

Sander stands up, says: *Go home, cat*. Then he asks me if he can carry one of the bags. I give him the lightest one. We turn around and start walking. It's not snowing, but the wind is sharp on our faces. The cat follows along behind us. The cat waits for us while we go up to the apartment with our grocery bags. When we let ourselves into the back yard, the cat slips past us, sits down, stares at us, and hisses. Then it butts its head against Sander's calf and rubs on his leg.

Why is it hissing? says Sander.

I don't think it knows that hissing is the same thing as being mad.

It's not mad, says Sander. It just hisses every time it sees us.

Exactly, I say. It's just a silly cat.

I don't think so. Maybe it's lost.


Sander dribbles the soccer ball with his foot. The cat sits and I stand against the wall and watch. You have to play too, he says. Come on, Karin. You have to play too. I can guard the goal and you can try to score. Sander makes a goal out of two frozen sticks and stands between them. I kick the ball a couple of times. I stumble in my long coat. I hit the goalpost. You have to aim at me, says Sander. I kick again. Miss. Maybe you should be the goalie so I can try, he says.

It's started snowing, but the snow is melting before it hits the ground.

I don't think I can play anymore, I say. I'm not very good.

We've only been playing for five minutes.

It's cold.

Just a little more. Please.

No, let's go in now.

All right.


The cat tries to slip inside the door this time too, tries to follow us up the stairs. But I shove it out with my foot. Go home, cat, we both say. The cat sits down on the ground and licks its paws, pays no attention to us.

Sander wants to draw. I take out some drawing materials and sit down on a chair and look out the window. In the living room there are three big windows facing the street. There's only half an hour left now before dark. Julie told me that when she was pregnant she used to sit in front of the window and watch the dusk arrive, watch how it touched everything outside: the treetops, cars, roads, people, and how everything simply vanished. It was more beautiful than a sunrise in the summer, she said. Sander is sitting at the dining room table and humming to himself. I get up and go over to the window, look down. The cat is still sitting there. I go out in the hallway, to the telephone, dial Anni's number.

She picks up the phone after one ring.

Anni.

I see her before me, sitting in front of the phone all day long. She's waiting. Every day she's waiting. I don't know what she's waiting for. The phone call that will change everything? She's waiting, and while she waits she tries to kill time. Maybe she tries reading something. Maybe she walks back and forth in front of the windows. Maybe she's counting to herself.

*When I've counted to three hundred the phone will ring.*

Hello? Her voice is eager and soft.

A voice doesn't change during a lifetime. The eyes change. The hands change. The hair changes. The area around the mouth changes. The body changes. The skin changes. Over time everything about a person changes. Except for the voice. Talking to Anni—it's as if I was little and standing real close to her with my eyes closed and thinking: Don't let me go now, don't let me go. The smell of her hair, the sound of her voice. But her face. It still hurts to look at her. There's nothing left, nothing to hold onto.

Hello? Is that you, Karin?

Yes. Hi.

What are you doing?

I'm here with Sander.

Have they gone yet?

Yes. They left this morning. They won't get there until late tonight. Julie promised to call.

Are they driving?

Yes.

Julie's not driving, is she?

I don't know.

Could you call me after they call, so I'll know they got there safely?

Sure.

Is it going okay with Sander?

Yes.

I take the phone with me over to the window. Look down. There's a cat sitting outside my window.

A cat?

Yes. It won't go home.

Maybe it's lost.

Yes, that's possible.

Will you and Sander come and visit me someday?

No, I say, I don't think we can. We have a lot to do.

Sander is done with his drawing. He comes over to me. I say goodbye to Anni, put down the phone, look at him.

He says: Do you want to see my drawing?

He gives me a sheet of paper. The drawing shows a soccer match between Juventus and Manchester United, with Alessandro del Piero in black-and-white stripes scoring the deciding goal. I know this because he has written it on the page, decorated with dots and arrows. I ask if I can keep the drawing. He says I can.

I tell him he's good with his hands.

I tell him he inherited that from his great-grandfather.
Great-grandfather Blom, he says.
Exactly, I say.
He was a tailor, says Sander.
Do you want to see a picture of him?
Sure. Okay.

Sander and I go into my bedroom. I open the wardrobe door and take out a cardboard box of old photographs. There aren't so many pictures of Rikard. Only one picture was taken of him before he went to America, it's a blurry picture of a thin young man wearing a new and ill-fitting suit.

I show the picture to Sander.

We sit on the floor.

Sander looks at the picture, holds it in his hands, says that in the olden days there weren't any colors. I say there were colors, just not in pictures.

Why not? he says.

Because they hadn't invented color film yet, I say.

Then I tell him, very proudly, that when I was little, and that wasn't really all that long ago, not in the real olden days—they didn't have VCRs or PCs.

Sander hands me the picture of Rikard.

I put it back in the cardboard box, take out another picture. It's a picture I found on Selma's nightstand after she died.

I hand the picture to Sander.

It shows five people: three grown-ups and two little girls. It's a bright and obviously hot sunny day during a summer long ago. They're standing in front of a gray monument.

On the back of the picture it says in green ink:

*The World's Fair in New York, 1939. Do you remember?*
*Everybody together. All of us.*
*In front of the Cupaloy.*

Sander and I bend over the picture.

I point at the woman on the far left in the picture. She's wearing a light-colored blouse, dark skirt, walking shoes, and a hat. The two little girls are standing in front of her, leaning close to her.

That one is June, I say. My grandmother, your great-grandmother. She died before you were born.

Rikard is standing in the middle, he looks a little like Jimmy Stewart, he has one arm around June, the other around Selma. He's smiling.

That's Rikard, I say. Your great-grandfather.

He's been dead a long time, says Sander.

He died only two years after this picture was taken. He died at the beginning of the war.

Did he die in the war?

No, actually he didn't.

So how did he die?

Nobody really knows. He died while he was eating spaghetti.

Was he allergic to spaghetti?

No, not at all. He ate spaghetti every single day, he loved spaghetti, but one day he fell off his chair and died—just as he was about to take a big bite.

Sander looks at the picture.

He points at Selma and asks who she is. Selma is wearing a blouse and slacks. She's smoking a cigarette.

That's Aunt Selma, I say. Mean old Aunt Selma. She died just a few months before you were born.

And who are the children? asks Sander.

The older girl there, that's Else. She lives in Wisconsin and is fat and happy with four grown children and a husband who's even fatter and happier than she is. The younger girl, the one who won't show her face, is Anni. That's my mother. And your mom's mother.

Is that little girl there Grandma?

Yes, that's Grandma.

I hand the picture to Sander. He looks at it. He turns it around. He hands the picture back to me.

►

*The World's Fair in New York, 1939. Do you remember?*
*Everybody together. All of us.*
*In front of the Cupaloy.*

The year was 1939. *Do you remember?* It was the year German troops marched into what was left of Czechoslovakia and annexed non-German population groups to the Third Reich. Duke Ellington and his men sailed to Le Havre—the first stop on a concert tour that took them to France, Holland, and Denmark. (The trip through Germany was described as apprehensive, since everybody knew that Hitler didn't like jazz.) In August, Germany and the Soviet Union signed a non-aggression pact, and in September Germany attacked Poland. James Joyce finished writing *Finnegans Wake*, the film *Gone With the Wind* was shown for the first time. France and Great Britain declared war on Germany. Three million people, including schoolchildren, pregnant women, the handicapped, and the blind were evacuated from the big English cities.

The year was 1939. A man named Grover Whalen is convinced that from now on everything will be fine. His dream has been fulfilled: On April 30 the World's Fair opens in Queens, New York, under the slogan: *We're Building the World of Tomorrow.*

Rikard Blom and his family make the trip on the El from Bay Ridge in Brooklyn to Flushing Meadows in Queens. The trip costs a nickel. The admission ticket costs seventy-five cents.

Several weeks earlier the ship *Oslo Fjord* sets off on its maiden voyage from Oslo to New York. Reservations have been sold out long ago. Among the passengers, in addition to the royal entourage, are the student singers under the direction of Sigurd Torkildsen, the president of the shipping line Gustav Henriksen and wife, managing owner Mrs. Michelsen, managing director Kloumann and wife, shipowner Klaveness and wife, managing director Backer-Grøndahl and wife—to name a few. Those who aren't going along themselves swarm onto the dock to wave the *Oslo Fjord* off with roses, carnations, lilies, and orchids. "It was as if spring itself had bloomed on all the little ladies' hats festooned with flowery veils in the most elegant of shades," wrote the newspaper *Dagbladet* the next day.

Everyone wanted to go to the World's Fair.

Everyone wanted to see what Grover Whalen and his men called the world of tomorrow.

It was also called the Emerald City.

Or the Land of Oz.

Straight, clean streets. Music on every corner. Splashing fountains and fireworks every night. An amusement park with roller coasters, a merry-go-round, live dance bands, skimpily clad girls, and an erotic cathedral created by Salvador Dali himself.

It was the year Glenn Miller recorded his "Moonlight Serenade."

Finally people were going to see what the future would look like, and the future was scientific, bright, fair, rational, safe, and rich. New inventions and ideas were presented—and Rikard Blom had never seen anything like them before: dishwashers, refrigerators, air conditioners, super-modern cars, a talking robot, Kodak color film, and nylon stockings designed by E. I. du Pont de Nemours.

President Roosevelt's opening dedication speech was transmitted via television—and that was the very first time the

American people saw their president on TV, and the fair hostesses, wearing scout uniforms, were the prettiest in the whole country.

The most popular exhibitor was General Motors with their "Futurama"—an amusement ride through the world as it was supposed to look in a few years' time.

After the ride everyone got a button that said: I HAVE SEEN THE FUTURE.

*Do you remember?*
*Everybody together. All of us.*
*In front of the Cupaloy.*

What's Cu-pa-loy? asks Sander.

A big shiny torpedo-like thing that some men lowered into the ground. A kind of time machine or time capsule made of copper, chromium, and silver—but mostly copper. They filled the capsule with things and lowered it into the ground. Then they decided that no one would be allowed to dig it up for five thousand years.

Five thousand years?

Five thousand years.

Why?

So that the people living in the year 6939 will find out what things were like for people in 1939.

The time capsule of Cupaloy is still buried in the Flushing Meadows park. The little monument is still there too, with its solemn, forgotten words. The rest of the World's Fair (except for a few symbolic structures) was demolished.

The time capsule contains the following:

Novels, magazines, comic books, and newspapers from the 1930s copied onto microfilm. Photographs of people, animals, houses, apartments, roads, and parks. Descriptions of the era's architecture and design, reports on scientific, medical, and industrial advances, depictions of a typical workday in offices and factories. Written greetings from Albert Einstein, Thomas Mann, and Robert A. Millikan. A copy of the U.S. Constitution, a Bible, and a glossary of the thousand most common words—in case the English language has been forgotten by the year 6939.

They lowered the Cupaloy into the ground and filled it with things, I say.

What kind of things? says Sander.

Lots of things. Things you would recognize. Things that Rikard and June probably had at home in their apartment in Brooklyn. An alarm clock, a can opener, a pair of glasses, a fountain pen, an electric lamp, a camera, a nail file, a safety pin, a toothbrush, a wristwatch, a Mickey Mouse cup, a pack of cigarettes, an electric shaver, a baseball, a deck of cards, a dollar bill, a lady's hat.

The men who lowered the time capsule of Cupaloy into the ground in 1939 wrote a greeting to the archaeologists who would dig it up in 6939.

A greeting that goes like this:

*Each age considers itself the pinnacle and final triumph above all eras that have gone before. In our time many believe that the human race has reached the ultimate in material and social development; others, that humanity shall march onward to achievements splendid beyond the imagination of this day, to new worlds of human wealth, power, life, and happiness. We choose, with the latter, to believe that men will solve the problems of the world, that the human race will triumph over its limitations and its adversaries, that the future will be glorious.*

The year was 1939. It was in May or June. Rikard Blom had bought a new camera, a Kodak model. Unlike his friends, he could afford extravagances like that. His costume shop was doing well, had always done well. Maybe because he was like Little Frikk in the fairy tale: Nobody could say no to the very first thing he asked for. And he didn't ask for much. Not now. Not on that day. He asked a young woman—maybe a tourist who had come from far away to see the World's Fair—he asked her to take a picture of him and his family in front of the time capsule of Cupaloy. She had to make sure they all got in the picture. His wife June, his good friend Selma, his daughters Else and Anni. We're from Norway, he said and straightened his shoulders a bit. The young woman said that of course she would take their picture. She thought it was exciting, she said, she'd asked for the same kind of camera for her birthday.

Then they posed. Rikard in the middle, with his arms around June and Selma; the children in front, leaning close to their mother.

Smile! said the woman, getting ready to snap it.

Of course! shouted Rikard.

t's almost six o'clock. It's dark outside now. Sander and I are going out to bury a treasure. We're going to take a short walk to a little park near where I live and bury a treasure. I've found a shoebox. In the shoebox we put things we like.

I don't want the treasure to stay in the ground for five thousand years, says Sander.

That's fine. It doesn't have to stay there that long.

So how long should it stay there? When can we dig it up again?

We can dig it up in a year, a couple of days before next New Year's Eve.

Okay.

We fill the shoebox with things: a picture of me, a picture of Julie and Aleksander, a picture of Sander.

I put in the box my old picture of Rikard, June, Selma, Else, and Anni in front of the Cupaloy monument. I don't really want to part with it, even if it's only for a year. It's a beautiful picture. They all look so happy. But Sander says that it's not a real treasure if we don't bury some special things.

We put a hundred kroner in the box. And a cork that Sander has in his bag. Sander goes to get a corkscrew, a spoon, and a green napkin out of my kitchen drawer. He puts all of them in the box. I ask if we should include the drawing he gave me, the one of the soccer match between Manchester United and Juventus. He says we should. We take out a book that we both like: *The Wizard's Hat* by Tove Jansson, and put it in the box. I get out a CD by Etta James (an old recording), a letter from Father, a lock of hair from Anni that I've kept since I was little.

I tell him to choose one of his soccer cards and put it in the box. One of the best ones he has. The one with the picture of Dennis Bergkamp.

He says no.

I say that it's not a real treasure if we don't bury some special things.

Maybe we shouldn't bury any treasure after all, he says in a low voice—holding his very best soccer card in his hand.

Oh, come on, I say. We can dig it back up in a year.

But what if someone finds the treasure and digs it up before us?

That's the chance we have to take.

Sander carefully puts the soccer card in the box.

We put on warm clothes. It's snowing outside now. The snow is sticking to the ground. I put on my parka, scarf, and boots. Sander puts on his down pants, down jacket, and waterproof shoes. I carry the hoe. Sander carries the shoebox. We go down the stairs, out the door. The cat is still sitting there. It hisses when it sees us. Then it gets up and follows us up the sidewalk.

There's practically no one on the streets.

We reach the park. It's dark, no street lamps in sight. We stop for a moment. The cat walks past us, turns around, sees us standing still, and sits down to lick its paws.

It's dark in the park, says Sander.

Are you scared of the dark?

No, he says. Just a little.

He takes my hand and we continue on. The cat follows us.

We head into the park and the falling snow makes everything a little brighter. We head into the park, a good ways in, until we find a fir tree, a wonderful big fir tree, almost like a Christmas tree. Here! I say. Here's where we're going to bury the treasure.

No, says Sander. Not here. We have to keep going a little.

Okay, I say.

We walk some more. Come to another fir tree. Here! says Sander. Here's where we can bury it.

No, I say. We have to keep going a little.

We walk farther into the park, the dark closes around us now, we walk farther and deeper into the park.

What about that tree there? says Sander.

The cat has already sat down.

All right, I say and wrap my scarf one more time around my neck. Then I start digging.

I hack at the frozen ground with the hoe. A thin layer of snow on top. I hack and hack. Clumps of earth everywhere. I tell Sander to stop me when he thinks it's deep enough. He doesn't say anything. Stands there with the shoebox in his hands and looks down at the ground.

Is this enough now? I ask and look at him. Drops of sweat are running down my neck.

No, you have to dig a little more.

I dig a little more.

Is this enough now?

Okay, he says. That's enough now.

We put the shoebox in the hole. We look at it.

It's going to get wet and crumble away in the ground, says Sander.

I brought a plastic bag along, I say. I forgot all about it. I take out the plastic bag that I had stuffed in my parka pocket. Maybe we should write something too, I say. A message, in case someone happens to find it.

What should we write? says Sander.

I find a pen in my pants pocket.

We write: *This is a treasure. Do not touch it until Sander and Karin come back to dig it up.*

Is that okay? I ask.

Yes, says Sander.

I put the shoebox inside the plastic bag, Sander puts the plastic bag in the hole, I fill up the hole.

We stand there for a moment and look at the mound of earth. Then we scratch a little mark into the tree trunk—in case we happen to forget exactly where the treasure is buried.

On our way back Sander says: You haven't forgotten that I get to stay up until Mom calls, have you?

No, I haven't forgotten.

Sander and I are eating supper in the kitchen. Slices of bread with banana and hot chocolate milk. We both jump when the phone rings. We look at each other.

I get up from my chair. I look at the clock. Almost nine. It's still a little early, but maybe.

I pick up the phone.

It's Father.

Hi, he says.

Hi, I say.

Have they left?

Yes, they left this morning.

What are you doing?

I'm eating supper with Sander. What are you doing?

I'm not doing anything. I'm waiting for that movie to start.

It starts at ten. I'm going to watch it too.

Can I come over and watch it with you? I'm feeling a little lonely. I miss Ingeborg.

Sander's going to watch it too.

Oh really?

You're welcome to come over.

Great, I'll leave right now. I'll be there in half an hour.

Fine.

I go back to the kitchen table. That was Grandfather, I say. He's coming over. He wants to see the movie too. Sander eats his slice of bread, doesn't say anything.

Father is out of breath. He leans against the wall in the hallway and pants heavily. He has drops of sweat on his forehead. His worn gray coat seems baggy on him. His pants are too big in the waist.

You shouldn't live on the fourth floor, he says. Too many steps for an old man.

Let me give you a light beer, I say.

Sander comes out to the hallway. Sander looks at Father. Father looks at Sander. They both have a kind of crook in their back that makes it hard for them to stand up straight. It's as if they're always having to duck, bend down—the way you bend down to go through a door that's too low.

Hi, Sander, says Father.

I'm allowed to stay up until Mom calls from Italy, says Sander.

Sure, sure, don't worry. I'm not sending anybody off to bed, says Father defensively.

Father is still standing in the hallway. He doesn't take off his coat. It's dripping on the floor. He looks at me.

When do you think they'll call? he says.

Before eleven. They had a long way to drive. But they'll probably get there well before eleven.

Julie's not driving, is she? Aleksander won't let Julie drive the car, will he?

I don't know, I say.

Father looks again at Sander, who's standing motionless and listening. Then Father hands me his coat and goes into the living room. Sander and I go into the bathroom. He's going to get washed up, brush his teeth, put on his pajamas.

I'm going to tell Mom when she calls that I'm allowed to stay up to watch a movie, he says.

All right, I say.

I like watching grown-up movies, he says.

I did too when I was little, I say. Father—*Grandfather*—used to let me watch movies on TV that I was too little to watch. Scary movies about scary things.

I look at Sander. Sander looks at me. We smile at each other.

We turn around when we hear a noise. Father is standing in the doorway. He looks a little uncertain. Sander is in the midst of pulling his pajama top over his head.

Father says: Did you know there's a cat in the living room?

Yes, I say.

Why is there a cat in the living room?

It's lost, says Sander. Tomorrow we're going to put up signs and maybe the people who own it will come and get it. And we called the police. They didn't think it was dumb that we just called about a cat—and not a murder or something like that.

It hissed when it saw me, says Father.

Don't take it personally, I say. It doesn't know that hissing is the same thing as being mad. It's just a silly cat.

I see, says Father.

He keeps standing there looking at us. Sander in his blue-and-white cotton pajamas. Me with a white towel in my hands.

I never thought I'd see you in this role, he says and nods at me.

I put the towel down on the edge of the tub.

We're getting along fine, I say.

We buried a treasure, says Sander.

Where? says Father.

In the park.

Father nods. We go back to the living room. The cat is lying on the couch. It's almost asleep. It doesn't even bother to hiss when it sees us. Just a little wheeze and then a yawn.

What's its name? asks Father.

Cat, says Sander. We just call it Cat.

I see, says Father. Do you thinks it's possible to ask Cat to move off the couch so I can sit down?

I put out a bowl of popcorn. Sander gets a bottle of soda. Father gets a bottle of light beer. I drink a glass of wine. The TV is on. The movie is going to start soon. We sit down next to each other on the couch.

It's an old film, I tell Sander, made by Alfred Hitchcock. Hitchcock made really scary movies. This one, *Rear Window*, is not so scary—just a little.

Father says: One time I dreamed about sitting like that, week after week, in front of a window and just looking at people—just like Jimmy Stewart. And now I have no choice, he says. Now I have nothing else to do.

One time I dreamed I'd wear dresses like Grace Kelly, I reply and smile.

Go ahead and joke, says Father. But now I don't have either a job or Ingeborg. It's depressing. Love and work are the only things that matter in life—and a really good cognac after a meal.

And then he says:

Don't you think I knew that nobody at the publishing company cared whether I did my job or not, that nobody really knew what kind of books I published, that management was just waiting for me to retire and take my pension because I'd become an expense they didn't want to bother with anymore? I knew. But you have to take your work seriously. Even if no one else does. You have to do your duty every day except Sunday, because that's a day of rest. The only thing you can be proud of when all is said and done is that you did your best and you were a hard worker.

Sander and I are silent. Eating popcorn.

Then Sander says: Do you want to see my soccer cards?

No, not now, says Father. Not while we're watching the movie.

I don't have the very best card anymore, he whispers. We buried it in the park. The one with Dennis Bergkamp.

Oh I see, says Father.

Father, Sander, and I watch the movie. A few times Father looks at his watch. A few times he looks at me, tries to catch my eye. I explain some of the plot to Sander, but not all of it.

I think about the photograph of Rikard Blom and it's true: He actually did look a little like Jimmy Stewart. Sander leans his head on my shoulder. Once in a while his eyes fall shut, but then he gives a start and stares at the TV screen again. His body is warm and heavy against mine, his pajamas are soft. His fine hair smells faintly of soap.

The night before Julie left for Italy with Aleksander she was allowed to sing to Sander before he went to sleep. Usually she wasn't allowed to sing to him anymore. The day before he turned seven and a half he said: I don't want you to sing to me anymore.

Julie tried a couple of times, but then he'd always say: Don't you remember the new rule? You're not supposed to sing to me anymore.

But the night before she left for Italy she was allowed to, and then she did what she used to do when Sander was little—even younger: She sang the four songs she knew. And then she said a prayer, the same prayer that Grandma prayed for her children and that our mother prayed for us.

I imagine her lying down next to him in bed, lying down close to him, and he doesn't push her away. She looked at him, kept her eyes on him, not wavering even for a second. She didn't see Aleksander come into the bedroom, didn't see him lean against the wall, without saying a word. She didn't see him, but she sensed that he was standing there, heard him whisper something. She didn't hear what he said, but it wasn't anything that scared her. It wasn't anything that scared her, because at that exact moment the walls were silent. At that exact moment everything was the way it was supposed to be. Everything was fine. And she closed her eyes and felt the presence of the others in the room.

Shhh, Sander, you have to be quiet now.
　　We're sitting in the living room.
　　We'll be up late.
　　Don't be scared.
　　The light's on.
　　You'll hear our voices.
　　And we won't go to bed before you sleep.

Sander wakes up on the couch after the movie is over.
Father has gone home.
Sander gets up, rubs his eyes, looks at me.
The cat is sleeping under the table.
I'm standing in front of the window.
What time is it? he asks, yawning.
Twelve-thirty, I say.
Did Mom call?
No, not yet.
She said she'd call before eleven.
She didn't say a specific time, I say. She didn't. She just said
it would be late.
She promised to buy me a soccer uniform in Italy, a real
one, he says.
I turn around to face Sander. He's sitting on the couch,
groggy and barely awake, with red patches on his cheeks and
hands.
Maybe you should go to bed and go back to sleep, I say
wearily. You can call them at the hotel tomorrow morning—as
soon as you wake up.
Can't we call them at the hotel *now?*
I just called, they're not there yet.

But I want to say good night before I go to sleep. You promised.

Sander looks at me.

You're right, I say. I promised. You don't have to go to sleep. I know what we'll do. We'll both lie down in my bed and take the phone with us into the bedroom.

We're lying in bed, Sander and I. The cat is lying on the floor. It's very quiet.

I look at Sander.

His face reminds me of Julie's face.

His thin body reminds me of Julie's body.

Those big feet.

His big feet remind me of Julie's feet.

Julie's big foot on the gas pedal.

I close my eyes.

Do you know what, Sander? I say.

What?

Do you remember that picture of Great-grandfather and all the others in front of the Cupaloy?

Yes.

Do you remember all the things inside the capsule?

Yes.

There's a story in there too.

A children's story?

Yes.

Why?

The people who buried the capsule probably wanted the people who dug it up in five thousand years to have something to read to their children. Do you want me to tell it to you?

Have you got it here with you?

No, but I know it by heart.

Sander doesn't say a word. I know he wants to ask why the

phone doesn't ring. He knows I can't answer him. That's why we don't talk about it.

Just listen, I say in a low voice, listen:
Once upon a time the North Wind and the Sun were fighting over which of them was stronger, and one day a man came past wearing a warm cape. When they saw the man, they said to each other that whoever was the first to make the man take off his cape would be, forever and always, the strongest. And the North Wind blew with all his might and all his strength, but the more he blew, the tighter the man wrapped his cape around him, and finally the North Wind had to give up—no matter how big and strong he was. Then the Sun began to shine, nice and warm in the sky, and the man took off his cape almost at once. Then the North Wind had no choice but to declare that the Sun was the stronger of the two.

Is that all? asks Sander.
Yes, I say.
Do you know any other stories?
Not really. No, I don't know any other stories.

Sander fights to stay awake, spits on his fingers and rubs his eyes.
But finally he can't do it any longer. He can't do it. His eyes fall shut. He knows that he can't stay awake. He whispers: If I fall asleep before they call, will you wake me up so I can say good night?
Of course I will.
Do you promise?
I promise, Sander.

But Julie and Aleksander don't call.
I sit down on the windowsill and look out. It's almost two o'clock.
I see them before me. As if in a film strip. The two of them

in a car on the road that will take them to a place they went to over eight years ago.

I think about Grandma.

I think that she probably didn't feel like smiling back in 1939 when the young woman was going to take a picture of her and her family in front of the Cupaloy.

There's no reason to smile, she whispers. *Do you remember what year this is? Do you remember?* It's nonsense what it says here, that the future will be glorious. It's all a lie. Can't you understand that, Rikard?

And Rikard turns around and says: You and I, June, we're going to stay on our feet until the last round. No one can knock us out. No one. Not even Al Brown. Do you know why? Because we love each other. That's why! Because we have love.

I see them before me.

Julie, I see you.

But the strip is getting narrower and narrower.

Soon I can't see them anymore, not the car either, only the road.

Sander is lying on his stomach, he's curled up on the bed, under the comforter, almost like a little frog. The back of his neck is sweaty. I listen but can't hear whether he's breathing. It's so quiet in here.

It's so quiet in here, and I have to hear whether he's breathing.

I bend over him, put my ear to his lips. Only then do I hear that everything is the way it's supposed to be. Everything is fine. Sander is breathing.

He's asleep now.

He sleeps the whole night.

Here, next to me.

Born in 1966, Linn Ullmann has lived most of her life in New York City and Oslo. A graduate of New York University, Ullmann has worked as a literary critic at one of Norway's leading newspapers since 1993. She currently lives in Oslo with her eight-year-old son.

Tiina Nunnally is an award-winning translator of Norwegian, Danish, and Swedish who has translated works by Knut Hamsun and Sigrid Undset among others. Her translation of Peter Hoeg's international bestseller, *Smilla's Sense of Snow,* won the Lewis Galantiere Prize, given to the American Translators Association.